*Praise for* The Shape of Her

'Rowan Somerville in...
desire. On a Greek isla...
idyll for two privileged youngsters darkens into dread and
recrimination ... unresolved trauma brings its danger to
this liaison like the jagged boat-wrecking rock that lurks
underwater beyond the golden beach' *Independent*

'Darkly erotic, offbeat holiday read ... an entertaining book
that while not echoing to
wouldn't be out of place in

'Confronts us with an exte
incomprehensibility surrou

'Somerville is clearly a thoughtful writer ... a rich plot and
some lovely vivid local colour' *Guardian*

'Deceptively simple in plot and singularly musical in its voice,
it is a study of the place where our past has become our
present. A summer read to be kept – and visited in the dark
days of winter' *Economist*

Rowan Somerville was born in London in 1966. He has worked in television, film and radio. His debut novel, *The End of Sleep*, was shortlisted for a Commonwealth Writers' Prize and the Glen Dimplex New Writers Award.

*By Rowan Somerville*

The End of Sleep
The Shape of Her

# The Shape of Her

ROWAN SOMERVILLE

PHOENIX

A PHOENIX PAPEHBACK

First published in Great Britain in 2010
by Weidenfeld & Nicolson
This paperback edition published in 2011
by Phoenix,
an imprint of Orion Books Ltd,
Orion House, 5 Upper St Martin's Lane,
London WC2H 9EA

An Hachette UK company

1 3 5 7 9 10 8 6 4 2

A CIP catalogue record for this book
is available from the British Library.

ISBN 978-0-7538-2859-5

Typeset by Input Data Services Ltd, Bridgwater, Somerset

Printed and bound in Great Britain by Clays Ltd, St Ives plc

The Orion Publishing Group's policy is to use papers
that are natural, renewable and recyclable products and
made from wood grown in sustainable forests. The logging
and manufacturing processes are expected to conform to
the environmental regulations of the country of origin.

www.orionbooks.co.uk

To my precious teachers: past,
present and future

*The past is never dead, it's not even past*

William Faulkner, *Requiem for a Nun*

Note

*Valentine* and its abbreviation *Tine* is the feminine of the name, rhyming with *queen*.

# One

Max struck out along the moving walkway. Despite the vigour of his pace, the bounce and swing of his shouldered luggage, the heat gathering under his clothes and the sense of excitement that filled him – brimming into a slightly asinine smile – Max did not progress in any way.

To move forward he must speed up, struggle against the flow of other passengers, face their disapproving expressions – and for what? Max had found a balance, an equilibrium, an easy and familiar pace that could be maintained without gaining or losing ground. But he stopped, allowing the moving walkway to drag him backwards, back to the point of departure, past the other passengers scorning him for his puerile game – back until the static lip of metal slipped under his heels and he was stationary.

He smiled, looking pityingly at the people around him, basking in the sense that life in the past month shimmered with extraordinary radiance. The source of such radiance was a girl so wonderful that every moment, every object, every thought, pulsed with the shape of her. He'd never been happier than right now. Never had more to look forward to.

His precious Valentine.

He looked around to see if the object of his thoughts had made it to the airport. His eyes pushed through a parting of the crowds, skimmed like the fingertips of a Braille reader over faces and bodies then lingered on a screen advertising a private bank, warning parents to prepare for the *best* days of their children's lives. The children in question, a schoolboy and girl staring out, in uniforms that would precipitate a stabbing in any British high street, their expressions a precise mix of vulnerable and impudent.

Max crossed the corridor and sat back at his place, heels hooked onto the chrome strut of the four-foot coffee stool. His cappuccino remained before him, untouched. He stared at the advertisement and wondered what Valentine had been like as a little girl – adorable certainly, fragile, tough – could you be both? The fluorescent light behind the picture flickered and died. As the faces faded into shadow a sense of unease crept into Max. He hardly thought about his schooldays now – never in fact – but he was sure that they couldn't have been the best of his life. The backlight flickered on again, flooding the little girl's face with a glow that was, for a moment, angelic.

Max smiled. It was a good omen. Any second now and he'd see her, hold her in his arms, feel her ribs through thin wool, see her pale skin, those frail lips, squeeze that tender frame until she disappeared in his arms. He wanted to consume her, bite her tiny ears, seize her earlobe between his teeth till she squealed. Perhaps he ... perhaps he was in ... well it was too early to say, but he was unaccustomed to feeling like this; not so it weighed in his chest, throbbing under his coccyx, straining his jaw, like an anxiety – but somehow exhilarating. It was like waiting for his Ma to take him home when he was a boy, standing at the boarding school gates, at the end of term. Waiting for his world to become whole again.

Max scraped away the cocoa topsoil from his cappuccino, and flicked it onto the saucer. He liked chocolate, he liked coffee – but together, why? The eastern European Barista behind the counter had taken his gesticulations for encouragement and unleashed an extra deluge of cocoa-flavoured dandruff.

He suspended his spoon over the flattened landscape of foam and plunged it onto specks of chocolate, pulling out peaks that hung and wilted before collapsing into arabesques like folding ballerinas.

'I don't know,' he'd sighed to his mother that morning, gazing about the drawing room of her house, wondering why only twenty-two minutes had ticked by when it felt like so many more.

She'd longed to know what he intended to *do* with his life, now that his education was long concluded. But he had no idea, no idea at all – other than to spend the summer with Valentine.

They spoke little; rehearsing the same questions, regurgitating the same answers – answers each had wordlessly consented to hear. Max was rarely in the family house, but the photograph of him, propped on the mantelpiece – scrubbed, combed and almost disappearing in a large school uniform – it had never left. Fused in time – a scared little boy smiling thinly in someone else's clothes – never quite losing faith in Mummy and Daddy's promise that everything was going to be all right.

'Must get to the airport,' he'd lied, pecking a goodbye onto her cheek. He had an hour to spare, perhaps more. His mother looked as though she might say something, her hand fluttering to reach out to him. But Max had turned and made for the door, promising postcards and a longer visit on his return. As he shut the front door behind him and paused on the doorstep, he'd managed to thrust away the approaching guilt and for a moment had felt ... almost nothing, nothing but a delicious longing for his Valentine.

Now, in the airport, he raised his cappuccino to his lips,

the foam, a strange landscape; alien tentacles, sea anemones, predatory, deadly.

Voided with a loud suck.

How would it be with her, with Valentine? He remembered that long weekend in Wiltshire; her best friend's parents away – Tuscany was it? A life immediately desired. Old house, Queen Anne they said. Light streaming through windows twice his size, people he'd never met, soon familiar as friends. Dinners, wine, weed, flashing eyes, touching feet. A huge table crowded with bottles and cups, coloured bowls smudged with coloured foods, ashtrays and flecks of bright green marijuana, with the twisted white tops of rolling paper strewn like dried-up cherry blossom. Lunches outside in warm spring sunshine. The sun, it seemed, those afternoons, shining just for them. Heavy purple flowers, crowded over the crumbling garden wall like bunches of grapes. Tennis and a pool, a private pool – what a thing. Guarded from gaze and wind by a maze of walls, ancient and red – a rich peoples' secret. Beautiful girls lying around, wearing so little. Where to put his eyes? The other boys seemed used to it, born to it. He could hardly hold on to normality.

A girl at three o'clock, sleeping by her freshly kissed boy-friend, covered only with wisps of violet in little 'v's, another at four-thirty, bouncing on the diving board in ironic leopard-print bikini briefs – like an arrow head, hardly bigger – pointing to that yearned for place. And Valentine's best friend, Hazel – she was under close and covert surveillance as she stooped to pick up a Frisbee and the candy-striped material of her briefs seemed to smile up her shapely rear like a joker's mouth. Hazel had turned, he recalled, her bikini top stretching like two nets held by tugboats, straining to contain the magnificent warm melting curves that begged to burst out and flood the universe with ... she'd seen him ... fuck ... he'd decoyed as if their eye contact was part of a normal sweeping of the vista. OK, she'd looked away. What did he think she'd do – he mused putting down the still warm cup – run away screaming pervert?

Her tits were probably too big for him anyway. What was one supposed to do with breasts that big?

Nice though.

Tine herself, she was the exception, the zenith of poolside glamour. An old one-piece swimsuit – from school … do you think it's too small? She'd smiled, hoiking it, oh so innocently by the shoulder straps, and twirling once before dropping on to her belly in front of him so they made a 'T' in the long cool grass. 'T' for her.

Everything for her.

Max found himself fingering foam from the rim of his cup into his mouth, his imagination opening her legs, examining this part of her, where the tight scoop of material disappeared between her thighs, sketching a loosely drawn 'Y'. What might he find when he was finally allowed to do, rather than think, to cross those intimate thresholds, to uncover, to touch, see, what letter would she be there? A scribbled 'I'? And when he turned her over, opened her … a shaded 'O'? Max stood, shaking his head to dislodge the letters, the images, a vortex of desire. He must act, do things, buy condoms before she arrived. Who knew if they could be found on this little island of hers.

That first afternoon, he had walked her home from tennis in Regent's Park. She was wearing a short and pleated tennis skirt – she'd claimed that it was club rules – which suited him. They walked side by side, he'd taken her racket, still warm-handled, and slashed it inexpertly through the air. Every few steps, the tops of their arms would touch. Her flatmate was out. She'd told him he could find a drink in the kitchen. She needed to shower, she'd said, turning and locking her eyes on to his. He'd been looking for an opening, a hesitation that might allow him to leap the space between wanting and having. Maybe he should wait, he'd thought, take her somewhere to dinner – they'd been to dinner. Should he just kiss her? Leap into the chasm? Too late, she'd left the room. He could follow her, walk straight into her bedroom and ... No, too rapist. Too rapist? Too embarrassing. She'd be undressing and assume he'd waited deliberately.

But here she was. Back. Walking into the kitchen, sweatshirt off, T-shirt and skirt, flick, flick. She needed a clean towel, she mumbles, opening a cupboard, stretching up, revealing a taut waist.

He's on his feet now. She turns from the cupboard. His head targeting hers. Locked on. Four feet and closing, three, two and a half, she's in retreat, she's moving. Abort, abort.

He's shot out a hand, a grappling iron of sorts. Flailing. Found an arm, hooked, tugged. Too hard, harder than he means to.

Abort? She's moving towards him, lips first, pulled by lips, lip to lip – they're touching – mouth, tongue ... She breaks, pulls back.

She's taken a step back, but does not turn away. She's placed her hands on her left hip and pushed the old-fashioned white button of her tennis skirt through its eye and stands looking at him as the skirt unwraps from her waist.

A thing sprung with magic. A slow spring.

Every time his friends asked him how the sex was with Valentine, he'd changed the subject or nodded his head in a way he hoped was both experiential and knowing. In truth, they had not done it. There had been no shortage of sexual tumblings, intimate moments – more intensely erotic and enjoyable than anything he had experienced – but she had not let him penetrate her, or even touch her down there. Not at all. Not yet. Despite hours of rubbing, of kissing, of grinding, of climatic sucking, she would not even take off her knickers. 'There's no point,' she'd say, 'it would be unfair to both of us, like serving up a delicious meal and then saying we can't eat it. When it's right, it'll be right and then I'll be yours.'

'Mine?'

'Yours. All of me.'

He wanted her, there was no doubt about that, every bit of her, everywhere – but almost more than being in her, he just wanted her naked, to look at. He'd seen women, of course he had, hundreds; four-inch, two-dimensional mannequins, pornographic images bristling with insertions, stripped, shaved and bent double. He wasn't a virgin. He'd been with a couple of girls, a few fumbled couplings; brief, unbearably exciting, embarrassing. But Valentine, when she had stood before him in her knickers that afternoon – like nothing was wrong – so real, so beautiful, so perilous, she'd tangled him up in a shame he couldn't understand.

'Max ... Max ... MAX ...' And there she was before him. Watching him dream.

Max leapt up, pulling at the tightened seams of his underwear, meeting her outstretched arms. Mute fireworks of heat thudded up his neck, blushes like smacked skin.

'Valentine,' he said, encircling her with his arms.

# Two

Unfairness on a universe-destroying scale. Two months in exile. My so-called holiday – prison sentence more like – my crime, total innocence – a lifetime of slavery to my mother. You should be excited, Triff says. Mortified more like, ruined, crushed. OK it will be hot and that's good and there's Angelika's yoghurt and Ionnes' honey and warm beautiful sea and Octopus Lemoni and a million things – but a girl has friends and plans and then they are smashed and beaten on pointy rocks like the poor Mr Octopus before lunch. I swear that Tash will drop me as her friend and I'll come back unpopular and everyone will have been slagging me off constantly because I've been away and missed everything and, of course, life in Year Ten will be tragic and my total world will surely end before it's begun.

I didn't remember the sun – not enough anyway how it shines on my shoulders and back, seeping into my skin, making my bones melt into goldenness. I lie on my belly, one eye open, and the white plaster of the porch like a beautiful pale planet, and there's a brave team of ants, a crust of Jojo's breakfast pincered above them, speeding towards my nose. Three parts to an ant; head, trunk and metasoma. Year Nine science. Mr Wilson, funny little piggy eyes and a bald patch like a monk. Tonsure, that's what it's called. Year Seven History, The Reformation – is it really necessary for a girl to know? One breath from me and Team Ant changes direction. The perfect marching band. Triff in the village buying lunch and Ithica is mine for the morning. Mine, mine, mine. Grown up at last, a teenager no less, and left on my own to swim and lie in the sun.

I see my sweat on the ground as I push up off the floor. Patches of damp shadow. Yuck. But exciting in a way. A few steps on the sandy ground, dodging the sharp pine cones and, remembering that right there – where anyone might think to dive – is a great sharp mountain of a rock, its point just under the water. I fly through the air like a gull, and into the sea. The water about me cool. Everything perfect and heaven – except the sea urchins beneath, shadowy torture bushes dotting the rock under the water. Maybe I'll get the mask and clear them ... The Triff will be pleased – though she'll want to eat them. I'd do it after lunch. Then their poor spiky lives won't weigh on my conscience.

I'm a hundred thousand light years away from that dork-king Devraj, who think's he's so cool sitting at the back of class with his stupid ear-stud and his spiky hair. There's not even a mirror at the house but when I stare at my face in the window of the pharmacy, my spots have disappeared, which has to be a good thing – though it doesn't even matter here with just the Triff and Jojo. I'm out and dripping into the sand and then onto the dusty leaves of the geraniums the Triff planted last year. They're dead almost. Already.

Someone else always used to be here. Never just me. If not the Triff then Dad. 'Going to the village for yiaourti do you want to come, Tine-bop?' Mum would call out hopefully. No, I didn't. I always wanted to stay with Dad. Whatever he was doing: going to the bar for a drink with Captain Maris, buying lime for the white plaster, going to the mainland to phone *L'Agent*. Whatever it was, I'd want to stay with Dad. Sometimes he'd stop me, prise my sweaty fingers from his giant hand. 'There's things a man must do alone, reallio, truelio my louloudi' he'd say. Then flipflop off to the woods for a scarily loud pee that I wished I couldn't hear.

He's doing a film, or play, or something, and in a way, it's a relief he isn't here. I miss him of course, but the Triff seems better now it's just the three of us. I asked if she was crying this morning as I rubbed the crusty sleep from my eyes. She said she wasn't. She never lies does the Triff. Not normally. She can be the most annoying tangly leafed Triffid-Queen of all time but she won't ever lie.

She was crying though. I swear it on Jojo's toes.

Dry already, flakes of salt on my arms, still pale but browning a little. Licked. Nice. Must put sun cream on, Triff says the sun will give me wrinkles, followed by hives, followed by terminal skin cancer . . . unless, unless. Cream must be applied, girls and cream like strawberries and dreams. Salty mouth. A fig's the thing, split it with my fingers and the sweet pippy pinkness within I'll toss into the sea, and then another fig too. Better not have too many or I'll pay later. In our tiny loo you can hear everything. I'd run outside when Dad went in, 'run for the hills' the Triff would cry and I would – but it's only me and Mum here so it doesn't matter anyway. We hardly close the door now Dad's not here – Jojo too of course, but he doesn't count. It's the only time Dad hasn't come on holiday.

Ever.

I wish he was here. I hate Mum to the point of death and beyond when she looks at him like that – all hard-lipped and like she might shatter – and then it's buckets of wine all round and long silences until Jojo screams, or I slam a door, or something like that.

There's that dog again barking somewhere up in the woods. We haven't seen it, but it was howling when we arrived last night. Rabies, Triff concludes with all-knowing ear. 'Beware!' cries the great carnivorous plant. Not for the first time. She's a great beware-machine, my Ma, and a Triffid too. Especially with Jojo. Attached to the Triff he is – just the way she likes it. Sometimes, I'll take him and then it's 'beware, beware, not too far, not near the water, not on your bike.' I wasn't going to take him far on my bike that time. I just wanted to see how he looked in the basket, all sat up like a puppy. Wheel him round a bit.

Sweet.

A splash. A great splash.

They're back. The Lemonade Rock has been thrown, the first of the summer and it's a good one. Triff can't throw. Not for toffee. Not for jewels. Not from the cliff. Dad must have arrived, just upped and come without telling anyone. I grab a T-shirt, ruffle my hair in the hope of feathering it like a Beautiful Person, and tear off outside so I can see them at the pass. Triff's first, I can make out the yellow mark of her embarrassing sunflower dress and her black scribble of mad-person hair and behind her is a man, it must be HIM, carrying something, carrying everything, on his back like one of those guitar and mouth-organ men with the big drum. What has he brought for me, my glorious old Pa with his lovely face and his great big nose? He must be thirsty, I'll make lemonade the way he likes it with two whole lemons and a great galoop of honey.

Three lemonades – like porridge for the bears – a tiny one in a baby cup for Jojo, a Mummy cup for the Triff and a great pint glass with a handle for Daddy Bear. The smell of lemons everywhere as if angels had just come in, and me never happier than here right now, everyone coming home and I'm all warm with my flip-flops kicked off and my bare feet scratching on the dusty plaster.

Triff is first round the corner, red in the face with a shopping bag, and Jojo clinging on and crying for all he's worth. I seize the pint glass and run out and there he is with an entire Gallepi of wine and twenty packages and plastic bags bursting with dishwashing liquid and nappies so you can't even see him. I throw my arms around his waist but it is not Dad. It is someone else, someone young, stinking of sweat. I jump back and he stares down at me, long hair falling over his face like he thinks he's an angel or something, and his mouth is smirking as if he wants to laugh at me but can't even be bothered. He reaches for the lemonade but it's not for him, it's for Dad, and he tries to snatch it and I throw it all over him and run off. He drops the bags in the sand and stares at me, a slice of lemon in his hair.

Triff shouts as I disappear into the woods and I run and run until a pine cone tears into my foot and I hear myself scream in anger and I smash a stick against a tree until it is nothing and this feeling too, is nothing.

# Three

There was an unsettling intimacy to travelling together that Max had not expected. A new obligation to question or alter habits and rituals. He had mentally prepared a list of twenty things Valentine might want to eat or drink or buy before boarding the plane. She wanted nothing. She saw no reason to progress to their departure gate until just before it closed, he wanted to go immediately so they could 'relax'. She reasoned with him; there was nothing to relax with, nowhere to relax, just an unrelaxing waiting room with parallel rows of unrelaxing chairs. These chairs were designed with minimum comfort in mind, she explained – otherwise, people with nowhere to go might arrive and set up home there. He only half listened, luxuriating in the line of her neck. In her ear, a tiny green jewel, like an atoll. He hooked his fingers through the handles of her bulging hand luggage and took the weight. She resisted for a moment, she didn't need help, she could manage – but then she submitted, skipping onto the moving walkway before turning towards him with a smile that drenched him with joy.

They were similar in age, not even halfway through their twenties, but so different, in size, in shape, in being. Perhaps they were not even the same species. Not just her and him, but women and men. Gender might be no more than a theory, a false one. Tine turned round again and Max allowed his eyes to trace her shape through her jeans. That he might soon reach round her waist and unbutton them, feel her belly against his flattened palms, hold her – it was better than anything. She stopped, turned again and smiled, stretching a hand back to him. He took it and pulled her into a kiss, the ground carrying on beneath them until they were tumbled off at the end, laughing at themselves as passers-by laughed at them.

Max scanned ahead for their gate number. The corridor stretched away like a first go at perspective, lucent yellow numbers shrinking until they became one, in a distant dot.

At their gate, they settled next to each other, on hard plastic moulds of chair that offered the discomfort Tine had promised and the view of a grey-carpeted wall. While Max examined the drab colours, wondering who had been paid to create such a thing, Tine spoke about her island. She told him not to expect much from the house – she'd been going there as long as she could remember. It was tiny and simple and they would not see another tourist because no one ever went there. There were no beaches and nothing to see, just olive trees and a turquoise sea.

'There's a village of course, a couple of tavernas, a general store, that kind of thing. It's quiet and ... well ...'

'What?'

'A bit strange. You might find it a bit strange. People do.'

'What d'you mean?"

'I don't know, the people are different, very different. It's a tiny village, maybe everywhere's like that.'

'And your mother?'

'It seems normal to her. She first went when she was twenty or something. That's how we got the house. Everyone knows her. She's like family there.'

'D'you go every year?'

'I haven't been for ages.'

'Why not?'

'I just didn't go back for a while.'

'Your parents' divorce?'

'Not really . . . maybe.'

She was silent for a few moments and then talked about the house and the mice and the heat and the thick, clear honey. Max kept her hand in his lap, exploring and squeezing it until their flight was called. He took her bag before she could argue and they sped down the plastic corridor. Lights glowed from the top and base of the wall, as if the corridor was blocking bright sunshine from outside, but as they came to the corrugated hatch leading onto the plane, they could see a strip of grey sky and the plane body streaked with rain.

Valentine was delighted by the terrible weather.

'*Schadenfreude*,' Max explained.

'What?'

'Delight in others' misfortune.'

'*Cloudenfreude* you mean,' she said kissing him, 'and the last ones we'll see for three weeks.'

Max opened his eyes. A stewardess rattled by. For a moment it was all so perfectly Disaster Movie. Tine was asleep, her forehead on his shoulder. He crept his gaze down the straight slope of her sweater, over the mogled ridges of a machine-embroidered thermal vest and down to the gap where her underwear snapped tight against her curves. He hooked his finger in the gap to expose more and her eyes twitched open. He snapped back his hand and squirmed in what he assumed was the accusation of her expression – but she said nothing so he smothered her with a kiss, descending onto her lips like a deflating balloon.

They slumped as comfortably as their seats allowed, flicked through a dog-eared airline magazine, kissed, ate every dull crumb of the chemically white, surgically sealed sandwich, sipped brackish coffee from cups the colour of prosthetic limbs, and then, with the snapping shut of tables, the righting of inclined seats and the broadcast of bilingual expressions of commercial gratitude, they landed.

As soon as they set foot on Greek tarmac Valentine took control, micromanaging each step with an authority that allowed no room for discussion.

At the passport queues, she demanded they race. He spied a shorter queue and took it, losing by several minutes.

'Rookie error,' she quipped, going on to analyse the failings of his strategy.

'You were just lucky,' he interrupted.

'No way Rookie-boy, the man ahead of you had a Turkish passport.'

Max attempted to regain some self-respect by producing a euro coin he had been saving in his pocket for the baggage trolley but she headed this off. They should carry their bags, she insisted. It wasn't far and the trolley dock was at the wrong end of the airport for the bus to the ferry. Max was about to explain that he was ideologically opposed to carrying bags when a trolley was available, but she'd already dashed ahead.

The bus arrived when Tine had said it would, crawling through the Athens traffic, coughing black smoke into the smog and depositing them at the ferry dock after a sweaty hour.

'Over here, we'll get on the boat quicker,' she commanded.

Max felt irritation rise in him but he covered it with a thin-lipped smile. They boarded the ferry, getting on first as she had promised. They sat out on deck, watching the craggy contours of the Greek mainland unroll like the flicking lines of a barograph.

The ferry neither tucked nor rolled, its bulk of riveted metal bulldozed through the mirror sea. Sticky-faced children chased between the seats; their mothers, shopping squeezed into bags, smoked and talked all at once, no one a listener. A covey of rich people broke onto the deck, cream slacks and yellow pullovers, crisp and clipped, tanned and flashing with gold.

Tine disappeared inside, returning with toasted sandwiches. Max took huge bites, hooking away strands of cheese with his fingers until he encountered a searing disc of tomato, which burnt his lips causing him to cough and splutter until he regurgitated a white and brown bolus of bread onto the deck, flecked with pink spots of chewed ham. The white-slacked sophisticates caught sight of the spectacle, frowned, fluttered and retied the arms of their cashmere sweaters. Max picked the wet lump of bread off the deck and threw it over the side. A gang of seagulls screeched and squabbled over it, one swooping up with the prize disintegrating in its beak.

Tine leapt up and pointed out a shape to Max. A rock like a hunched animal, the back of a pig perhaps, its outline feathering in the heat. Max's fatigue and hunger, and even a certain anxiety that he had glimpsed but not acknowledged, disappeared as they pulled into the harbour. She dragged him away and marched him along to wait at an exit deep in the ship.

'First off the boat?'

'You're learning,' she replied.

They disembarked through the bow, gaping open like the mandibles of an immense beetle. Max was disappointed. In front of them was a jetty like a crooked concrete arm, featureless but for a portakabin café with bolted down rows of orange plastic seats. Next to them was a smaller retired ferry, green with years of algae, bobbing like a mad pensioner in the waves of the larger vessel.

'I meant to tell you not to look,' Tine said from a few steps in front, 'it's the new port – for the big ferry. It's hideous but it's the only ugliness you'll have to bear.'

Max marched behind Valentine as she hurried across the concrete. They walked a few hundred yards on a road cut beneath a cliff. Max stopped in a shadow and looked up at the cliff above him, crusted yellow like clotted cream.

'Come on, look at the real port,' Tine called from the corner.

He followed her to where old buildings were freshly painted in ochre and cream, with whitewashed windows and doors barely a body-length from the water. Fishing boats crowded side by side – mostly wooden – but here and there was an inflatable rib, or a moulded plastic hull. All the vessels gently bobbing as water flooded and ebbed, flowing between the protective arms of the harbour, rising and falling like an old man's chest. No one was about and the taverna they passed was closed, a menu held by a rounded sea rock fluttering in the breeze, which, somewhere out of sight, tapped cables against masts.

They turned into the main street of the village. Tine announced that they would buy what they needed to last them until the next day, then they would come back and shop properly. Two ancients walked close by the walls, a child followed, straining with a huge bag of oranges. A radio chattered from some open window, a machine tool whined from a village house, loud then silent.

It was late in the afternoon, hot and somnambulant. The shop was shuttered and draped against the sun, dormant like its owners. A taverna stood before them, its whitewashed walls glaring in the sun.

Tine stopped and put down her bag. Max observed her sweater hanging round her hips, a ribbon of waist exposed, a strip of underwear creeping up. Her thermal vest was darkened under the nape of her neck, her hair damp against her precise skull.

'Oh drat – I forgot – everything's shut till evening, straight to the house then.'

'Drat? Where did that come from? Anyway, how far is it?'

She shrugged. 'Two miles.'

'Let's have a drink, in the taverna,' Max suggested.

'No, let's wait till …'

'I quite want a drink.'

'It'll be closed.'

But Max had gone, striding across the road towards the taverna. Tine called after him but he ignored her. He pushed open the blue-painted gate and crossed the courtyard. It was deserted but for the heavy wood and wicker chairs and a disorder of tables. Max called a greeting through a doorway. There was no response, no sign of life except for the acrid scent of yesterday's grill. As he headed back towards the gate, he heard a voice uttering entreaties to the entire canon of Orthodox saints. An arthritic grandmother followed, rubbing her hip and yawning pointedly as she approached.

'Sorry to wake you, I was looking for a drink … water or maybe a Coke?'

She looked at him with a frown. Waiting for him to speak proper words. Greek words.

'Apologia,' Max attempted, then remembered that this was something to do with philosophy.

The old woman seemed curious and her eyebrows climbed up the wrinkles of her forehead.

*A drink?* Max mimed.

She studied him and issued another phrase in Greek which sounded like one very long polysyllable.

'A beer?' Max ventured.

As he looked around the taverna for inspiration the woman grasped his forearm with a darkly spotted hand and spoke at him as if revealing the final instalment of a prolonged and intricate story. She took him to a table and sat him down, patting his cheek as she spoke. Tine appeared at the doorway and requested that they set off. The old woman released his arm and fixed her with a Gorgon stare, before trudging back into the restaurant.

Valentine scurried over to Max.

'Malgortzata. You're lucky to be alive after waking her up. What a cow. She can't stand my mother, or me – don't know why, probably thinks I am her. Used to pinch Mum's legs when she first came. Come on, you'll never get anything out of her.'

Max was about to shoulder his bag when Malgortzata reappeared with a large bottle of beer, a single glass frosted with ice, and a plate of tzatziki. She set these in front of Max, pouring the beer and almost cooing to him while motioning that he should eat. She ignored Valentine and when Max passed his glass of beer to her without even sipping it, Malgortzata tutted, shook her head and shuffled to the kitchen.

'That's amazing, I can't believe it, she's been cursing us ever since I was old enough to notice and now you've got her bringing you treats – it was like that with my Dad.'

Malgortzata reappeared with a second bottle of beer, which she left unopened by Max before palming his cheek once more and whispering something which Max swore was *what are you doing with the skinny witch?* Then she departed.

They both laughed and Max opened the beer on the side of the table.

# Four

The Triff was so angry with me for the lemonade scene. I'd got the whole you-want-to-be-treated-like-an-adult-but-you-behave-worse-than-Jojo speech. Such a hypocrite – she was crying this morning. Is that adult? She wouldn't even let me open my mouth before she started with the you-don't-know-how-hard-it-is thing. Like I asked to be born. I want to tell her that I am sorry about the lemonade, and Pa and everything, but she won't listen. Can't listen. Her Triff head is too full of hating me. I didn't carry Jojo once the whole way from England, she said. I didn't help. I never help – such a lie. As much as it's possible for a girl to do. I ignored her, inspected another ant as he trundled by, dug into the sand with my toes. She went on and on until her face – which is not a bad face normally – turned all red and blotchy like when she's drunk. I'd dug right down to the corally rock underneath the sand and there was nowhere else to go with my toes so I kicked my feet up and the sand went all over the terrace she'd just swept. Which I didn't exactly mean to do.

'You made me come to Greece,' I said when I'd finished sweeping, 'I didn't even want to be here.'

'Do you think I do?' she said, 'with a screaming infant and a permanently pre-menstrual teenager.'

That was it.

I hated her. It was time she knew. She already knew Dad hated her but I thought she should be told again.

That's why Dad wasn't here.

Because of her.

So I told her.

She called me 'a little shit' and stormed off.

I was right to say it. She knows I'm the only girl in my year who hasn't come on yet. Not that I care.

I can hear her sobbing in the house and Jojo is screaming. I sort of wish I hadn't said that about Dad so I pick Jojo up and take him to the water to look at the sea.

The sea is flat and beautiful and a seabird is floating all alone without any friends like me. Jojo stops crying and looks at the bird as I point. He gurgles and then shows his understanding and depth of personality by peeing on my arm. I hold him over the edge and clamber into the water. He smiles and waves his pudgy hands as I dip him, My baby brother and me. We bounce and sing until I climb out and wrap him in a towel and we lie together in the shade of the carob tree and fall asleep.

She must have seen us as we slept all sweet and innocent and had a rush of Triff-Guilt or Maternal Love although they're probably the same thing. When I wake up the sun is setting and she's taken Jojo out of my arms and put him to bed. Everything's pink and hopeful and sad in a beautiful way and as I walk into the house we hug and she says she's sorry for what she said and all the shouting – and I whisper sorry for saying I hated her and about Dad and everything. I ask her to brush my hair because I know that for all her be-an-adult talk, she misses that. And I still like it.

A bit.

As for the stranger, his name is Khalib, she'd met him, she said – taking a monster gulp of retsina and pulling her old black brush through my salty hair – shouting at a group of men in the village square. They didn't want him in the village and he was arguing with them. When more men arrived, they'd begun throwing things at him.

'What things?'

'Lemons . . . rocks.'

He'd sworn at them, *Arhithopiti*. Probably.

Now that I think of it, perhaps she didn't tell me that he had used that word, *Arhithopiti* – but it's the word she might have used. Almost certainly, it was her favourite word that summer. She wouldn't tell me what it meant at first. She actually blushed when I asked her. The Triff. God knows what she has to blush about, walking about in her embarrassing clothes and practically demanding stares from the fishermen doing their nets and then lying topless every afternoon in front of Ithica so that people could easily see her from the top of the cliff if they had binoculars. 'No one WANTS to see them Mum,' I'd shout. She's so proud of them, everyone's so obsessed with them, 'they're just breasts, Mum, get over it.' She's such a hypocrite.

'*Arhithopiti!*'

Khalib ran away from the men and the Triff ended up chatting to him outside the village. I knew *-opiti* was pies, like *spanokipeta* was spinach pie and *tiropita* cheese pie (my favourite) but I didn't know what *Arhith* was. I asked Christos – the nice one with eyelashes like a bushbaby whose father took us on the fishing boat when I was six and threw up on Dad's head – and he just ran away. A few days later his jerk friend Risto came up when the Triff was gossiping to Angelika about the price of yoghurt or something equally exciting. He asked if I had found out what *Arhith* meant. I told him I hadn't and he said he'd show me. He was being all nice so I should have been suspicious because he's one of those boys who only have a jerk gear. I wish I'd known because as soon as we were round the back of the shop he grabbed my hand and pulled his privates out of his trousers and made me touch the bag bit. I screamed and ran. He laughed. He was still laughing when I walked past the next day. He pointed at his trousers, showing off to his friends. I walked past him like I didn't care, then turned and shouted *Arhithopiti* right into his face. His friends fell about laughing. At him, not with him – it was great. Triff told me I shouldn't use that word – but she thought it was funny, I could tell. I didn't tell her about Risto's ball-sack though, too embarrassing by ten million miles.

I don't really care about Risto's silly trick because every last person in the world knows that all boys – except my Dad and Jojo – are morons, including this Khalib friend of Ma's who walks about like he owns the island. As for Risto, he will be known as 'Ball-Pie' for ever more and he deserves it for being so disgusting.

I keep thinking about that soft bit though, like the dangly bit on a turkey.

# Five

A bottle of beer down and then another, and Malgortzata appeared again with a *skordhalia* dip of such brazen garliciness that it burned their ears. She clucked about Max, her back presented to Tine like a baboon's buttocks. To Max, her language seemed familiar but exotic, with 'k's and 'l's, high notes and glottal growls, syllables interlinking, polished and stretched. As she rumbled back into her kitchen like a creaking war machine, Valentine jumped up and swung her bag onto her shoulder.

'Let's get out of here,' she demanded.

'But we've got beer and this crazy garlic stuff . . .'

'We need to go.'

Max took a swig, the bottle between his lips. He stared ahead as he drank and there was something so cold and angry in his gaze that Tine dropped her bag and sat down again.

'I'm being bossy, I know . . . it's Malgortzata, she makes me want to scream.'

Max didn't reply. He placed his beer on the table.

'Look I don't mean to be like this,' she said, 'it's just . . . I want everything to be right for you, for us. I've seen things here. I want it to be right for you.'

She looked at him again and it was as if he had returned to his body.

'What?' he asked.

She stretched over the table and kissed him. She held his head in her hands and took his tongue with her lips tasting the flavours of his mouth; garlic, lemon, bread, beer, boy.

Max leaned towards her pivoting on his hands. He could not move to reach for her, show her the desire of his tongue, his hands were caught beneath him, his tongue trapped in Valentine's mouth. She slipped her hand on his neck, into his shirt, onto his chest. He arched his back pushing his chest towards her. From the kitchen, a plate was dropped – perhaps tossed. They pulled apart, flushed like children woken from the heavy sleep of a hot afternoon.

Max sat back into his chair. Tine filled his gaze. Caught in his eye, she was his. Soon, later, he might unbutton those tiny white buttons on her thermal vest, unbutton them down to her belly, one at a time, and then tug the shirt down over her shoulders so it contained the top of her arms, binding her. He might drift his lips down the sloping trapeze of muscles above her collar bones.

The idea of her physical delicacy emboldened him. Untouched, perhaps even virgin. Could she be? Was it fineness or weakness he saw? Submission or surrender? He wanted it to be surrender. He felt powerful in his skin, within his arms and legs, his hips, in the hard muscles of his jaw.

He finished his beer.

# Six

*Remember, O most loving Virgin Mary, that it is a thing unheard of, that anyone ever had recourse to thy protection ...*

The ground looked cold and hard under his knees. Was cold and hard under his knees. Soon it would be the sprint up the spiral staircase, pulling on the banister, his hand already gripping the same places each time; that rivet, that notch. His feet stamping on the cut stone, each step worn smooth by centuries of sprinting feet. Then pulling off shirt and jumper in one – why everyone hadn't worked it out he did not know, off in one, on in one. One hundred and thirty voices echoing round the school. He felt in his pocket: a comb, a three-day-old tissue and what was that? Solid and promising – a square of chocolate sullied with lint and grit. Too late tonight to perform the necessary surgery ...

*... I fly to thee, O Mother, Virgin of Virgins; to thee I come, before thee I stand, a sorrowful sinner ...*

He prayed for a moment as he always did to Holy Virgin Mother – Virgin because she did not have sex to make the baby Jesus. Sex was a sin. In all cases. Except if you were married – she was married to Joseph so it would not have been a sin anyway – but she was 'blemishless'. White. White because she didn't have sex. Pure. The Fathers didn't have sex either. They wore black with a white ring round the neck. Black for the sin of the body, the white for holiness, a halo, like the saints, but not above the head. Round their necks, to stop the sin coming up. His Mummy must have had sex to have him,

27

but that didn't bear thinking about. She was many colours, warm colours. It was not a sin because she was married, but it was – what had the matron said when Linnet had done a fart? – 'unsavoury', that's what it was. If Mummy had been like the Virgin Mary, and not had sex, then she would be a better person. Just that bit.

*... implored thy help, or sought thine intercession, and was left forsaken ...*

He hoped the Holy Mother would keep him forsaken from ghosts and rats with glass teeth and the Spanish boy with the funny arm in the year above ... and mostly that she would keep him forsaken from trouble. He felt in his pocket for his MCs. If you did something wrong you got an MC, which stood for mea culpa, and he already had three: one for running in the corridor, one for talking after the silence bell at dinner, and one for not having a comb on him, which was a School Rule. Seven more MCs and he'd have to Report, and then anything could happen. Seven in twelve weeks ...

*... Despise not my words, O Mother of the Word, but graciously hear and grant my prayer. Amen*

Everyone broke ranks and charged off, two hundred and sixty shoes – Clark's Commandos mostly, except for the overseas boys – clattering on uneven wooden floors, on worn stone stairs, a hand bell flinging out a warning to the Mites.

Ten minutes to tear off your clothes, wash your face, brush your teeth and get into bed. No Talking.

Bodies smashed into the metal plates of wildly swinging fire doors, feet slap slapping on the linoleum. Crashes, zips, rush. No Talking.

Not a word.

# Seven

They kissed and explored each other until Malgorzata's broken crockery and the force of their desire raised them to their feet. Max left some money, swung the bags onto his shoulder and strode out into the main street of the village. Tine followed, emerging from the bathroom, shaking her hands dry. She ran up to Max, stole back her bag and rushed ahead.

Max caught up and wrapped his free arm round her waist. As they left the village, dry scrub took over from the glare of white buildings. To one side, a hill of rocks stretched up, dotted with a few scraggy trees and the plaintive bleat of sheep; to the other, a cliff reached down to the sea. They walked, his hand on her waist, their hips bumping, stopping every few steps to kiss.

'It's a long way,' she said, pulling away.

He ventured his mouth to hers and his tongue into her mouth and pulled her close. He licked the salty sweat where her neck met her torso, edged towards her breast, stayed by the buttons on her shirt. She held his hand as he moved to release them.

'Not here, it's a conservative country. Very. You can't imagine. We'd cause a scandal.'

'Who's going to see us – the goats? Someone's probably having sex with one right now.'

They followed a slow curve round the hill where the cliff dropped away vertically, threatening to collapse their path. He was relieved when the cliff became a slope again, dotted with olive trees and sharp bushes. Tiredness, heat and alcohol had never felt so good. Her hand was slippery in his. A car clattered round a corner, hooting a greeting and trailing dust like cans behind a wedding limousine. A truck followed as if in pursuit, edging onto their path, sending up a storm cloud. They leapt away onto the steep slope, coughing and laughing. As the air cleared they slapped dust off each other. Tine combed her fingers through his hair, ploughing out the grit and wiping his forehead with a tenderness that for a moment made him want to cry.

'The path's round the next corner.'

She smudged his eyebrows with her thumbs, pressing down over his eyelids as if painting a stripe down a clown's eyes. She pushed her thumb between the cracked, dust-caked split of his lips and into the wet of his mouth. She spread his spit over his lips, then hooking her thumb in his mouth, pulled him to her, stretching open his mouth and licking in it. He raised his hand between her legs and drew her to him, his fingers searching up through the dampening fabric. She pressed herself down on his hand, making his body rush with blood. He tautened his wrist as she rocked back and forwards, riding the knot of his knuckle. Her hands around his neck, her eyes closing, her bottom lip caught under her front teeth, her expression set. Moving, bearing down, reaching as far as she could at each swing, like a cellist's bow sawing back and forth, producing a low moan from her chest. He moved his free hand round her hip and hooked his fingers around her cheek. He released his wrist, dropping the hand she was straddling, his fingertips now pointing towards the ground behind her. She moaned, widening her stance, pushing against him. He caught her rhythm, pulling and releasing, cradling and crushing; pushing up his fingers with each swing, mining up, like an otter through wet sand. Her sounds shifted from moans to grunts, insistent, almost desperate cries from the throat. An external noise, a screech like a drill, shattered their dream as a motor scooter tore around the corner, sounding its horn in boorish triumph at the discovery of their clinch.

'God . . .' she breathed, 'I'm so turned on.'

She broke away and rushed down the slope, dislodging rocks which overtook and tumbled past her. Max followed, scrambling and slipping, until they met at the path which doubled back to the sea.

'Do you see?' She pointed down the path. 'It takes us to Ithica, and nowhere else.'

'Ithica?'

'That's what the house is called, our name, anyway. The villagers call it "The English Woman's House"; but Dad always called it Ithica.'

They charged down the dusty path, skidding where it steepened, walking side by side where they could, arms interlocked, hampered from further intimacy by their shouldered bags. Clumsy like amorous snails, they rested hands on each other's thighs as they rose and fell with each stride, both of them attuned to the tightening and loosing of muscles, the mundane enlivened by desire. Tiny rocks slipped under their feet, delicate sparse strands of hair-thin grass poked between, grouping in places, like an old man's pate, olive trees stood by with gnarled stumps out of which arrow-straight shoots of new growth had sprung. She pointed to a patch of white between the trees on the edge of the shore.

'There it is, do you see it?'

She ran ahead and Max caught up with her in front of an old building, whitewashed with lime. A weather-worn front door sealed the house, held fast by a rusted chain and padlock the size of Max's hand.

Valentine scanned the ground, frowning.

'It's been swept.'

'That's good isn't it?'

'Someone's been here. There should be a year's worth of leaves, cigarette butts, scratched graffiti from local kids ...' She paced around like an animal searching for a scent.

'Local gesture?'

'Not a chance. The Triff must've paid someone to do it and forgot.'

Valentine stepped off the terrace and began digging at the base of one of the young trees that struggled, with a dozen others, to delineate a path.

'That's weird too,' she said, producing a key from the ground. 'Normally it's a real operation, like unearthing a fossil – but it was right near the top and the soil was loose.' She brought the heavy iron key to her mouth and blew off the sand. Her pursed lips made him want to kiss her again. She unlocked the padlock, removing the salt-corroded chain, and began worrying the heavy wooden door open, pushing and pulling, grunting as she had against Max's hand.

The door gave.

Everything within was so still and untouched that for a fleeting moment the very air seemed caught from decades before, laden with the hopes and fears of childhood. Then it crumbled, vanished, with light and the hot breeze from the sea.

Max followed her into the house, darkened by shutters, scented with figs and mice. He rested his hands on her hips and paused, turning her to him, kissing and climbing his hands up her back, drawing her to his torso and squeezing until he could feel the light give of her ribs. He covered her mouth with his and she sucked at him, the smell of him filling her. He unbuttoned the front of her shirt and pulled it to the side so that her breast was uncovered, her nipple poking out, upturned like the nose of the loveliest nocturnal animal, sniffing the night. He took it between his lips and sucked the salt from her. He hooked his fingers into her waistband, caught the elastic of her underwear and began pulling down. The knot on her light cotton trousers held fast as the fabric reached the curve of her backside. She twisted from him and stepped back.

'I want to suck you,' she said, descending. A part of him wanted to resist but he could no more stay her descent than the vague sense of disappointment that was arising in him. He wanted her this time, not to be consumed, but to take. She loosed his trousers, pulled away his underwear and gripped him with fingers tender enough to hold a tiny bird.

As he felt her mouth's engulfment, he acquiesced, disappointment melting like ice in hot cream.

# Eight

It had become clear to everyone that Weld's inability to write legibly – or even at all – was not, as had first been diagnosed by Miss Trench, pure idleness.

'He's a quiet boy, clearly not entirely stupid, so his nursery school scrawling and ... tribal' – there was a twitch of her retroussé nose at the utterance of this word – 'spelling is clearly a question of discipline. These boys I take in Lower Elements are barely off their nanny's knee.'

'I think Miss Trench,' Mr Jackson – Rufus 'Dam' Jackson – of bow-ties, neon V-neck pullovers, adventurous facial hair and the mouth of an American beaver, interjected from the beverage table. He was stirring three teaspoons of Super-Valu instant coffee into a cracked red mug resplendent with maple leaf and the legend: *3rd Ecumenical meeting of Catholic School-masters, Toronto.*

'I think Miss Trench, you will find that these days it's all au pairs.'

'You would know so much better what is à la mode than I, Mr Jackson. The point is,' she said, rubbing at her hands with an antiseptic tissue she had extracted from her bag with a whip-like crack, 'some of them are barely house-trained. Some of them can't speak English, and that boy Weld, despite being able to read rather well – suspiciously well in fact – can hardly write his name.'

Miss Trench's announcements in the staff room were invariably complaints. It did not matter to whom the speech was addressed because the other members of staff present – one reading the *Telegraph*, one the *Racing Post* and one working his way through a pile of exercise books with extraordinary ferocity, as if slashing at the Devil with a cracked red biro – all of them had heard versions of the same complaint on many occasions. Despite the frequency with which Trench had repeated her message, and the ingenuity with which she dressed it up in new costumes, not one of them listened, sympathised or even bothered to recognise the leitmotif in what she was saying. Miss Trench's point was simple: every member of staff, clergy and lay, should be grateful to her, because it was she who made their jobs possible, schooling as she did the new entries to St Xavier's; twenty-two seven- and eight-year-old boys from the better Catholic families of the world. It was she, and she alone, who battled with the soft clay of childhood and compacted it into the cement of civilised Catholic men. Of course, English boys would always have a head start, they knew the language and presumably their fathers were gentlemen (and if not, as sadly seemed to be the case these days, at least they had pretensions towards being so). But even those from Good English Families had been mollycoddled and left to their own devices to such an extent that their first months at Francis X would be, she liked to think, the very making of them.

'Give him a few weeks to settle down and then if he won't raise his game, MC the bugger.'

'Mr Jackson!'

'Apologies Miss Trench ... I do forget myself with you. What was I saying? Oh yes, if that doesn't work, toss him to Brother Noonan. He's been known to keen up a weak boy's concentration.'

Trench, although not a liberal – God forbid – did not altogether approve of Brother Noonan's methodology. While effective, she did not consider it necessary to go through the archaic hullabaloo of physical punishment – an experience that boys soon hardened to – when a few well-chosen words could shatter the confidence of any boy in her care. Nevertheless, she felt tempted to follow Jackson's advice. She was exhausted, bereft of the usual verve that a month of brass rubbing and cycling in Belgium usually gave her. And then there was the awful mess with Celeste and the disappointing diaspora of her bi-weekly Geology group – no, maybe a short, sharp shock from Brother Noonan might cauterise the boy's insolent lethargy.

Weld's trip to the lion's den was as good as booked when the quiet francophone tones of Father Le Saux rose up from the time-ravaged Chesterfield by the window.

'Forgive me for overhearing, Mlle Trench, may I add to what has been so thoughtfully expressed?'

Trench and Jackson were surprised, as were the other staff members in the room. All stopped and attended; Miss Trench ploughed the antiseptic wipe into every joint and wrinkle of her hands. It was not so much that Fr Le Saux rarely spoke, but his silent presence and octogenarian form had been entirely invisible in the seat and until he unfolded his crossed legs (a habit he had carried from the Indian missions) and levitated from the chair like a particularly underfed genie, no one had realised he was there.

'I think back to my own childhood. It seems like so long before . . . indeed seventy years or more. I recall great difficulty in the forming of letters. Of course, I did not have the benefit of such wise and experienced teachers as you Mlle Tranche or you Monsieur Jack-sone. The good Fathers of my school sought, at a cost of much physical effort to themselves, to drive the incompetence from my young body through regular and *furieux* application of the stick.'

'Exactly what I was suggesting Father,' Jackson burst in.

'But it did not help, *mon cher professeur*,' Fr Le Saux replied quietly. 'I required my lessons a little more slowly, or perhaps even from a different *point de vue*.'

'I am sure in your day, Father, there was time for such luxuries,' Miss Trench interjected, 'but the world has become quicker and much, much, more competitive. I have a class full of children, barely civilised children, who would rather play about in the dirt like common pigs than have me inculcate the values of this school, indeed Father, of your sacred Order into them. Nobody seems to understand the raw material I am faced with. I simply don't have the time ...'

'Perhaps I have more time than you and might offer my assistance,' the ancient Father offered, leaning lightly on the arm of the sofa.

'Out of the question,' Trench erupted, with more vehemence than she had intended. The last thing she wanted was Fr Le Saux prying into her methodologies, making all sorts of, no doubt, *eastern* comments – of course by his very intervention implying she was incompetent. She'd seen it all before. Everything. Often. And none of it was satisfactory.

'I could not countenance taking up your precious time, Father. I know you are busy upholding the spiritual life of this institution.'

'*Au contraire*. I have almost nothing to do but watch and contemplate.'

'Oh, well ...'

She was stumped for a moment until Dam rescued her like the hirsute courtly knight he – particularly when slashing at nettles with his walking stick, or riding his bicycle back from the public house of an evening – believed himself to be.

'Why not send the boy to Beaufinn for extra tuition. Even if it doesn't solve the problem, one can be sure Richard would be grateful of the ... haha ... fiscal bonus, what with his hip and all ...'

'Excellent idea, Mr Jackson,' Miss Trench trilled. 'Of course, I am not convinced of Mr Beaufinn's methods either – if indeed there is method,' Trench quipped, folding the now soiled tissue into ever decreasing triangles. 'Those who hope to be both credits to this school's values and ... popular are expecting something which never has, and never will, happen. If the good Father insists on this course of action, then naturally I will obey, as in all things – but not on my timetable, I beg you. There's so much to get through. Some of the boys are as wild as savages and if we are to herd them away from certain failure, then there is no time to lose.'

But Father Le Saux was no longer in the chair or indeed the room. He had disappeared as soundlessly as he had remained.

Trench looked up and found Rufus Jackson looking at her with a distasteful yearning in his eyes. She gave him her back and deposited the soiled wedge of antiseptic tissue into the wastepaper basket.

# Nine

Khalib appeared more and more that summer and what with the Triff telling me to feel sorry for him because he lived alone and had no friends, and Dad not being there, I suppose I did get more used to him too. Everything: school, rain, sun, even breasts become normal after a while and I stopped thinking of Khalib as this twenty-something-year-old man or whatever he was and thought of him more as one of those things that are part of reality – like an annoying relation. Sometimes when the Triff wasn't drinking wine with him or teaching him English or just staring at him, he would show me interesting things on the island like birds' nests or a slow-worm or a secret swimming place with a cliff to jump off.

When Dad was there, he and the Triff would drink gallons of retsina every night of the holiday and I would lie in my tent next to the tiny white house listening to the murmur of their talk and the sudden bursts of laughter like the alarm calls of tropical birds. Once there were guests: this actor friend of Dad's called Ozzie and a classmate of the Triff's – I can't remember her name. I was little, and that summer was the best ever.

At first anyway.

Ozzie crowned me Poet-queen, Rubbie Burns, Ruler Of Suntan Potions and my sacred task was to select and apply the right suncream for each person. Ozzie had brown skin even when he arrived, so I'd use oily stuff on him that smelled of yellow flowers. His skin was so dark, he must have been foreign – or maybe his mum or his dad were.

'More!' he'd shout.

'It's covered!' I'd shout.

'More!' he'd demand.

I'd tell him he'd had enough.

'A hundred drachma for ten more minutes,' he'd beg.

'Deal,' I'd squeal and rub his dark shoulders. I would have done it for nothing because he was so nice.

The Triff's friend was different – white as a witch with red hair like leaves blown in autumn. I used the white baby stuff on her; she'd whisper from under her hat that if the sun so much as looked at her she'd burn right up. She didn't like to be touched really – not by me. Putting cream on her bony white shoulders was like dusting my granny's glass animals. I had to pretend to love them because it was a grown-up thing to be allowed to touch them – but I didn't. The curved neck of the swan with its swirling colours and the legs of the golden flecked giraffe that you could snap in your fingers, they scared me in a way. It wasn't that I thought they would break, it was that somewhere in me, I felt just like them. Sometimes, I'd wake up and my own fingers would feel so fragile, like those bread sticks in Italian restaurants or those glass legs, but I still would clean the animals every time I visited my granny, and I put cream on the white woman just the same.

I have not thought of that woman for years, but now it's just the Triff, Jojo and me, I am thinking about her again. There was a lunch one afternoon and everybody had eaten a fish Captain Maris had suddenly appeared with. I remember the grown-ups shouting and laughing so I suppose they must have been drunk. Mum and Captain Maris fell into a red-faced sleep on either side of the olive tree and Dad and the white woman disappeared for a walk.

40

I didn't follow them. Actually, I suppose I did – but I don't think I meant to. Sometimes I was a sprite; so light as to be able to fly on the back of a bat, to wisp through the trees on a breeze, to lie along the stalk of a sunflower, my neck tickled by petals, but above all, my greatest power was to tread without a sound. This last I could really do well, certainly enough to surprise Dad, who was rubbing something – cream I suppose – all over the white woman's front.

'What are you doing creeping around?' he shouted, wiping his hands and pulling up his swimming trunks. Scaring me with his angry face.

'I thought she didn't like potion there,' I said in confusion, watching the white woman scrabbling to pull up her swimsuit.

I looked at his expression and it changed from fierce to smiley, like a toy I used to have with a round hat and you'd turn it to make it happy or sad.

'Well she was burning and you weren't here,' he said. 'D'you want to put some suntan potion on me?'

'No,' I shrieked and ran back into the forest.

I said nothing to the Triff. Something must have sent it out of my mind, a certain food for dinner, a dolphin sighting, fear of tidal waves – whatever it was, I didn't say anything and I can't remember why. But I do remember that the next day Dad took me to town and bought me an even bigger ice cream than usual and then, after he had finished telephoning L'Agent, he asked me if I wanted to talk about what had happened.

I shrugged.

He asked me, did I still want to get my ears pierced?

Did I want to? Fireworks exploded in my belly. More than anything, more even than wanting to be a forest sprite. I'd been begging him and the Triff but they'd said I had to wait till I was fourteen 'minimum'. I'd told them it was *so* unfair, two other girls had pierced ears in my class. I didn't tell them that they were the twins from Spain, where you have them done when you are no years old, literally. But both the Triff and Dad said 'NO WAY'. And yet here he was, standing in front of me, asking me if I wanted them done.

He pretended not to know where the shop was, but I knew exactly. He walked with smaller and smaller steps which is a silly thing he does to be funny but I skipped ahead and pulled him. When we were in front of the shop he let out a big pretend sigh.

'Are you sure you want this done? Wouldn't you prefer a few hours in the Museum, rumour has it they've found a new pile of broken vases?'

'Come on,' I begged.

'Do you know, I think I've forgotten my wallet.'

'COME ON.'

I did it.

It hurt more than anything ever before and I fainted when they pierced me and then cried and wished I hadn't done it, and Dad cried too when he saw the blood trickle down. But there they were: two gold studs in my ears. And me ... as grown up and pretty as a princess.

The Triff went bananas, of course, trulio, crazio, bananas, giving me the whole arm yank treatment – tug, tug, tug with each question. When her Triffid brain finally understood that it was Dad who'd offered, that it was his fault, then things actually got worse. She grew two hundred and fifteen feet and sprouted invisible deathspikes dripping with anti-Dad poison. I ran out for a walk, and then another, but even by the sea, I could hear her giving Dad The Full Treatment.

I wished I'd never got them done because the Triff didn't stop being angry with Dad after that. It didn't help that the holes went bad and poison oozed out and I couldn't even swim for weeks.

It was funny, my pierced ears closed up on their own as if they wished they'd never been done.

I never saw the white woman again.

In some ways, although that was years ago and I'm more grown up now, it's all a bit sad with just me, Ma and Jojo here. But the shouting and the pretending to be happy, that was even worse.

Ma seems to like Khalib being around this holiday. He is certainly strong, clearing rocks away between the house and the sea, some of them huge. He even stayed underwater for ages without a mask and collected every single sea urchin from the huge underwater rock where we swim. He cut them open and fed them to the Triff. She tried to get me to try one.

'Go on darling, they're delicious.'

'Sure, for people who like orange fish-snot.'

Dad wouldn't like them, I know.

Khalib smells of fish. Triff told me off – of course – when I said that to her, but it's true. He smells like dried fish or old prawns with curry spice or something. The Triff watches when he takes off his shirt to go swimming. She says that he looks like one of those statues in the museum. I said he doesn't. First, because he's got two arms and none of them have, and second, because he has lines on his back and marks on his skin like knots in wood. She told me that these were scars from people being cruel to him his whole life. She told me his father was a sailor from the village but his mother was from Algeria in North Africa. His dad came back from the ships with little Khalib, but then he drank too much ouzo and dropped dead. Fr Dennisos looked after the boy and Khalib served at mass

43

and did odd jobs around the church until he did something terrible and was thrown out.

'What did he do?' I demanded.

'Something disgusting,' the Triff replied, with her that's-all-I'll-say voice.

'Like what?'

'Like you don't want to know.'

'Like you aren't me,' I said, 'so how do you know what I want to know?'

'Well, I'm not going to tell you, I don't even want to think about it.'

'Please tell me. Please!'

'No means no. You can sit here all day, but I'm not going to tell you.'

'That's not fair.'

'Nor is life.'

'Life with you certainly isn't. Give me a clue ... is it disgusting, in a sort of boy way?'

'What do you mean?'

'You know the way boys do disgusting things.'

'Like what?'

'Like making you touch their ball-sack.'

'Their *what*?' She put down her retsina and leaned into me. 'Has someone been making you touch them?'

Her voice was all spikes and danger.

'No ...'

'Listen to me Valentine, this is very serious, you're to tell me right now. What's been going on?'

'You wouldn't tell me about Khalib.'

But I saw the pulse begin to throb in her neck like those lights in an atomic power station saying emergency, melt-down, so I told her about Risto and the 'ball-sack pie' episode. She was shaking for a moment and I thought it was too late and she was about to explode – but then she burst out laughing and pulled me into a full Triff-hug and told me not to worry. Boys were like that, she said, but I was never to let anyone do anything that I didn't want. Did I understand?

We hadn't had a chat about sex and things since her incredibly embarrassing 'tête-à-tête' about the birds and the bees and the bees and the bees and the birds and the birds. More recently she kept trying to ask me about my period – or lack of it – but what was there to say? I'm a freak: other than the class genius who's two years younger than everyone else, I'm the only one who hasn't come on. Yes, I know that some people don't until they are fifteen or even sixteen, but some people have eleven toes and do you think telling those poor multi-fingered freaks that there are people out there with fourteen makes them feel any better?

NO.

Was there anything about sex and things I wanted to talk about?

'No – like triple, skinny, decaf NO, with frosted sugar and wings.'

'Do you know what fellati . . .'

'No, Mum, yuk. I mean yes, of course I know, but I don't want to talk about it. There is one thing you could tell me though.'

'Yes?'

'Do you swear on your mother's life?'

'Your Granny is dead. I hope you don't swear on my . . .'

'OK, then, do you swear you'll tell me?'

'Of course darling, if I can.'

'What disgusting thing did Khalib do?'

I'd won.

She told me.

But she was right. It was disgusting and I wish I'd never asked.

When he was a teenager, he smeared crap all over the walls inside the church. Not donkey. Not dog. His own. Fr Dennisos threw him out and the villagers would not let him stay in the village from that day on, so he lived on his own, in a ruin of a house somewhere.

Of course, the Triff was right, it would have been better not to have known, because now the whole story with full colour pictures and Smell-O-Vision took over half of my brain – that's 500 billion brain cells minimum. When I next saw Khalib, shit, shit, shit, it was all I could think about – at least, until he showed me a tree with hard berries that smelled like Dad's gin and he took me to a sweet little animal hole with tracks going in and tracks going out. Then I almost forgot.

We stood staring at the tracks for a long time then Khalib took a stick and pointed.

'*Mama,*' he said, tracing a line alongside the tracks.

Crouching down again he pointed to a tiny track next to it, so faint it was hardly visible.

'*Nipio.*'

'What?'

'*Micros y Mama.*' He bought his first finger from his left hand and his little finger from his right in front of his face.

'Baby?' I ventured. 'Baby animal and mother?'

He nodded and linked his fingers to show togetherness, the little finger all hunched and snug under the big. I suddenly realised that Khalib had never even had a mother or anyone to wander about with and then, as if that wasn't enough, I looked up at his thick scarred hands and twitching blue eyes and noticed that he was missing three fingers from one hand.

I looked away from him and then looked back because I didn't want him to think I was disgusted by his stumps. The truth was I felt sorry for his missing fingers and his being all alone – but he had walked on ahead, pushing through the bushes as if he was too proud to accept they existed.

As we were walking back to the house something must have caught his attention because he stopped dead. I didn't make a sound and stood very still. I could hear my own breathing, smell the hot dry smell of the forest and feel the rubber of my flip-flops pushing in the space between my big toe and the next one. After what seemed like ages I opened my mouth to whisper to him, but before I had even formed a word, his fingers pinched my lips closed. My nose was almost touching the side of his finger and all I could think of was that I didn't want to smell his shit – but I sniffed anyway because that's the thing with disgusting things: you don't want to know, but you have to know. Then whatever it was he'd been listening to exploded out of the bushes with a snarl. I screamed and jumped onto Khalib and he roared at the thing, which was only a half-starved dog, and it must have run away because when I untangled myself from him, it had gone.

He didn't smell crappy – just a bit like a fish.

The Triff was out when we got back. She must have taken Jojo for an evening walk because the door was open. I made Khalib a lemonade in Dad's big glass, not because I liked him but I thought it was possible, or even certain, that the dog would have followed us and would come to get me as soon as Khalib had gone. Each time Khalib looked like he was leaving I'd hold him back for a few minutes by telling him something or bringing him more lemonade. He loved the Triff's fashion mags from England and sharpening his penknife on the sharpener that would sharpen things in three or four sweeps.

Somewhere in me I knew I was being silly – and, of course, the Triff wouldn't have gone that far carrying Jojo – but I couldn't help being scared of the dog, which seemed to get bigger and bigger in my head every moment the sun went down. Khalib did not seem to care or even notice and he ripped out a whole page from a magazine (without even asking) and folded it into his pocket. He was just getting up from the so-called bench Dad had made – really just a wooden plank across two tree stumps – when there was an evil rustling in the bushes. Of course, I grabbed him and wouldn't let go even when he tried to leave. He must have wanted to get back to his shack before it went dark as there's no electricity but he felt sorry for me I suppose, because he sat down again.

I am not afraid of dogs – really I'm not – but the Triff had put this whole rabies thing in my mind and Devraj from school told me that there were loads of rabid dogs in foreign countries – India especially, and if you got bitten by one, even a tiny little scratch, you would start frothing in the mouth and trying to eat people you loved. Literally tearing off their flesh like zombies. The only cure, he said, was to have massive injections in the stomach twice or three times every single hour for a month at least. This was the most painful place to have an injection, he assured me. More than the eye? I'd asked, and he'd laughed and called me a madhead because no one had injections in the eye. He told me his uncle had been in India's Special Forces and had often endured terrible torture without a whimper, but he had cried like a baby when he had a rabies injection.

Of course, Devraj lies every time he breathes – I swear his uncle is a postman or computer programmer or something – but Dev does know about diseases because his mum is a doctor and *so* nice. I wish she was my mum sometimes. She's beautiful, and at prize-giving she wore a lime-green sari that was beyond loveliness.

Soon there was another noise and, of course, it wasn't the dog, it was the Triff with Jojo, strolling back to the house without a care in the world. She was in a full bloom mood and gave me a big kiss which I didn't really see the point of. She even leaned in to give Khalib one and he looked almost angry. She spoke to him in Greek and he answered her in his gruff single words, shaking his head when she offered him some wine. I told her about the dog and she told me not to worry, but she looked worried and I'm sure she was grilling him about it because she is the biggest worrier in all the plant kingdom. Then she told me to get wood for a fire and I said 'no way, I'm not your slave' and she smiled like she knew I'd say that. She and Khalib did some whispering and she laughed, and then they went together and were quite a long time so I ate three figs and put Jojo to bed.

She came back alone, opened up the retsina and sang to herself as she poured a big glass.

We never even had a fire.

# Ten

Max woke into a dream so hot and strange and beautiful he knew it could not be real. Beams of sunlight slanted though the dim shade. He could smell the sweetness of the wavering bushes outside which scratched at the shutters like old women's fingernails, and through it all he could smell his body, sticky and damp like an over-ripe fruit in the early evening heat. His trousers were bunched by his knees, his underwear slanted on his thighs, his shirt rucked under his arms. A curious but half-remembered nakedness, infantile, exciting. He touched himself, remembering where he was, pleasures past and future. He slid his feet onto the floor and pulled his shorts and trousers up as he stood. A curtained arch separated the bedroom from the kitchen. Flowers were everywhere, in mugs, old bottles, cups and jam jars. The heaped scree from a sweeping lay next to a witch's broom, dust still clinging to slants of light. His eyes, tranquil with sleep, were drawn to a startled mouse, unaccustomed to intruders in its solitary domain – it disappeared in a swift dark line. A crinkled plastic bottle of water, its label faded and tattered, gnawed away perhaps, lay in the sink. Max opened it and sucked at it, allowing washes of sun-warmed water, musty as attics, to flood down his throat. He pulled off his socks, feeling the air between his toes, the uneven softness of the plaster on the soles of his feet. He bundled the socks and tossed them over his shoulder into the room, unaware that he would not think of them again for weeks, that for his feet at least, a liberation of spaciousness was beginning.

He found Tine outside watering the feeble palms, her hair damp from a swim, her dusty travelling clothes discarded and replaced with that same swimsuit he had seen in England, now partly covered with an Indian wrap.

'I woke up in a state of undress,' Max said to her.

She faced him, shaking away tails of hair from her face.

'You looked sweet, asleep with your knickers down. I wanted to have you like that for ever ... innocent as a little boy.'

'... blown like a sailor,' Max replied.

Tine laughed.

'What's with the "knickers"?' Max asked.

'What do you mean?'

'Men don't wear knickers.'

'Pants, underwear, you know. There was something so adorable about you like that. I wanted to remember you exactly as you were, asleep. Mine.'

He liked this, but something about it made him uncomfortable.

'Take a picture next time,' he said.

'Yes.'

'Did you?' he asked, suspicious.

'Of course not.'

She returned to her plants. They watched as a moat of water round a flaccid young tree drained away into the sand.

Max looked at her body; he wanted to fuse her in his memory as she was now. He traced the arc of her in the sand as she bent over the plants. He neared her and put his arms around her waist, crossed them around her hips and, resting his lips on the back of her neck, kissed the knot of vertebra that appeared as she bent her head forward. His elbows pivoting at her hips, he raised his hands, feeling the ripple of her ribs and bringing each palm flat onto a breast.

She placed her hands over his and turned.

'What's wrong?' he asked.

'Nothing,' she replied, breaking away.

It was already a familiar game. She disliked the question; he still did not understand the *nothing* in her answer.

'Hold on, Tine. I want to tell you …' Max spoke to her retreating back '… when I woke up, I felt so … I don't know … pretty much as good as I've ever been.'

She paused and looked at him.

'The thing is,' he made himself go on, 'I've never really said this before … I like you and when I look at you …'

She turned and walked towards him. Max scanned her smiling face for signs of mockery. She took his cheeks in her hands and tilted her lips, stretching them open and covering his mouth, taking Max's tongue and pulling him into her mouth. He gripped her shoulders and they rocked back and forth, pushing into each other as if trying to disappear down the other's throats. Max hooked his thumbs in the shoulder straps of her swimsuit and pulled them down. Over her arms, her waist. When she dropped her hands from his head, it was to allow the looped straps free, and excitement surged in him like heat. She tugged at her wrap and shook it to the floor. She arched her back as he peeled the damp swimsuit over her backside like the finest skin of an onion. He worked the suit down over her thighs, pushing the clinging material as far as he could stretch without breaking contact with her mouth. He didn't want her to change her mind, to stop him, come to her senses – whatever it was that had prevented her before – but she did not; she encouraged the suit down her legs with one squirming shiver of her hips and tossed the skein of material to the side with a flick of her foot. She was naked at last. He dared his hands to the soft rise of her hips, he cupped the muscles of her bottom, hardened by tennis and youth.

He delved between the cheeks as he angled his hands down, edging his fingers deeper, wanting to reach her but primed for her retreat. His fingers found a silky undergrowth and furrowed on into the plump rise of the swell between her legs.

She angled her hips away.

'Let's swim. You haven't even been in the sea,' she said, spinning from him.

Annoyed, he watched her walk off. So he scrutinised her nakedness with as much onanistic pleasure as he could, mapping the shape of her as she walked – if she would not give him what he wanted, he'd take what he could, bank it. She paused at the water's edge, no longer, it seemed, aware of him but contemplating the sea. She was beautiful naked. Even better. She said something to him, but he was not listening, his eyes campaigning over her buttocks, willing her to expose more of herself, his toes digging into the sand as she dived into the water.

She moved through the sea with elegant, effective strokes. When she was fifty metres out, she stopped suddenly and turned to him, shouting – to catch up or something – but he had needed no inducement and was already without clothes, sprinting towards the edge. He thought her shouts were encouragement but recognised they were screams as he launched himself into the water. When he surfaced he saw her hands scissoring in panic. Max slapped his way to her as best he could, making up for his lack of technique through sheer effort and adrenalin.

His body soon met hers.

'Are you OK?' she said, her face taut and flushed.

'What are you talking about? I'm fine. You were the one screaming,' Max panted.

'I was shouting stop. There's a massive rock just under the

water. You can't even see it. I thought you'd break your neck, you were right there. I'm such an idiot.'

Max tried to hug her but she shook him off and swam towards the shore with hard, fast strokes. Bewildered, Max followed her as best he could, alternating between his clumsy crawl and an ungainly, exhausted backstroke.

She was waiting for him where the water shallowed. She grabbed his leg as he passed. Shocked, he blundered backwards, exclaiming with fear and then anger.

'Fuck. Don't do that,' he snapped.

'I'm sorry.'

He saw that her face was taut with emotion.

'I'm so stupid, I meant to tell you when we arrived,' she said, her voice strained. 'I kept meaning to tell you.'

He kissed her and put his arms round her, squeezing her naked body to him, wondering if it would be inappropriate to try to touch her again.

She pointed out the underwater rock.

'It's so dangerous. Sharp, huge, bigger than you'd think.'

Max glanced at its dark mass, its point just under the water. Curious that something so large could be invisible.

'I don't know how I missed it,' he said. 'I must have been so close.'

'You would have smashed your head or ... what would I have done? There's no phone here, no electricity. Sometimes the water's clear and you can see it but sometimes – most of the time – it's hidden. I fucking hate it.'

'We're OK, I'm OK. Nothing happened.' Max put his hand over her mouth. 'Enough of this. We're on holiday and I'm hungry. So hungry that, for the first time today, I am thinking more about food than kissing your tits.'

He dropped his head onto her breasts, but she slipped away from him again and swam back to shore.

Max followed her, sinking to his ears in the water and scrutinising her body as she clambered onto the land. As she stretched one leg onto the rocky edge and slowly pulled herself out, he hungrily inspected the places she so diligently hid from him, relishing images he had seen magnified in so many different shapes from so many angles in pictures. She turned round as if feeling the intrusion and he snapped his eyes away and submerged.

She'd disappeared by the time he'd reached his clothes and he wondered for a moment if she had seen something in him, some truth that had made her retreat. He peered down his nose, following a drop of water until it fell and stained his dusty jeans with a dark smear. He wrapped his T-shirt round the front of him and went into the house to find a clean pair of trousers. Valentine was in the kitchen, burrowing in a cupboard under the sink; objects – a faded plastic sandcastle mould, cleaning products, a deflated beach ball, a cardboard box full of old tools – scattered behind her like debris outside a badger's set.

'Aha,' she announced from within, emerging with two bottles of wine and a couple of unidentified cans. 'Saved from starvation and, more importantly, thirst.' She stood, re-tying the wrap round her waist, a man's blue shirt – her father's – hanging over her hips, torn at one elbow, open low at the neck.

'I like your outfit.' She nodded at his miniskirt and rubbed her hand down his chest and belly. She closed her hand around the knot of the T-shirt and pulled him gently towards her. 'How does it work from behind?'

'You tell me,' he said, feeling himself turned.

'Less is most definitely more,' she said. The T-shirt covered

55

only his front, leaving his buttocks comically bare. She ran fingernails over each cheek, exploring him with an attention that surprised and excited him.

He enjoyed her scrutiny but he worried he should turn and kiss her.

'No, please,' she said, staying his hip, keeping him where he was. She loosed the arms of the T-shirt from the tight knot, and let it fall, baring him completely. He felt her lips slide down his spine, felt her squeeze each cheek of his backside with an intensity, a hunger that astonished him. The idea that she might want to see him, touch and explore him with a desire as strong – perhaps stronger – than his own, arose in him a sense of balance that he had never before considered. He put both hands on the wall when her mouth reached the base of his spine. He moaned as he felt her take hold of his hips. For Max the idea of this vulnerability, of nakedness – while she was clothed – of being kissed, being touched, being the object of pleasure, it was exciting in a way that was overwhelming, and then a voice in him asked him how he appeared, if this was suitable for a man, and he tried to turn.

She held him.

'Please, let me, I want you. I'm so wet.'

He acquiesced – what did it matter? Who could see? And as he felt her tongue delve into him and her hand reach between his legs and grasp his penis, appearances dissolved and there was no space for whispering voices. He leaned his forehead on the wall, surrendering, gasping and pushing against her tongue. She turned him then and took him into her mouth and he saw that her wrap was now bunched up by her waist and her hand was in her knickers, pulsing like a beating heart. Thoughts of delaying himself were overcome by the sight of her squeezing and rubbing between her legs, and he collapsed against the wall and ejaculated with three low moans. Tine doubled and trebled the speed and intensity of her movements but even with the taste of him in her mouth, she could not catch up with her desire and could do nothing but pant as it faded out of reach.

# Eleven

So it was that Weld found himself following a narrow path behind the gymnasium.

Brambles towered on either side of him, darkening the path ahead, and he reminded himself that, had he not been so particularly brave, he might have found it frightening. He quickened his pace anyway, relieved when the path opened up into a clearing where a smouldering fire of rubbish filled the air with the reek of metal and plastic. Bonfires could be amongst the most exciting things in life, and this grey heap of ash, although unprepossessing, was still a bonfire. Weld drew a stick from its scabbard of brambles and delved into the ash, uncovering a blackened can with jagged teeth and a clod of damp and smouldering rags. Another poke disturbed a column of unburned tiny triangles which fell like geometric snow and curled up in the hot ash – hours of dismal maths homework gone, pencilled numbers and red ticks disappearing for ever.

A bell sounded in the school building. There were so many new and unexpected ways to get into trouble at St X's but something as exciting as a fire was sure to be against any number of rules – particularly, Weld reminded himself, when he was meant to be having extra tuition. He dropped the stick and rejoined the path.

After lunch that day, Miss Trench had summoned him and pointed out the way.

'Do you see that path?' She had knotted a tight rope of

sweater in the space between his shoulder blades and thrust him towards the path in question. 'Go along it till you get to the house with the green door.' With each phrase she gave him a push and then pulled him back as if he had been trying to escape. 'Do not leave the path for any reason. Because if I find out – and I will find out – it'll be an MC straight away. Do not dawdle. Do not be late, and one other thing, the most important thing, Mr Beaufinn currently has a handicap. Do you know what a handicap is, young man?

'No, Miss,' Weld had answered reflexively.

'It means, DO NOT STARE. If I find you have been staring, and believe you me, I will find out, then, woe betide you.'

Thinking of Miss Trench's 'woe' and her 'betide' encouraged Weld to run until he might escape the very idea of her. He followed the path as it skirted an enormous field, the gate posts shooting past him at speed, until the path veered off and disappeared before a run-down garden gate amidst a great walled knot of honeysuckle. Weld halted. There was nowhere to go but through the gate – a gate, not a door, and brown not green. He stood on tiptoes but could not see above it. He looked at the ground and then behind him, wondering what he should do. Anything could happen if he went through the wrong gate, and in his recent experience, anything was invariably bad. He checked behind him again, but there was nothing, no sign, just the path he had come on and a glowering sky. He nudged open the gate, ready to run away, and to his relief, there, at the bottom of the most overgrown garden he had ever seen, was a green door. He approached it and rapped at its flaking paint with his soft knuckles.

'Key under the flowerpot, let yourself in,' a voice bellowed from within.

Weld saw the flowerpot immediately; it was cracked and contained the skeleton of some long-dead plant. He pushed it to one side and five gunmetal woodlice scampered over his fingers. He flicked his hand and made a shivering sound, then wiped his fingers and went back for the key. It was cold as only metal can be. He pushed it into the lock and turned.

'Come in, come in, I'm here.'

Yellow paint hung off the wall in a galley kitchen. A sink, old and stained, one saucepan, one almost full bottle of whisky, three empty bottles, one plate, a knife and fork drying in the washstand. There was no oven, just a hotplate. He found himself unnerved by the dirt and sparsity of the place, by the cold and the damp. He passed through the kitchen and into a dark corridor where a golden line of light framed a door.

'I can hear you, so why don't you come on in,' the voice roared.

Weld pushed at the door, but to no effect. He patted for a door handle but found only a rectangular indentation. He put his fingers there and tried to pull, nothing.

'What can you be doing?' the voice demanded from the other side of the door. 'Come in child.'

'I . . .' Weld placed his palms flat on the door and pushed to the left and right; the door slid open on oiled coasters.

'Ah-ha, good lad, you've passed the test. Excellent. I can't bear stupid people. Perhaps it's wrong, I might have been one myself. In truth there may well be thousands, hundreds of thousands, no my boy, millions, bloody millions of people who might, quite possibly, make even me look a dullard, had I the good fortune to meet them – but seeing as you performed so well on the sliding door, I don't suppose I will need to explain further. The world, my dear boy, is full of 'poops – don't you think?'

Weld had no idea what he meant, but he was fascinated, and a little repulsed, by the sound of it.

'That's what I call 'em, nincompoops, the world is teeming with 'em – not their fault, but my friend, remember this, not our bloody fault either.'

Weld stood in the doorway, gazing at the bulky cardigan-clad shoulders wedged in a wheelchair and the mass of speckled grey and leather-brown hair that had delivered this monologue with not even the slightest effort to turn round.

'Static little fellow, aren't you? I presume little ... what did they say, first term here ... eight ... seven?'

'And a half, sir,' Weld announced before he could stop himself.

'Seven and a half, there's an age. First off we will have to attend to this Sir business. Sir indeed. My father was called Sir, Sir Bernard Beaufinn. A nastier man you couldn't find, couldn't pay to see, not even in the circus. So I tend to discourage Sir as it reminds me of that drunken bastard – ha ha, excuse my Saxon.'

Weld smiled at the daring use of 'bastard' which followed not one, but two 'bloody's', and then not liking your father – openly – wasn't there a Holy Commandment Of God saying that was a sin? Weld breathed the musty strangeness of the room deep into his chest, ransacking its corners with his eyes. Never had he seen so many books, such intriguing chaos. Mr Beaufinn was seated in front of him before an electric fire in which three bars blazed. Shelves covered either side of the fireplace, packed with books, and all around columns of volumes rose from the floor like stalagmites. Amidst the books and papers, on the floor, and even balanced on some of the book towers, were half-constructed home-made electronics, with wires and graphite strips, multicoloured resistors, two-way switches, tiny light bulbs and exciting little dials –

fascinating objects that lay about the room like the skeletons of robotic rodents. Most exciting of all, on the wall behind the teacher, there was the stuffed head of a wild boar, moth-eaten but still ferocious with its mouth open and one enormous tusk sticking out like an afterthought.

'Take the back leg off an elephant with one charge, that beast could. Still, unlikely he would ever come across one, *Elephantidae* and *Sus Scrofa* not being found on the same continent – except in a zoo, of course, ha ha ha.'

Weld wondered what would happen if he came across such a beast on the way back to school.

'Come, come my young friend, we are not going to achieve any of the dizzying heights of scholarship that are no doubt the ambition of your parents whilst you dally in the doorway. There is more to me than the slightly balding back of my head and furthermore you are encouraging an exodus of heat particles to dilly out the room on a Judaic scale. Dallying and dillying classic 'poop behaviour. Shut the door and come over here. As you may have deduced, being the intelligent young fellow that we now both know you are, I cannot easily turn round as I have cracked my pelvis thus making me entirely non-operational, no more use than that blasted Nazi wireless over there.' He pointed to the corpse of a radio on a chair in the corner of the room, its back off and wires spilling out like entrails.

Eager to obey the tiny portion of this speech he could understand, Weld slid the door closed and approached. He wondered when The Handicap would become clear and hoped that whatever it was, a rash on the skin, or a nose like a rotting mushroom, it would not cause him to stare. Weld offered up a prayer and stepped in front of the wheelchair.

But it was a man, just a man. Quite old in fact. There was even something of the Father Christmas about him, or Father

Christmas' brother, younger but fatter. A mass of beard that smothered his cheeks, mouth and jaw and tapered like melting wax around his plump face. There was no sign of the teacher's mouth until he talked, and then it was a wet and lightless hole. His fleshy skin was surprisingly pale although his nose was quite pink, almost red, but not as red as the rims of his eyes, eyes that were tightly closed. Perhaps, Weld thought, this was The Handicap.

'In front of me at last? Good, and as you can no doubt see if your eyes are open, which would be more common, mine are not. Forgive me, but there are so few surprises these days and I am *relishing* this one. Who would have imagined as this week made its cold, wet and bloody depressing beginning, that I would encounter a problem as entirely unexpected as you.' He reached out his large hands and grasped Weld by the arms, feeling his way down as if checking the boy was real. Then he rubbed one hand over Weld's face and the other over his head, and ran his hands over the boy's shoulders and down his back, palpating him like a piece of meat.

'Not much to you is there. Introduce yourself, dear boy, come on,' he said, letting go.

Weld reached out his hand towards the man as he had been instructed to do since the age of four.

'How do you do sir? My name is Weld.'

'Richard Beaufinn.' He snapped open his eyes and seeing the frail hand before him fell on it like an eagle on a vole, pumping it with unbridled vigour.

'Pleased to meet you,' he replied with a roaring. 'Now what will you be calling me. You know the boys call me Beef – behind my back – perhaps you haven't heard them yet, as you are only a Mite?'

Weld shook his head emphatically.

'Could be worse, of course. Jackson's known as Dam because

63

he looks like a bloody beaver and then there's your fragrant teacher, Trench-Foot, that's hardly flattering. God knows what others have sprouted since I've been off with this blasted fracture. Now, Mister Beaufinn is a bit of a mouthful but it's acceptable and better than sir, so if it's just the two of us you can call me Beau – but that's our little secret.'

Weld nodded.

'Look at you, not at all how I expected.' He reached over and gave Weld a shake. 'A largish sneeze from me might blow you clean out of the window – an act called defenestration. Are you really seven and a half?'

Weld nodded.

'And what is defenestration?'

'Being blown out of the window?' he replied.

'Very good. FULL MARKS.' Beaufinn bellowed with such a force that Weld felt he might well have been blown out the window had it been open. He had never met an adult like this, like someone out of a story, but much better.

'Now you reprobate,' Beaufinn said, scowling, changing his tone unexpectedly and moving his wheelchair half a foot closer to the boy. 'It's time to explain why you are so bloody late.'

Weld looked down at the floor, his story shattering, disappointment flooding his pores.

'Tardiness is a well-known feature of 'poops. Are you a 'poop my boy?'

Weld wondered whether perhaps he was.

'I don't want to be, sir.'

'Good ambition boy, good ambition. Now it's past four thirty, you arrived at four twenty-one. In the future, it is better you arrive at four on the dot. Do you know why?'

Weld shook his head without looking up.

'Four o'clock is Tea Time – a unique moment in the life of an English Gentleman. A time designated in all likelihood by

God (an Englishman) and all his holy angels (Englishmen too). Thirty-six minutes ago all the saints and dearly departed sat down for a cup of single estate, hand-picked Darjeeling with the Creator and all our ancestors and there is no reason why we should do any differently. Do you drink Tea, Boy?'

'Yes sir.'

'Good – but desist with the sir or I shall be obliged to hack you into pieces and stack you in the wood pile – which, between you and me, is full of little chaps like you. Or perhaps if I am feeling particularly brutal, I will feed you to Fynton.' He gestured to the wild boar. 'He can be woken you know.'

He looked at Weld for a while then gave him a large and knowing wink. With a sharp reverse tug on the wheel rims and a powerful push and pull action, he spun the chair a hundred and eighty degrees and whizzed out of the room with impressive speed, hardly slowing to open and close the door behind him.

Weld sat down on a stool, swept the room with his eyes and smiled for the first time in weeks.

# Twelve

The sun had set with a radiance that glorified every object and made them seem even more intensely wonderful to each other. For those moments when they were drenched in its pink light, it seemed that everything was unobstructed, full of beauty, and the promise of beauty. Max gathered the dry wood that was scattered all about from winter storms and constructed a fire. Tine unearthed heavy salt-bleached rugs and cushions from a chest that scurried with spiders, and constructed a luxurious outdoor den in front of the house. The wood caught with dramatic snaps as if it had been yearning for years to release its energy. Tine dotted the sand about them with thin golden candles which she lit with a taper dipped in Max's fire.

Max succumbed to the cushions and rugs, his hands behind his head, his eyes wide to the stars. He was pleased and he wondered if now, instead of being apart from everything, he was a part of everything. At last, he could join the tribe of everybody, this group that never seemed to pick him for their team. Perhaps this was love. He had finally made it to love. In so many stories, in so many films – nearly all of them in fact – this was the qualifier. The point where ever after began.

But there was something in this paradise he could not quite pin down – a worry, like fear, but not fear. He was happy – who wouldn't be? Excited too, but it was an excitement that was almost indistinguishable from anxiety. Perhaps it was the way Tine kept slipping out of his grasp at the last moment, always defining what the last moment was. He wished she would let him . . . *act*. Not simply descend and take him in her mouth, suck at him like a vampire. Of course he enjoyed it, he had no choice but to enjoy it, like ducks have no choice but to sleep if their heads are tucked beneath their wings.

He wondered if he was doing anything wrong, putting her off in some way. Perhaps he should be more forceful, or more gentle. Did she find something about him unsettling or even disgusting; his penis, was it disappointing, ugly? He suspected it was ugly, so why shouldn't she?

He expelled air through pursed lips.

No.

She had asked him on this holiday. She smiled when she looked at him. She must like him. Perhaps she'd never done it, never had sex. That was the reason, it had to be. He'd let her take her time. It should be her decision what she did with her body and when she did it. And what a body it was. He replayed the sight of her pulling off her swimsuit, of her fingers pushed into her knickers, of her climbing out of the water. A part of him wished he could possess this image, turn it, magnify it, contain it . . .

'You look absorbed,' Valentine said, startling him as she appeared from the shadows. 'Have you moved my swimsuit?'

'What?'

'My swimsuit, have you seen it?'

'No. Not since you last had it on.'

'It's weird. I left it on the wall. Are you sure you didn't take it.'

'Actually, I'm wearing it under my T-shirt.'

'I bet you'd love to. Boys always secretly want to try on girls' clothes.'

'Girls always want to get boys to dress up like them.'

Tine laughed.

'What were you thinking about?' she asked. She stood over

him clutching one of the bottles of wine and the dented cans she'd unearthed from under the sink.

'You naked.'

'I am naked,' she joked, descending to him, 'under my clothes.'

'You're never naked, that's the problem,' Max said.

Valentine stood up again as if pulled. 'What do you mean?'

'Nothing.'

'You can't say that now. I took everything off this afternoon, didn't I? I was naked swimming. What d'you mean?'

'Nothing, it's nothing really.'

She stepped away from him. 'Just say whatever it is. You can't say something like that and then pretend it's nothing. It's not fair.'

'Look ...' he said to her back. 'It came out wrong. It's just that whenever we are doing anything, you know, sexual, it's amazing and I am there ... and I feel you are too, and it looks like we are both really getting into it. I mean we should be by now, shouldn't we? But then you just stop or pull away.'

'I make you come.'

'Yes. It's just that ...'

'Don't you like it when I suck you?'

'Of course, it's just you don't let me ... We're on holiday together, I've never even ...'

'What? Stuck your fingers in me? Your cock?'

'Look, I'm sorry I mentioned ...'

She paced off into the darkness and there were no further words but the wood in the fire snapping and cracking like the thoughts in their minds.

After a few minutes Valentine came back into the light and crouched down in front of Max.

'I fancy you more than anyone. I've never done it like this, you know, slowly, I mean ... usually I ... look, it's not just for me Max, it's for both of us. I'm sure all the other girls you've been with have been ... you know, much more, well ... I am trying to do it this way because I want it to be different.'

'Of course, I'm sorry. I'm really sorry.' Max opened his arms and they hugged each other.

'Valentine,' he whispered.

'Yes?'

'I really haven't had many gir—'

She sealed his mouth with her hand.

'I don't want to hear about your filthy history. Let's have some wine.'

Max held her hand on his lips and breathed in the perfume on her wrist: sandalwood or some night- blooming flower. He slid her hand across his mouth so her fingertips were beneath his nose.

'I can smell you.'

'My perfume, it's ...'

'No, you. I can smell your pussy on your fingers.'

She squeezed his nose between finger and thumb.

'Stop it, you disgusting boy, and get that wine open.'

Max worked the cheap and brittle corkscrew into the tight cork and levered it out with a pop that cleared the air. He sloshed the wine into two thick tumblers and they toasted each other.

'*Lochaim*,' she said.

'Oh really.'

'It's Jewish.'

'Jewish? I don't know that language.'

'Israeli then, Hebrew! I don't know, my friend Naomi says it when we are in the pub. It's lovely, it means *to life*!'

'Yes, I know,' he said smiling. '*Lochaim*.' They clinked glasses. Tine knocked her wine back in three forceful glugs – surprising him.

'What d'you mean, you know?' she asked, refilling her glass.

'What?'

'*Lochaim*,' she repeated.

'My father was Jewish,' Max said.

'I'm sorry.'

'That he was Jewish?'

'No silly.' She touched his leg. 'That he's *was*.'

'Oh yes, thanks.'

'You've never mentioned him.'

'I must have ... didn't I?'

'No, I supposed he must have left or something.'

'No.'

'So does that make you Jewish?'

'It goes through the mother. My mother's Catholic.'

'But surely you're half Jewish.'

'I was brought up a Catholic.'

'But if you could choose?'

'I've never really thought about it.'

Max found himself wondering about it though, how it might have been.

'How were they?'

'What?'

'Your parents?' Valentine asked.

'Oh fine, you know, I've got nothing to complain about. They sacrificed a lot and all that.'

Tine surveyed her glass. It was already nearly empty.

'You need to catch up. Come on,' she demanded.

They clinked again and Tine threw her wine back and Max finished his, and for a few moments they were both coughing and laughing as the rough wine soused their throats.

She refilled both their glasses and took a gulp.

'Wow, it doesn't really improve with age – no wonder it was

70

under the sink. Maybe it's to unblock it. The retsina's better I swear, drink up.'

'I need food,' Max said.

'Eating's for poofs,' she said.

'Oh so that's what a poof is,' Max laughed. 'I thought it was more to do with my wish to have my arse fucked.'

'Do you?' she asked.

'Want to eat? Yes. Want a cock in my bum? Definitely not.'

'What a pity.'

'What are you saying? Would that turn you on?' Max asked.

'Well,' she laughed, 'you do have a very sweet little bottom.' She reached round and cupped a cheek.

'And it's going to stay that way,' he said turning over. 'Now where's the food?'

Tine dashed off to the house, returning with the two tins, forks and a pair of pliers.

'There's no key ...' she said, gripping the metal tongue of one of the tins with the pliers. 'Some sort of fish I think.' She twisted the metal lid off with practised skill. 'Oooh, it's a winner, ladies and gentleman. For one night only, I offer you ... Musky Octopus ... dig in.'

She passed the tin and fork to Max.

'Is it safe? It stinks.'

'Musky Octopus never smells good. Even to another Musky Octopus.' Tine took another gulp of wine.

'Is it off, or just repulsive?' Max asked, forking a dirty pink segment of tentacle into his mouth. 'It's not too bad at first,' he said chewing tentatively, 'and then ...' He spluttered, spitting bits of chewed octopus out into the sand, 'kind of disgusting.'

'That'll be the musk you're enjoying,' she said. 'Try the other tin.'

Max gargled some of the wine and spat it into the fire. Then he took the pliers and opened the second can. Tine snuggled up to him and peered into the container.

'Oh my God,' Max said, peering into the can in the flickering light of the fire. 'What now, eyeballs in tomato sauce?'

'No, you fool,' Tine said, reaching over and popping one of the spheres into her mouth. 'They're meatballs and delicious.'

Max tried one and whooped.

'Food at last,' he said, chomping away. 'Do you want any more?'

Tine shook her head and sipped her wine, watching as he upended the can into his mouth, welcoming the loosening she could feel in her body from the alcohol.

There was a cub-like quality to Max as he excavated the remaining sauce with his fingers and swigged his wine with a loud and happy slurp. She found the stain of tomato on the side of his mouth either endearing or repulsive, she was not sure which.

He smiled at her, noticing the focus of her gaze. Then he was on her, tumbling, brutal and intent. He lost himself in the consciousness of his tongue, entwining in her mouth until she angled away.

'Let's have more wine,' she demanded, examining the now empty bottle.

'You do it.'

She stood, ignoring the impatience in his voice. She uncorked the second bottle, glugging a quarter of it from the neck. She proffered it to Max. He shook his head. She looked at him lying beneath her. She took another swig. Then she fell onto him.

Max tried to ignore the sudden brusqueness of her movements, tell himself this is what he wanted, convince himself that she was simply being decisive. Her body felt tough and

72

sinewy, her movements hard and insistent. She tugged at his hair, dug her nails into his scalp. When his leg was between her thighs, she scissored her legs open as if he'd released a spring-loaded catch. She pushed herself against him, rubbing her pelvis on his thigh as if trying to reach an itch. He was about to pull away from her when she pushed his hands up her shirt, placing them on her breasts, her nipples hard in the middle of each palm. This silenced the chatter in his brain. Focused his intent.

She put her mouth onto his ear.

'Fuck me.'

Now? he thought.

Suddenly, he was not quite ready. He wanted to be ready. He wanted for it to happen, it was the next step, it was what people did. But he'd thought it would be ... more of an unfolding, more because he was desired, because of something *he* would do ... something that grew, ripened.

This was wrong, like a fish slapping panicked on the bank of a river. But he knew he must act. That's what men did.

He pushed his mouth against hers, filled her mouth with his tongue. He wrapped his arm round her back, angled his leg away to find purchase on the ground, and clutching her to him, turned them both so he was on top of her. Her eyes widened at this. Panicked. He wondered if perhaps he had misinterpreted her, misheard those words, or she hadn't meant them, or had wanted him to, but not *now*. She hadn't said *now*. He was the one who'd seized *now*, leapt on her. He did not have his condoms anyway. Now he was soft. He moved his weight onto his arms and arched away from her so she could escape – but she did not. She yanked at the rip cord of her trousers, tugged them down, tugged her underwear down, pulled up her knees, flicked her clothes away.

He looked. Mesmerised.

Naked from waist to toe, a faint wedge of paleness from a few hours in the sun, streaked with shadows in the candlelight; the triangle of pubic hair, blond, a thin line bunched darkly, like desert vegetation following an underground stream. He placed his hand on the concave stretch that was her belly, letting two fingers rest in the yawn of her navel. He slipped downwards, grazing the tight skin of her waist with his fingertips. He reached her hair line and the muscles of her belly hardened as she raised herself up onto her elbows. She stayed his hand and drew him, yanked him, into a smothering kiss. She released his hair from her fingers and twisted onto her belly like a fish flipping itself, her movement so brusque his chin bounced off her head.

She lifted up her hips in front of his face.

'What about ... protection?' he ventured desperately, confused by her sudden assertiveness.

She looked round at him, as if from afar.

'What?'

'Protection, birth control ... condoms.'

'Just fuck me,' she said, sinking her face into the pillow.

The sight of her made him hard, drove away all confusion. Her hand appearing between her legs, a finger following the line of flesh, beaded and uneven like a drip of wax. Her fingers withdrew and he heard a quiet spit before they were back spreading moisture.

'Fuck me,' she repeated.

He worked his trousers over his erection, pulled off his T-shirt and tossed it away. It landed too near the fire. He crawled over to it and pulled it free, scuttling back: naked, erect, ridiculous. Valentine remained, her pelvis in the air, her face in the cushion. Max manoeuvred himself behind her, brushed sand off his knees and knelt, pushing the head of his penis at the snug of her.

'Wet,' she ordered.

He licked his hand and coated the head of his penis until it glossed in the firelight. He tried again. Pushed it into her. She was tight, the opening of her clinging to him as he pushed. He spat on his hand and covered as much of his penis and the stretched split of her as the moisture would allow. He sucked his cheeks in, drawing saliva into his mouth and applying it in the dry night air.

He edged in and out. He worked his way deeper, deeper until she began to slick and give. As soon as she felt him, the slide of him, she smashed her hips to him. She hooked her forearms under the cushion pressing her face down, clawing through the blankets into the sand. Each thrust from Max made her grind her face further down as if she were trying to break through the surface tension of the ground and submerge. Max rocked back and forth within her, as if worrying a loose tooth, burrowing down the sand under his knees. Then he was as far into her as he could go, she was crouched tight so the bones at the top of her thighs pointed through the stretched muscle of her buttocks. He placed his arms around her waist and held her to him. She cried out, a moan – pleasure? Her arms were clutching at the back of her head, a thick twist of her hair in each hand.

'Are you OK?' he asked, rubbing the steep slope of her back in a gesture devoid of all meaning except the desire to continue.

'Are you OK?' he asked, wondering if he was causing her pain.

She surfaced from the pillow and pushed herself back on him.

'Go on, go on,' she gasped.

He grasped the side of her hips, pushed her away and pulled her to him with a slap. Again and again with more force and velocity. Tine pressed her face deeper into the cushion, grunting into the foam at each thrust.

The wet friction of her, tight around him, the sight of her open, stretched around him, the cleft of her body, it tore a climax out of him with a final lunge. Like a lepidopterist mounting a tough-skinned insect with a too blunt pin he screwed himself into her.

He collapsed on her back and they toppled to the ground, Max's penis softening in her, one arm wrapped around her chest, the other around her thighs, keeping his pelvis hard against her. Scared of what would happen when they parted.

She made a noise like a cough or a cry.

'Tine, are you OK? Did it hurt? I'm sorry.'

She turned to him, her eyes dead.

'No it's fine. It really is.'

# Thirteen

Bells marked the movement of time at St Xavier's but for boys who had lived fewer years than they had fingers this offered little sense of progression. Time looped, until an end was in sight, or until the more advanced skills of institutional life could be learned. As in hospitals, the military service and prisons, there was only one goal: going home. To hope for, even to consider this, too early was a strategy fraught with incapacitating repercussions.

'Lights out,' came the nightly call.

Weld stared at the light blue curtain at the end of his bed, drawn as far towards the end of the cubicle wall as would balance the security of there being a world outside – where, somewhere, lights would be burning – with the privacy to allow whatever unguarded thoughts possessed him. Lying in his cubicle with Heavy the Bear, he attempted to calculate a conceivable amount of time until the end of term. It was still September, after that would be October; a good month usually because it held his birthday, like a huge oyster might hold a pearl. He wondered about pearls for a while, his Ma had a string of yellowy white ones he used to grasp and suck when he was little.

They were 'fake', he now remembered her saying. The word had had a magical sound, like something that glittered. Then he'd found out that there were real things and there were fake things – although at the time, he'd suspected fake was better. Real pearls must be wet or messy, or smell bad, or live under the sea. He had a fake fried egg that had come with his toy oven. Its yolk was so yellow, like the best colouring-in pen ever. He wished he had a colouring-in pen that could make all that yellow in one stroke. A corner of the egg was chewed away where he had fed it to Boris the dog, before Boris had gone. A real egg fried, or scrambled egg for breakfast was one of the worst things ever, so a make-believe egg, a fake egg, was better. Most likely it was the same for pearls, he'd thought now he was older he knew. Fake was bad, a grown-up make believe when something real could not be found.

Ma did have a real pearl he remembered. It was dark and silver and big like a blob. A black pearly, she had said, like a pirate would have. Owning such a magical thing confirmed a specialness in her which − although he did not need confirming − he loved to consider. Especially at the beginning of night when the hope of light was so distant. He thought of the morning when everything would be reborn with one flick of a switch. He wished there was a night-light, like at home, even a small one, burning away like an echo of love. He turned over in the creaky iron bed; yearning for light brought the terrors of the night, as sure as bleeding brought sharks.

September−October−December, then home. They were already a little into September and they went home a bit into December, so these two chunks probably made a month and then there was October, that meant two months, which was eight weeks. Eight weeks could be seen as four, two-week parts, so by this time next week, there would be less than two of what he had already done ... and his birthday period hardly even counted as proper days, in the way of things to dread ...

Then the terrible abstraction of November appeared,

swimming up like the shadow of a fish, intensifying until it crashed onto hope like a falling anvil ... unless ... could November have been before September? No, he realised it could not; before September was summer, and obviously November wasn't after December, and now he remembered, his Pa's birthday was in November because he and his Mummy had made a cake last year and he had licked the buttery brown mix straight from the bowl and wondered why anyone even bothered to put cakes in the oven ... that had been November and it was cold, freezing cold ... so November was real and that meant ... three months ...

Despair.

No.

Duvet over head. Trapped in a cave hundreds of feet beneath the ground. Explorer. Weld Of The North. No one knows. Air running out. Brave explorer. Alone. Not even a Bear for company. Breathe, Weld, breathe. Solid rock above, solid rock below, too much – even for the Brave Explorer. Seven more breaths. One ... two ... three ... four ... five-six-seven. Freedom. Sweet fresh air. Cheering crowds. Reunited with his Bear.

Weeks could be considered, a month perhaps – but not months. Better to think about his toy box: Meccano sets III-VI (missing the essential pulley his cousin had lost), Lego in all its magical forms, a tank that had never worked, powered by batteries which had leaked a green toxic crust, a leather shepherd's hat from Peru, Justin Time the stuffed hedgehog. He'd tried to love him, really he had, but he never could – that's why he was in the toy box, not here on his bed like Heavy, who was Pooh Bear's brother. Actually, Heavy had been Pooh Bear, but he got worn out and his Ma had re-covered him in a darker material and at first Weld had been very upset because he had not minded the worn-out Pooh Bear at all. He had not minded the holes and he liked pulling out the fluff and stuffing it back in. But now Pooh was gone – a whole part of his life taken away for ever. One moment he was there and then gone for ever, without him being asked – what else might happen in this world? His Ma had told him that Pooh was still here, but with a winter coat. She was upset, he could see, and he didn't want to make her cry, so he'd pretended that he didn't care, but the fact remained, Pooh was gone and he didn't touch the re-covered bear for a long time – not until it occurred to him that the newly covered bear was not Pooh, but his long-lost brother, Heavy. That was why he was with him now – even if all the things he loved were far away, he still had Heavy because he needed his protection. Weld gave the bear a squeeze and thought of bears and Beaufinn's inventions, and his Mummy's hugs and Fynton the Boar ... and sleep took over his thoughts and time paused until the inhuman clatter of brass that was the wake-up bell yanked the school awake like an electric shock.

When a day started well it was a general sign that something awful might happen. For reasons he had never questioned, Weld had taken to interpreting any vicissitudes in the school's incrementally detailed routine as meaningful omens. If there was golden syrup instead of sugar on their porridge that was a good sign; wearing his nicest socks before Thursday was inviting trouble. A particularly weighty and complex omen lay in the choice of Eucharistic prayer during morning mass. There were four in all, each of different lengths – obviously the shorter Eucharistic prayers, III and II, were the best; II was the shortest, then III, I and IV. However, if Fr Le Saux was saying mass, everything changed – even if he chose Eucharistic Prayer Number IV, which was the longest one, it did not matter because he spoke the words with such astonishing speed that it was only possible to hear certain parts. As a result, Weld and many of the boys listened to those parts and sometimes found themselves praying during them. In the hands of Fr Le Saux, Eucharistic Prayer Number I was also exciting because it was used only on special occasions and contained strange names such as *Melchizedek* and *Perpetua* – like characters from a magic book.

Weld hoped, as he sat in Morning Studies before prayers, that the prefect who would stride into the classroom with the post would be wearing a bright red V-neck pullover. This would be a good sign for the day, very good. Prefects could MC you whenever they felt like it and wear whatever colour pullover they wanted – as long as it was not light blue or green. These particular shades were called *colours* and were reserved as awards for boys who had done something special in rugby or cricket.

When the prefect strode into the class, Weld saw he was wearing a pullover the colour of sand – which was probably a bad sign: brown would be OK, yellow excellent. The prefect lounged by the door and snapped the elastic band off the uneven wad of post and doubled it over his wrist in a clever, grown-up way. There were rumours of a bundle of elastic bands bigger than a football in the prefects' common room, hundreds of thousands of them, maybe a million. It would be a wonderful thing to see. The prefect flicked through the post calling names in his nearly grown-up voice and passing out letters. Every boy listened for the sound of his own name while the prefect gloried in the importance of his voice amidst the hush of the classroom. It was a terrible thing to share a name with a boy who got loads of post. And a trick too low – even for Linnet who had a brother in the top year and was the worst tormentor in the class – to pretend to someone that they had received a letter, or worse a parcel, when there was nothing.

Weld found his attention drifting away from the prefect's voice, which was good because hoping for a letter would make anyone sad. Instead he emptied out the pencil shavings from the inkwell on his desk, and constructed the sort of fortifications that might hold off an attack from Julius Caesar's Fifth Legion. Caesar was preparing a merciless bombardment of banana-scented rubber crumbs when it became clear to Weld that everyone was looking at him and laughing.

'Weld!' the prefect bellowed.

His name. A new name. Weld.

Before it had belonged to his parents but now his own name was lost and this was him. Christian names were not used at St X's, even amongst friends. They were for home and, like goodnight kisses, were not part of school life.

'Earth calling Weld, come in Weld.'

A riot of laughter, sallies of grunts and insulting groans. Weld flushed with embarrassment – but before the rush of inevitable tears, the prefect restored order.

'Settle down, you Mites,' he demanded, clapping his hands.

As the lowest of the low, they were called Mites. As well as being a name that indicated insignificance, there was also a certain degree of protection that came with the title. It was not *on* to bully a Mite and certain forms of intolerable behaviour – particularly any sign of 'wetness' such as homesickness – might be forgiven in the first term, with the explanation: 'He's just a Mite.'

Weld swept away his battle re-enactment as the prefect neared, but instead of a rebuke, the boy delivered a letter. Weld's eyes widened with pleasure. He hadn't dared to hope for a letter so soon as he'd already had one the week before. The bell went for morning prayers and he lingered with his letter as his classmates charged towards the door. His name and address were cramped on a parchment-effect blue envelope of the type that came in a boxed set with a see-through plastic lid and a strip of navy blue ribbon. He pushed the letter into his pocket and caught up with the end of the queue which was marching into chapel.

As his knees pressed cold against the wooden kneeler, he thought about his letter and allowed his imagination to bask in the warmth that lay within the folded pages, radiating against his hip like a pocket warmer. The last 'Amen' of morning prayers heralded a stampede to the refectory, where beside a bowl of porridge, a rasher of angry pink bacon lay like an isthmus in a sea of watery tomato.

After breakfast he wandered down the long corridors, turning over the letter but putting off opening it because he wanted to savour the anticipation. It was only as the bell for class sounded that he realised he had delayed too long because now he would have to wait until First Rec. He rushed to the classroom and folded the letter back into his pocket.

Miss Trench proceeded into the room at the very moment the final bell sounded, and the wall clock clicked to nine. She did this always, everywhere she went, so it was natural for the boys to suspect that she possessed some sort of dark power, or even a remote control in her bag. When Trench entered the pupils jumped up with an alacrity that tended to send a book or pencil case crashing to the floor and earn the offender, and all those in his vicinity, a tirade of humiliation. Today nothing fell, but rather than walk to her desk and arrange her educational instruments, Miss Trench paused at the door.

'I am standing here asking myself if you are either the least intelligent class I have ever taught, or the most idle. It is far too dark for any boy to do any work in this room, be it reading, arithmetic or writing. This little switch here activates the electric lights. Surely this is not news to you. Can anyone inform me why the lights are not on? Perhaps you have already mastered reading? No longer need classes in basic arithmetic? We shall see. If only you understood the difficulties you create for yourselves ... this is precisely the sort of lost opportunity boys like you, who are so far behind where you should be, simply cannot afford.'

It was a dark morning, but no one had dared consider the possibility of being allowed to switch on anything as significant as a light. The Mites were beginning to understand that it was wiser to keep one's head down and stay within the herd. Trench swept her gaze like a searchlight over each of the boy's faces, seeking out signs of guilt or rebellion. Finding none she sighed, flicked on the light and walked to her desk.

The first period was Reading and she had started them with *Oliver Twist*. 'Great Literature for Small Boys,' she had called it.

'It seems unlikely this morning that anyone will have prepared chapter 3 as I instructed yesterday. Why is it unlikely Davies?'

Davies was almost Weld's friend – at least as much, or even a bit more than he was anyone else's. He lived on an island at the other side of the world and had arrived at the school as dark as the gravy that covered their lunch. Each day that passed, he became paler.

'Because it was too dark to read properly Miss?'

'Exactly. Now tell me Davies, since you are so clever, if you knew it was too dark why did you not turn the lights on? You did have lights in your classroom in the Cook Islands?'

'No Miss.'

'Don't you no Miss me. Of course you had lights. Was *The Island School* not a Catholic establishment?'

'Establishment Miss?'

'Institution, Davies, or in this case school. Was it Catholic?'

'Yes Miss, I think so.'

'You think so . . . well then I can assure you it had lights.'

'No Miss.'

'Don't you lie to me, boy, or I'll have you standing outside this door before you know where you are and woe betide you when Brother Noonan finds out you are lying because one thing he *won't* tolerate is a liar.'

'I'm not a liar,' Davies said simply.

That was the thing about Davies, he was dark and compact and had confidence in what he was, and what he was not, so he sometimes said things in his soft and certain accent that made you think he might not be your friend.

'There's no lights at my school, Miss – my old school – no electricity, no classroom. We sit every day under palm thatch beside the banyan tree – except in the rainy season – and then we go home.'

'Well you can thank the merciful Lord that you have come to a proper school with walls and electricity. Sit down Davies and stop smirking.'

'Miss?'

'Sit down you tiresome boy. We will now begin with reading and I hope for your sakes that you put in some preparation last night.'

Trench was a woman who believed in order and routine, but she liked to hone the idle inclinations of her charges by setting as many traps as she could muster.

'Arlington.'

Arlington – bespectacled, eager, terrified – was ready, desperate not to let his equally bespectacled and eager father down, to fulfil the myths of midnight-feasting, heroism and derring-do that Mr Arlington had fabricated to disguise his own decade of terror from his family, his colleagues at the bank, and most of all, himself. Arlington's book was open and he had been fearfully rehearsing the first sentence of the piece throughout Miss Trench's diatribe. As soon as he heard his name he launched into the first words, like a novice parachutist who leaps out the plane rather than suffer a moment more terror.

'Silence. We will *not* commence with you today, Arlington. We will begin at the end of the alphabet . . . and since we have no Zebardee, no Xenon, and mercifully, no Yavov, we find ourselves with you Weld. Begin.'

Weld was surprised, but not panicked. He had not been able to prepare any of the reading because his entire study period had been taken up by copying out his essay, entitled *Where I Live*, attempting to wrestle legibility from a hand that seemed not his own, a limb in rebellion, swooping, dancing and shaking with ungovernable energy. Reading, he could always do. It was something he remembered rather than learned. Words were unified objects to him, independently recognisable; he no more saw them as being built of letters than people recognised each other as particular compilations of vein, muscle, bone and blood.

Weld opened the book and flashed his eyes over the words. He was a little frightened to see three unfamiliar shapes – *sinecure*, *impious* and *profane* – but he began anyway, hardly hesitating as he came across the first curiosity:

'. . . would not have been a signcure.'

'What is a signcure Weld?'

'I don't know Miss.'

'Neither do your classmates, I presume. See-nay-cure is the word and it is uncommon, I'll admit. I won't ask if anyone knows its definition, because you will not know and I'm certain none of you idle creatures will have bothered to look it up. A *sinecure* is a paid position with little or no work – precisely what you wretches hope to find in the hard world of employment that awaits you. Unfortunately for you boys, a *sinecure* is awarded for merit rather than idleness – at least, that is the case in what remains of the British Empire. Resume Weld.'

He read on, keenly aware of the proximity of *impious* – a word that looked not only unlikely, but impossible, a word designed to fell him; *impi* and then *ous*. But just as Weld was about to fall before it, he caught sight of *pious* hidden within, like a nocturnal monster that is only a chair with a shirt on it when the light comes on. He ventured *im* and then *pious* and it seemed to work. *Profane* he leapt over like a low fence and galloped through the rest of the paragraph without incident.

'Impressive, as always, Weld. Your reading is among the best in this class. What remains unimpressive is why the rest of your work cannot be of this quality. We know the answer, of course, do we not Weld? Idleness, sheer idleness. Urquhart, begin.'

Weld looked down at his text, relieved the attack had been so swift, and for the next thirty-five minutes he surrendered himself to the exhilarating woes of poor Oliver's life.

With the noise of the bell fading and perhaps a twitch of pleasure, Miss Trench announced that their next adventure would be Double Mathematics. For Weld, this was a cold world once known as *sums*, but even with the more mysterious name *Mathematics*, it was no better. As sure as the grey streaks of rain slashing down the windows on this depressing morning, it would be a particularly slow and disagreeable stretch of time.

Numbers had no colour, no characteristic other than being right or wrong – and the curmudgeonly thing about them was that so many more of them were wrong than right. For Weld, they were dark and negative things.

He considered that it would be more than an hour before he could open the letter in his pocket and suddenly he yearned for his mother, yearned to hear her voice in her writing, imagine her hand scratching out the words for him. Perhaps she would have a surprise for him. His greatest hope, more than anything in the whole world, was that she might tell him that it had all been a terrible mistake and he could come home. But he knew this would not happen – because if it were possible, he would never have been sent to St X's in the first place ... no, he must dream of something easier, flying or being invisible, presents waiting at home, a new dog. He hoped she would not write that anything had changed; been painted or thrown out, or even moved about. It was essential that at home everything stayed the same.

He could not resist any longer, he slid his hand into his pocket and allowed himself to feel the paper smooth against his knuckles. He grazed the other side of the envelope with his fingertips; indents of his mother's pen under his fingers, his name, his real name, in her hand. He knew the pen. It was silver and heavy, covered with patterns of flowers, and was meant to live in a smart leather box, but most of the time it was lost between the piles of papers and bills that crowded her desk. He delved his fingers deeper, tracing the address of his school on the envelope, tiny crests and folds made by her ... and then ... something wet ... stickiness like an open wound. He snatched his fingers out of his pocket and passed them under his nose – melted chocolate. He pulled out the letter, horrified, desperate to wipe it clean.

Miss Trench, keen as a sparrowhawk, caught the movement. 'Weld, what's that? Bring it here.'

The static terror of prey. He tried to hide the letter but once Miss Trench had locked in, there was no chance of escape.

'This instant.'

He shuffled towards the towering desk, head low. He turned the letter to hide the smear of chocolate.

'Tell me, young man, indeed tell all of us, what happens to any *distractions* in my class?'

'They will be confiscated Miss.'

'That is not what I said, but idle boys like you are too busy fiddling and wasting their time to attend to me. Anyone?'

An eager hand shot up to the sky.

'Yes Linnet.'

'They will be ground into the ground Miss.'

'Exactly Linnet. Well ... hand me that *distraction* this instant.'

'Please, Miss, it's a letter.'

'No Weld, it is not a letter, it is a *distraction*. If you wanted it to be a letter you should have kept it out of my sight. My classes are not an opportunity for idle boys to read letters.'

'I wasn't reading it. I was ...'

'Did anyone in this class hear me ask this boy a question? No. I gave him an instruction did I not? One he would do well to heed. Weld, you have distracted not only yourself, but the whole of Lower Elements with your fidgeting and letter reading. You are ruining everyone's chances and I shouldn't wonder if the entire class were to fail henceforth, not just at this school but in life. When you boys leave this establishment, you will discover that your future will be competitive and hard. Of course you are a baby now, Weld, your mother's milk barely dry on your lips – don't snigger class – but once you grow up, you will find the outside world is full of short, sharp shocks.

And when you all find yourselves abandoned, hungry and humiliated, you will all know who to blame will you not? Yes, you WELD. Come on boy, stop wasting time, give me that *distraction.*'

He could not betray his mother to the force of destruction before him. Instead, he stood staring at the splits in the wood of the parquet floor – breaches like lightning, forking this way and that. He wished he could sink into such a crack and hide there.

'Well, Weld, we are all waiting ...'

A mayday call from his deepest being trembled inside him, mounting in intensity like a siren. Somewhere Miss Trench was telling him off but he was closing to the world, a tin soldier being wound up, springs tightening till they were strained beyond endurance. The ground before him began to quiver at the corners, like a mirage, things dissolved in the liquid pooling in his eyes. He was hardly aware when Trench reached over and snatched the letter from his hand, and he did not even register her scream as her neurotically clean fingers encountered the faecal smear of melted chocolate. Bursts of terrified laughter erupted from his classmates as Trench's handbag was upended in the scramble for disinfectant wipes, creams and other unnervingly female artefacts tumbling onto the desk and floor.

Now Weld found himself standing in the corridor gazing down the moss-green walls, seizing at breaths through a nose blocked with emotion. There was worse to come, he realised, as the black- clad figure of Brother Noonan turned the corner. The Brother's crepe-soled shoes squeaked with each step, but he seemed not to have noticed Weld as he neared the Lower Elements classroom. Maybe, Weld prayed, he was insignificant enough to be invisible and he might make it to First Rec – after which more than an hour would have passed and everything might be forgotten – but no, Brother Noonan stopped and examined him with eyes magnified by thick lenses.

'What do you think you're doing outside your class?' Brother Noonan asked, in the first real Scots accent that Weld had heard outside of the television.

The coil in Weld wound another notch, tightening from the base of his spine to his throat, squeezing tears out of his eyes like a twisted toothpaste tube.

'I was ... Miss Trench ...' He extinguished a sob, smothering the words he was trying to communicate.

'We haven't met before, am I right?' Brother Noonan asked, a grey-flecked eyebrow raised above black horn frames.

Weld managed to shake his head.

'You know what happens to boys who misbehave so badly that they are sent out of class?'

Weld nodded, though he did not know. He did not want to know.

'I beat them, if that is what they deserve – and nine times out of ten they deserve it. Now tell me, is that what you deserve?'

Weld shook his head and with as much struggle as he had ever known, explained about the chocolate and the letter and how he hadn't meant to look at it – but did not want it ruined by the chocolate, which he hadn't meant to put in his pocket, but he'd forgotten, and how he hadn't wanted to give his letter to Miss Trench because it was from his Ma, but Miss Trench had taken it and said she would grind it into the ground. Each explanation required a heaving breath to keep himself under control but this seemed only to stoke the intensity of emotion until it flared up and overcame him, exploding through his eyes, mouth and nose.

Brother Noonan again raised his eyebrows and then stooped to the boy's level.

'In my experience laddie – which I can tell you is extensive – you'll find that this is not the end of the world. I've seen every sort of boy and every sort of problem and they are usually quite similar. Let me see your pocket.'

Weld pulled out both pockets, one marked with a smear of melting chocolate.

'I see. Follow me.'

Weld kept up behind the dandruff-flecked black suit, punctuating every few steps with a sob. Strips of fluorescent light shimmered in the oily shine at the suit's shoulder. At the end of the corridor, instead of taking the right turn that would lead to his office, the suit made for the washrooms where fifty sinks were arranged in rows. The suit turned and a large and well-used handkerchief was removed from a pocket and dampened under the tap. Weld was dragged behind the dirty pocket towards the sink, and the stains of chocolate were wiped with hard, efficient strokes. When most of the matter had been removed, the pocket was dragged to a damp communal towel festering on a wooden roller and rubbed until it approached some semblance of dryness.

'Now explain to me laddie, what was the chocolate doing in your pocket?'

'I had it in my tuck box, because I didn't know we weren't allowed, and Mr Jackson confiscated the big piece but I still had one bit left that I was saving ... and I forgot it was in my pocket.'

'Aye, well now you know why it's not allowed and even if you were allowed, would your wee pocket be a good place for it?'

'No Brother.'

'No Brother, indeed.'

'Do you know what MC stands for laddie?'

'Mea Culpa, Brother?'

'Indeed, Mea possessive pronoun – feminine – to Culpa, first declension Culpa, Culpai Culpam, "fault" or "guilt" – feminine, of course, like Eve in the Garden of Eden. Now, "whose", cuiud cui – possessive pronoun taking dative feminine, but in this case irregular, so ending is ius – "fault" Culpa, thus, "whose fault" – cuius culpa – is it that the chocolate was in your trousers?

'Mea culpa,' Weld answered.

'Exactly. Good lad. I will let you off this time because you are a Mite and you seem to be listening. Now return to class for the last ten minutes before Recreation. Off you go now.'

Weld scurried away.

'Laddie,' the Brother called after Weld as he scurried back down the corridor, 'when the bell rings for the end of class you let Miss Trench know that I spoke to you. Understood? You will tell her you are sorry for being a distraction. Got that?'

'Yes Brother.'

'And you may politely ask her to return your letter so you can read it in the break. Off you go, and don't let me see you again ... no running laddie.'

Miss Trench did not acknowledge Weld when he crept back into class. His classmates were fizzing with curiosity but they dared not look up from their sums, and inclined their hunched bodies away from Weld as if they feared being implicated in, or even catching, his misfortune. When the bell sounded for the break Weld remained in class, planning to apologise as instructed and request the return of his letter.

Miss Trench ignored him, making a great show of being absorbed in her diary – her evenings were now quite empty since the mutiny of her geology class and the contretemps with Celeste. After a pause designed to impress upon the boy his essential irrelevance, she peered over her glasses.

'Please Miss, I am very sorry for having a distraction in class. Please may I have my letter so I can read it in First Rec?'

Trench raised her eyebrows in mock surprise and informed him that boys who wished to keep their possessions, whether they be a letter or a sack full of precious jewels, should not play with them in her class. She flicked her eyes back to her empty diary and then back to Weld, whom she dismissed with a sharp monosyllable.

'Out.'

The playground was an expanse of slate grey concrete topped with a sparse layer of gravel. Where the gravel was thickest, the boys exploited its lack of purchase by running as fast as they could and stopping suddenly, thus sliding in an ungovernable and impressive skid that was the cause of constant festering injuries to knees and hands. Various parts of the playground bore the faded remains of painted games: goals, shapes and numbers in circles, long forgotten and as indecipherable as the ancient signs of extinct civilisations on the planes of Peru. Weld sometimes paced these lines, imagining them to be vertiginous paths between enchanted mountains, or jungle trails to unimaginable treasure. Today, he followed the line in a sort of dazed reverie. At first he had been mobbed by his classmates, who'd bayed for details of his encounter with Brother Noonan and then abandoned him in disgust when he revealed that he had not been beaten or savaged in any way.

Now he walked alone, desolate at the injustice of it all,

finding solace in the creation of elaborate tortures that would make Miss Trench realise how evil and unfair she was. He was hammering the last of twenty-two thousand silver nails into a coffin filled with scorpions and biting millipedes, and of course Miss Trench (now begging for mercy), when he caught sight of an older boy running towards him. It was too late to escape so he stayed where he was and did everything he could not to look scared.

The boy skidded to an impressive halt inches from him.

'You're a Mite aren't you?'

Weld nodded.

'Are you Weld?'

Weld nodded again.

'Trench-Foot said to give you this.' He held out the letter.

Weld reached for it – but too eagerly – and the boy snatched it out of reach and dangled it over Weld's head.

'Give it to me,' Weld begged.

'Urgh ... it's got crap on it,' the boy said turning over the envelope.

'It's not crap, it's chocolate,' Weld insisted.

The boy brought the letter up to his nose to confirm this.

'Who's it from then, chocolate face?'

'Ma ... my mother,' Weld replied, screwing up his fists.

'All right then,' the boy passed the letter over, recognising an artefact from the sacred territory of home.

Weld let out a little cry of victory and ran to the perimeter of the playground. He sensed, without knowing, that contact with the letter would make him cry, and he knew not to let this happen in as exposed and dangerous place as a play-ground. The bough of a sycamore tree which stooped almost to ground level provided the cover he needed. Weld leant against the tree, placed the letter against his face and for a moment dissolved wholly into the memory of his beloved mother.

# Fourteen

Max didn't know quite where he was as the sun rose and his consciousness sharpened around the world that following morning. The jumble of cushions, the feather of a fly buzzing near his lips, the hardness of the ground, the lap of the sea and the sweaty knot of body beside him divided into separate entities as his eyes flickered awake. As the warmth of the rising sun registered on his sandy feet and he began to understand the elbow and leg against him, he experienced a pleasure that reminded him of a precious memory of boyhood when he would wake up, a few days into a school holiday, with the illusion that he was not only still at school but in some sort of trouble, caught out by one of the hundreds of ways it was possible to break a rule. Then, as he felt the soft cotton of home under his cheek and heard the noise of traffic in the street and the quiet murmur of his father's radio downstairs, he would realise that he was at home and would experience an explosion of pleasure like the blooming of a sky-wide firework.

Max's relief that first morning on the island might have lacked the desperate force of his younger days but he was aware of a new type of ease as he worked his arm under the sleeping Tine and pushed his thighs under her naked hips, pulling her close. As he drowsed he calculated the weeks left of their holiday, converting them into days and then snuggling into Tine's neck as his calculations dissolved into the smell of her hair and the rise and fall of her chest.

The first few days passed in a lotus rhythm of sleeping,

swimming and sensual exploration. A glass of wine was never far from their lips and Max's penis more often in Tine's mouth than the food they spent hours preparing. Now that Tine had granted Max the visa he so fervently desired, his hands were constantly on her: cupping, pinching, delving. His fingers would slip through the neck of her T-shirt as they walked, the tips of his fingers brushing across her nipples. When he stood behind her as she strung the morning's crop of shells onto the rotted garden twine that had long since lost its battle taming the bougainvillaea, he would slip his hand into the bikini bottoms that had replaced the missing swimsuit and, when she would let him, curve a finger between her legs.

They walked to the village and back, stocking up on wine, olive oil, cans of fish and other supplies. They read for hours on cushions and rugs on the powdery white terrace. Max immersed himself in the family copy of *Gormenghast*, its pages having endured so many years of summer sun and winter mildew that the paperback had developed a potent must and golden mottled patina – as if the imaginative world in the novel could no longer be contained within its covers and was leaking out into the real world. Tine read whatever came to hand, twelve-year-old Sunday supplements, her mother's fashion magazines, bits of beach novels, the remaining two thirds of *Northanger Abbey* – but mostly she read Max's *Gormenghast*, peering surreptitiously at it from his shoulder, trying to contain her enthusiasm for whatever was about to happen next, and so often telling him that 'one of her absolute favourite bits' was coming up. After a dozen such interruptions Max would accuse her of being 'an impinger' with feigned irritation, and demand that she find her own book.

Their skin darkened, and even the pale strips about their hips found colour as they were both more often naked than clothed, more naked than Max had ever been in his life. Their sexual life seemed to Max almost childlike, exploratory and playful. Much of his satisfaction came from being able to look and examine, to follow the labyrinth of his curiosity – but often, as soon as the inevitable arousal was achieved and his desire moved to penetration, Tine would make him come. It was not that difficult, she was expert in the precise frictions that would bring him to orgasm without the need to delve into her.

In truth, Max was now less preoccupied with penetrative sex – what he considered sex to be – now that they had 'done it' or, as he sometimes said to himself, 'performed the act'. Nevertheless, at certain times, he might propose it, he might want to see himself 'in her' and then Tine, having thrown back glass after glass of wine, would crouch on the floor or lay a towel over the rough outdoor table and herself over that, or kneel on the bed with her head in a pillow, or on one or two occasions, stand out in the sand in front of the terrace and hinge herself over the low wall putting her hands and forehead on the soft roughness of the lime while Max, lost in his excitement, worked away behind her.

And after the act ... Max might drop unconscious, or stare at the sky through the trees, or the lizards disappearing into the cracked ceiling and ask if she was 'OK', and wonder if he had been 'OK'; if this was how it was meant to be. And Valentine would get up and shower, or turn away and close her eyes, forcing herself to lean into his reach but desperately wanting some volume of air between them. And she might return to find him standing, or doing something with brisk movements – or one night she caught sight of him through the bathroom door, cleaning his teeth with harsh twists of the brush, as if trying to rip away his gums. She had scratched on the door and he had shouted to her through the rabid froth of toothpaste that he would be out soon, but she'd slipped in anyway and put the lavatory seat down and placed her hand on his, and gently eased the toothbrush from his mouth. She'd pushed him down onto the seat and brushed his teeth with gentle strokes, holding the back of his neck in her hand, wishing she could gentle away his jagged thoughts and her own half-remembered history.

The next morning they separated for the first time. Max set off to the village for supplies and Tine tossed and turned in a chaos of cushions in the shade of a walnut tree by their favourite swimming spot. Earlier Max had dragged rugs, carried cushions and peeled fruit for her, laying out magazines and a cup of tea while Tine remained in bed, her abdomen swollen and her lower back echoing with menstrual cramps. She had then reclined in what Max had christened The Recovery Room although she seemed vaguely irritated by his impotent fussing, as if he could, through some sort of *doing*, save her from the hollow ache of her cycle. What she really wanted, and what she planned to do as soon as he was on his way, was return to her bed.

As Max sweated his way to the top of the cliff he looked back and saw the tiny flick of blue that was Tine in her wrap, scurrying towards the house like an iridescent ant. He assumed she must be heading in to use the lavatory and hoped with a sentimental throb of compassion that she would soon feel better.

As he joined the road, it occurred to Max that he was alone for the first time in days and this afforded him the opportunity of luxuriating in the idea of Valentine. She was his girlfriend, he could say that now, his lover ... beautiful and clever, the embodiment of everything he desired. A real, proper, woman. Anyone would want or admire her. She was the sort of girl he had seen so many times, walking with another man, always with another man, hand in hand, kissing, being at ease, normal.

He had never acknowledged his yearning as something ordinary, immersing himself instead in scourging condemnations; there's something wrong with me, I'm wrong – and although he was not sure what exactly was wrong in him, he suspected, knew, in his deepest places, that something was disfigured or shameful, or even disgusting – his isolation had been proof enough of that.

Tine was perfect, everything about her was the best it could be. Even her hair – something he had never considered in a woman – was a hundred different things, forever falling into beautiful combinations: natural and blowy, twisted up with a stick from their souvlaki, swept back and held with elastic, plaited, free, wet, styled; each novel shape a thing to admire and glory in.

Her top lip swelled and replicated itself over her bottom lip, making him think of a dark dimpled mountain reflecting itself in a Scottish loch he remembered. Above her mouth was an indent, a cushion for something precious, a golden grain of rice. Her nose was small and pronounced, slightly pointed and simple, like a triangle. Her ears were tiny and her skin so fine it was almost translucent. The whole effect of frailty gave him a confidence, a strength he had never known.

And this beautiful weave of humanity, this woman, had chosen to wind her way around him, plait herself into him, allowing him into her heart and body, and in doing so, she gave him a value he had never allowed himself to consider. He stood, luxuriating in the way she looked, the way she tied her wrap, or wore her father's shirt, or adored *Gormenghast*, or craved bed, or fell on food. He thought of her body – hardly curved, vulnerable, slight, everything he had ever yearned for in a woman. It was almost as if he had put her together himself, pieced her together and breathed the life into her, the very life that he loved. He had to protect her, he knew – from what, he did not know – something that needed his protection, something dark and malevolent. Something familiar.

He yawned. Despite their incessant languor, he was hardly sleeping, and never for more than a few hours, dropping his head onto her breast or cradling her head in his arms. Strangely, it was when she was asleep, or out of sight, as now, that he felt an easier sense of her. The very moment the vision of her had shrunk into the distance, he was able to realise that what he felt for this girl, this woman ... it was nothing less than love. Now that she was gone he knew, at last, that he was in love with her.

He could not wait to tell her.

He loved her.

He loved her.

He loved her.

At last he could be part of it.

He stood on the edge of the cliff and shouted his triumph towards the house, hoping it would bounce down the cliffs, reach her and echo back to him. But there was no echo. The great expanse of water absorbed the sound and Tine, now in her bed, heard nothing.

# Fifteen

Weld stood by the smouldering rubbish heap behind the Gym, clenching and unclenching his swollen hands, shock raw in him.

Miss Trench had encountered Brother Noonan in the staff room during the recreation period and had been infuriated to discover, not only had the clerical brother spared the rod with the miscreant child, but he had promised the miserable wretch the return of his letter. It was yet another slap in the face for all her hard work. How was she to impose discipline on these clueless pups if she was to be overruled at every turn? The staff, particularly the clerical community, did not understand the trouble she took, the sacrifices she made, to rinse the savage out of these children.

Of course, she shared none of this with Brother Noonan. She thanked him, forcing a tight smile over the sharp bones of her face, before gaffing the nearest boy and despatching him to locate the reprobate and return the soiled epistle.

Mercifully for the Mites, the classes after First Recreation were the peaceful refuge of Double Religious Doctrine with Fr Le Saux. The aged missionary's belief in the absolute truth of all aspects of Doctrine had, over the years, melted away in the searing heat of India, and instead of working through the catechism, he had held the class's attention with a story about dislocating his shoulder in the Himalayas and being rescued by a long-haired Hindu holy man besmirched with cow dung and wearing only a handkerchief in front of his privates. The boys were riveted to the tale, in particular the burning eyes of the holy man and the sickening crunch as Fr Le Saux's shoulder socket was clicked back into place. They were disappointed when the lunch bell rang early. Of course, the bell was not early – never early, never late – but the boys of Miss Trench's class had not yet been rinsed of their immature relativities of perception.

Weld had all but forgotten his dreadful morning when Miss Trench, with a stack of exercise books under one wiry arm, marched into class on the three o'clock bell. The compositions she had set, entitled *Where I Live* were, she announced, of a disappointing standard. Boys would need to pull their socks up if they were not to find themselves a long way behind when the introductory year – 'Mitedom' – came to an end. It would not be Miss Trench's fault if they entered the main school in a state of confusion and humiliation. In less than five years' time, she shrilled, they would sit their Common Entrance Examination and the way they were proceeding, she expected them all to fail. Did anyone, she asked, happen to know what happened to a boy who failed his Common Entrance Examination? She would tell them, because she had seen it before, many times. If you failed your Common Entrance Examination, you would not to get into a 'Proper School' and if you failed to get into a 'Proper School' ... well, you might as well give up, as you would be cleaning lavatories for the rest of your life. Is that what they wanted?

There were a few titters at the mention of lavatories. This was tinder to her fire.

'You may well giggle like schoolgirls,' she hissed, 'but when you are faced with a lifetime of destitution you will be crying, crying like babies, babies in their nappies on your mummy's knees.'

She walked in between the desks, taking pleasure in the

effect created by reminding these boys of the all too recent humiliations of infancy.

'Some of the compositions are better than others,' she allowed, picking up the exercise books. 'Most are worse.'

She dropped them back on the desk with a jarring thud.

There followed a slow and tortured exposition of each individual's errors − with an occasional acceptable sentence read out. Spelling mistakes were chalked briskly on the blackboard and boys instructed to look up each word in compact dictionaries whose tiny letters, to Weld at least, shifted and disappeared like a circus of fleas.

He was surprised that his composition was not nearer the top of the pile. He had envisioned the home of his imagination with an intensity of fantasy that had completely absorbed him. He had uncovered exotic new words like brightly coloured shells, constructed turrets and dungeons, hauntings and histories, a menagerie of pets which − led by a white and black spotted Great Dane called Boris and his best friend, a Russian Blue cat − stampeded en masse down passageways the length of roads.

As more and more of the class's work was reviewed, Weld's nervousness and disappointment turned to hope. Miss Trench must be saving his essay for special mention. Everybody else had restricted themself to repetitive lists of rooms, fields, gardens, pets, staff, lawn mowing and predictably irritating sisters. Weld was excited when his was the last book left on her desk.

'And now your effort, Weld. Remind me, what was the title I gave for this composition?'

'*Where I live*, Miss,' he answered brightly.

'Indeed. And the place described within these pages, is it where you live?'

He had not been expecting this question and had no idea what an appropriate answer might be.

'I am waiting for a reply young man, is this where you live?'

'Sort of Miss,' he replied.

She then asked, in an acidly comic tone, if in his family home, along with Boris the dog, there was a blue cat called Younghusband?

He shook his head.

In his parents' small house in London – for it was a house, was it not, in Paddington rather than somewhere between Buckingham Palace and a chocolate factory, unless she was mistaken – were there a number of lofty towers, a moat and an indoor pool full of golden fish?

'But Miss . . .'

'Were there?'

'No Miss.'

It was not simply his singular decision to indulge in creative whimsy that was unacceptable, Miss Trench declaimed to the class, there was a time and a place for whimsy, and some of it, Mr Dickens for example, was very improving. Of course Dickens, unlike Weld, knew the difference between fact and whimsy. And Dickens, unlike Weld, would have produced a composition acceptable in terms of spelling and handwriting, but this flight of fancy, this mess . . . she opened the exercise book and held it up to the class. A sycophantic murmur of giggles met the expressionist frenzy of his composition which was flogged raw and red with crosses and slashes. Weld dared not look, keeping his eyes focused on the banana-shaped eraser on his desk whose once sweet smell now made him feel sick.

Some people were blessed with less intellectual ability than others, she went on, and that was a burden they all had to bear and a weakness that might be tolerated, but Weld's work was marked out by a carelessness that was close to vandalism.

Every other word was spelt wrong – words even a nursery school child knew. Words they had all heard Weld read aloud.

'Tell me Weld, the word *t-h-a-y*, is it in the dictionary?'

'Yes Miss,' Weld replied, mistaking this question for a narrow foothold of hope.

'If you would be so kind as to look it up, perhaps you could elucidate us as to its meaning.'

'It means ...'

'I'm sure you think you know what it means, but humour me. Look it up.'

Weld dived into his dictionary and scanned for the word – anxious, like any young animal, to please his carer – but he was astonished to find it absent. He searched and searched, panic increasing as he wondered if there was some sort of misprint, or his was a trick dictionary – but no, it had disappeared.

'I can't find it Miss.'

'Of course you can't because there is no word spelled *t-h-a-y*. The word is *t-h-e-y* as well you know.'

He had never questioned that 'they' should be spelt with an *a*. After all, it was a word that announced its letter in the saying of it, how could it be spelled any other way?

'I thought it was Miss.'

'Oh did you? Don't you dare play the fool with me boy. You aren't at nursery now. Your life has started and although I cannot entirely prevent you from tossing away the opportunities offered to you by your parents – who I know are sacrificing a great deal to have you here – I will not allow you to drag the rest of the class down with you. If you think you can play the fool with me, you'd better think again.'

It was almost unimaginable that things could get any worse. But they did. Trench wrote each of his spelling mistakes on the blackboard, pronouncing them phonetically to the increasing amusement of the class. When she asked him what he meant by 'the reeson why the ceiglin was hiye' a tornado of mocking laughter tore into his ears and through his internal landscape, causing him to scatter his books and pencils into a wide arc on the floor before his desk. There was a moment of utter silence, like a vacuum, like the pause between a flash of light and the roar of an explosion.

Then came the aftershock.

Now he stood kicking at the mud ruts of the path behind the gymnasium, his hands still swollen and red. Everyone in his class had heard about the Ferula, but Weld was the first to see it – a shining wand that cracked as it came down on his hand. It had filled his world with a new level of pain. He'd thought that Brother Noonan was his friend, but the holy man had not even paused to talk to him this time. He had seen Weld standing outside the classroom door and had marched straight past him into the classroom. Weld had supposed he was telling off Miss Trench for being so nasty, but the Brother wasn't telling off Miss Trench and he wasn't Weld's friend. He was his Worst Enemy In The Whole World. The Brother had returned and dragged Weld to his office by his arm. He made him hold out his hands and Weld was thinking about Oliver asking for more food when the first blow fell. It was as if the air had been sucked out of him and been replaced by a red flash of pain, but before he could cry out the Brother had grasped his other hand and struck it just as hard.

Weld could not scream or even make a noise, he just gulped air like a landed fish, his hands squeezed tight under his armpits. Pain, shock and confusion had exploded through him with an intensity that brimmed, stretched and tore at every membrane in his little body, then burst out with such force that a part of him separated from himself.

An older boy passed later and seeing a sobbing wretch

outside the Brother's office, had guided him to the washrooms and filled a basin with steaming water. The boy forced him to unclench his fists, and held the clawed fingers under the hot water. As soon as the first flash of agony passed, Weld felt some of the terror begin to ebb away.

'You're a Mite, aren't you?' the older boy asked.

Weld nodded.

'These your first?'

Again he nodded his head.

'Bad luck for getting them off the Noonatic, his are the third worst – some say second, but I think third. What d'you do?'

Had the boy not been only four years older, Weld's staccato explosion of phrases hiccupped with captured sobs would have made an unintelligible narrative, but the boy understood everything and delivered his considered judgement on the information provided:

'Trench-Foot's a fucking bitch.'

Such a potent mantra provided more relief than fifty sinks of hot water and a smile crept across on Weld's face.

'Here's some advice.' The boy crouched down to his eye level. 'Next time you're hit, warm your hands on the radiator first – and whatever happens, *don't cry*. However much it hurts, *don't cry*. The hurt goes away, but people thinking you're wet, that never goes away. You don't want people to think you're wet do you?' He turned and began to walk away. 'Not to worry though, I won't tell anyone – and anyway, you're just a Mite.'

Weld realised with a sense of anxiety, as the elder boy disappeared down the long corridor, that he needed to go to the lavatory. He poked his head round the corner of the stalls and saw to his relief that they were empty. Going to the loo with older boys hanging around meant inviting Torment; the door could be kicked, loo paper or water thrown over, an ambush prepared – all sorts of terrible things.

Weld found a cubicle that was not too filthy – stuffed with paper or with a seat carelessly splashed but above all with a door that locked. He pulled down his shorts and pants and sat down on the cold seat. When he'd finished, he pulled up his shorts and saw that something had fallen onto the floor. It was his book of MCs, partly lying in a splash of urine. The idea of someone else's pee filled him with revulsion but he took the book by the other corner with his still swollen fingers and rushed to the nearest sink. With careful application of water and the communal towel he was able to wash the plastic folder. Losing your book of MCs was a crime that elicited a merciless quantity of punishments, climaxing, he was sure, in a barrage of ferulas.

A few hours on, standing before the charred refuse and acrid fumes of the bonfire, he felt bereft. He gazed at his once new shoes and thought about the moment when he had tipped them out of their box in his bedroom. He had been disappointed to find, amidst the wrapping of army-style camouflage paper, only three commando stickers rather than four, or sometimes – it was rumoured – five.

Weld kicked the ground in disgust; a missing commando sticker, a broken toy – now such misfortunes seemed unimportant. A pile of ash and scalded rubbish collapsed, releasing a weak plume of grey smoke. It was a fire that burned without colour, without warmth. Weld's throat began to ache. Months to go, so many weeks – even an hour seemed long, a day endless. It was too much to consider. He had never had to conceive of such a long amount of time and now it separated him from everything he loved. Weld dreamed of how it would be when he stepped through his front door at home; the darkness of the corridor, his mother's perfume trailing her like a lazy shadow. He obliterated a crusty escarpment of dirt with his toecap, exposing the softness underneath, the mud splattering his shoes and socks as he kicked at it again and again. Tears welled in the corner of his eyes, campaigning down his cheeks.

The faint clang of the four o'clock bell startled him. Tea time, he remembered. With one sweep of his arm, like the arm of a knight sheathing his sword, the same arm that had scattered his books, he wiped his nose on the sleeve of his blazer and sprinted to the house with the green door.

Mr Beaufinn was raising a cup of tea to his thin lips as Weld stepped in and slid the door closed behind him with a plastic 'clack'.

'Ahhhh,' he bellowed. 'Not perfect, but you're getting nearer. Look at you standing there like a mud-bespattered waif. Take your shoes off before you come any further and sit down this instant. We're on the Assam today, bloody strong it is, brutal even. I'm sure you'll want some sugar. I had two heaped teaspoons and it's better for it in my opinion. Much better, there you are, only two? Have three. Good lad.'

When tea was done, Beaufinn reached for a battered book from a tower next to him.

'Listen to this my boy: *the woods are lovely, dark and deep, But I have promises to keep, And miles to go before I sleep.*'

Weld wondered what he meant by promises. The idea of woods being both dark and deep was quite frightening, and not at all lovely; the sort of place where Sir Fynton might lurk, waiting for a boy walking back to school on his own.

'*And miles to go before I sleep*, yes indeed. Frost – strange man, bloody good poem. Now settle yourself down and get ready for a little dictation. I'm sure you are familiar with the idea. I read each line and you write it down. Here we go. *Whose woods these are I think I know ...*'

Weld attempted to arrange himself in front of the paper as if he were at his desk, but the relationship between the stool, the table, the paper and his sore hands was so confusing and new that the notion of actually managing to write was beyond him.

Seeing that the boy had not yet begun, Beaufinn read the beginning of the poem again. Although Weld could hear and understand the words, translating them from speech to script was a dimensional shift too complex for him, with too many forces campaigning for dominance in his brain.

When Weld heard Beaufinn say 'horse' he understood precisely the word's relationship to that four-legged beast. Were he to read the word, *horse*, Weld would not only have known what was meant, he would have been able to sense the quadruped near him, pawing at the ground, full of movement and a darkly knit smell of hay. But to write down this sound, this idea, with marks on paper and coordinated movements of his hand, was an altogether different matter. There were so many letters to choose from, so many orders in which they might be arranged. It was like ordering him to make bread because he knew what bread was.

'Come on my lad, I haven't heard your pencil so much as scratch the paper.'

Beaufinn repeated the first line again, and then once more, his voice growling with irritation: '*Whose woods these are I think I know.*'

But Weld was thrown by the first word *whose*. How could such a thing be approached; an *h*, an *o*? As Weld pictured the word, it voided itself of meaning, so he skipped *whose* and went on to the next, *woods*, in desperation creating his own sentence about being in woods. Beaufinn grunted when he saw the pencil move, satisfied that at last progress was being made. Once Weld had started writing he kept going, making up a sentence each time he heard one read out. When it came to the end of the poem he handed over the sheet of paper, hoping, with the unique optimism of boyhood, that everything would turn out all right.

'What the bloody hell's going on here?' Beaufinn demanded. 'Are you demented?'

Weld froze.

'Look, here's *wood* and *horse* and *snow* but that my friend, is where the similarity ends. What in God's holy name did you think you were doing?'

Weld could not explain what he had done, nor the nature of the confusion that had caused the problem. He did not understand it, the problem lived in a place where there were no words, just a tight feeling in his throat and a fog in his brain.

'You have written *I went along the path allone* and then . . . what's this? I can't even read this, it's so bloody garbled. Here, you read it.'

Weld slipped off his stool and retrieved the paper from the thick and mottled fist. He gazed at his own uneven letters which, unlike printed text, tamed their meanderings for him like a crazed dog for its master:

'*I went along the path allone / except for beests that have no home/ Like bees and flys and tiny things/ which washed me pass as high they flown*'

'Give it here.'

The paper was snatched back and re-examined.

'It says *washed me past?*' Beaufinn commented, his voice a mixture of curiosity and disbelief as he combed his beard.

'I meant, *watched me pass*, sir.'

'Anything but sir. *Watched/washed*, *watch* with your eyes, *wash* with soap . . . but the point is, this nonsense is not the dictation I gave you. Why did you not write what I said?'

Weld could not answer.

'Did you understand what I was asking you to do? Or are you trying to be clever?'

Weld did not move.

'Look, you young bugger, you'd better not be trying it on with me. I can smell boys trying it on, I assure you of that, and you don't want to be around when I smell a boy trying it on. Why are you shaking, what's wrong with you? I'll rattle you if you're not careful. And crying now, what's the point of crying?'

'No, sir, I'm not ... it was the bonfire sir, it made me ...'

Beaufinn threw down his hands and thrust his chair over to where the small boy was gripping the stool like a fledgling bird on a wind-blasted rock. He grasped the boy's shoulders with his heavy hands, his thick fingers meeting behind the bony back.

'Look at me. LOOK at me,' Beaufinn ordered.

Weld raised his eyes from the carpet to the bedroom slippers crammed with misshapen feet, resting on two metal plates, dark thick trousers with thighs like minced meat stuffed into sacks, a cardigan, dark with blue and green-black diamonds, stretching over a swollen trunk. Weld's gaze travelled up the great mass of contoured facial hair, the thin mouth, then stopped before the eyes.

Beaufinn looked serious, but not unkind; a friendly ogre perhaps ... Weld risked meeting his cement gaze.

'There's not a thing about you I don't know, every inch of you is exposed, unclothed, naked. I've been teaching boys like you for thrice as long as you've been alive. Now I know that sometimes you have to tell fibs to get through the day, to survive. But here, boy, in this house, with me, you will tell the truth. ALWAYS. Now you stay here and I will get something to make you feel better.'

Beaufinn then sped out and returned with a cup of the strangest and sweetest tea Weld had ever drunk. When he'd drunk the last drop he gathered his courage and recounted what had happened that day but despite his efforts his throat tightened and as his throat tightened tears leaked out of his eyes. He managed to splutter enough of a narrative to describe his trauma before emotion swamped him and he stood, his shoulders heaving up and down as he twisted his fingers in the blue wool of his sweater.

He felt his cheek being wiped with large and calloused thumbs, and then he was picked up and hugged so hard he thought his bones would crack. He was overwhelmed by the intimacy of the teacher's grown-up smell, the feel of his cheek and lips squashed into the man's cardigan, and the tenderness of the great hand stroking his head made him feel safe and at home. Soon his tears ceased and he melted into safety and drowsiness. He felt himself being placed somewhere soft. He hoped dreamily that perhaps he would never have to go back, that he could stay here and be cared for. Then, leaning into the softness of a large and stained cushion depicting a needlepoint design of the dragon of St George devouring a tiny human, he spiralled down into unconsciousness.

# Sixteen

Jojo found it – of all people. He didn't know what it was, bless him. Well he probably knew what it was, but he was too young to know the difference between dead and alive, or that the sticky stuff he'd got all over him was blood.

I'd never imagined the Triff – or any human being – could make the kind of noises she did. Jojo's crying must have woken her and when she realised that he wasn't in bed, she stumbled into the kitchen. That was when I heard the first sound, deep in my sleep. It was a slow scream, like a heavy river looking for the sea. She'd seen his little handprints on the limewashed wall beside the front door, two perfect little hands, like on the side of houses in Egypt when we went on holiday that time – but these, Jojo's I mean, they were real blood.

He must have toddled into the kitchen, his face, hair, hands, all thick with blood. It was the scream that woke me. I'd been asleep in her bed, too frightened to sleep on my own. I leapt up and found Ma holding Jojo, naked and bloody, under the tap in the kitchen sink, rubbing away at him, saying 'oh my baby, oh my baby' in a low mad voice.

She couldn't find any wounds, of course.

Not on him.

It was me that discovered it. Covered in flies, its skull smashed in, dark blood oozing in a black syrup puddle. Paws crossed front and back, ribs like a shark – what are they called? Gills, that's it. Tail pointing down. Forever now. It must have been that one from the woods. I didn't see it then, not properly, but it must have been the same one. It was dead now. Poor thing.

Khalib soon turned up. He grinned at the battered animal – pleased with his work, I bet. He must have thought the Triff was rushing towards him to thank him, maybe even kiss him again. Amazing that her expression did not get through to that thick yoghurt of his brain. I'd have run for the hills, but he's so full of himself, he just stood there smirking.

The Triff shouted at him to 'bugger off', 'leave us alone', and if I hadn't been so disgusted by the battered dog, I might, for a tiny moment, have felt sorry for him. For his disappointment, I mean – he'd only been trying to help. Khalib shrugged as if to say 'what did I do?' and Ma shrieked and pushed him away. He froze and everyone stopped, even the sea stopped, everything went still and dead, as dead as the dog. Only the swarm of flies was moving, dipping in and out of the smashed skull. Then Khalib looked at the Triff with such a look of sadness, or something more, betrayal maybe. That's it. Then he slunk off into the forest.

I noticed the Triff was shaking as I tried to give Jojo back to her. She waved her finger as if to say 'no, no' and stared into the woods. I wanted to run into the house and lock the door and hide with her – or maybe close my eyes and just start the day over again. Neither of us could walk past that dog again. It was almost as if, along with the blood and brain ooze from its smashed-open head, a spirit of death had leaked out and neither of us wanted it near – especially not near little Jojo.

After a while she looked at me and said: 'It's time for a swim.'

So we did. Naked like we used to, Mama, Jojo and me. The

warm sea washed away the blood and the fear. Mama and me held on to each other, sandwiching little Jojo in the warm saltiness. I felt a closeness and a force that was beyond anything we could have had if Dad was there. Like me and Mum were strong as the sea, and Khalib and Jojo – and even Dad – were as fragile as can be, with all their noise and killing of dogs and playing in suntan lotion and blood.

I came out from the water after the Triff, and as I walked towards our clothes I saw her staring at me, at my body, with such a frowning look of Triff love.

'Oh my darling, you've . . .'

'Oh Mum,' I grabbed my wrap.

As we approached the house, bodies already dry from the sun and still cool from the water, the Triff stopped.

'Oh God.'

'What?' I asked

'The dog.'

Jojo complained as he was squeezed in the crook of her arm.

'Wait here,' she said, handing Jojo to me.

'What are you going to do?'

'I don't know. Stop it Jojo.' She reached over and released my hair from his fist.

'I'm coming too Mum.'

'No.'

'I'm coming.'

'OK then.'

We walked up to the house, moving closer to one another until we were nearly touching. Her hand was swinging close to mine and, almost accidentally, I took it.

She liked that.

'Let's leave Jojo here,' I suggested. I looked around. 'He needs something to lie on.'

'Hand me your wrap,' she said.

Swimming naked was one thing but this was too much.

'OK then.'

She untied her wrap and flicked it out until it lay flat on the ground. Her Triff breasts hung like the bags of sand that keep the scenery in place in the school play. Her bush, thick and dark. The white of her bikini mark wrinkled as she bent down. I put Jojo on the material and he's happy to be free of us. I held her hand again and we move to the house. We're about to climb the two steps onto the porch.

'Hold on,' I said.

I untied my wrap and let it drop. We're both naked.

The dog was still there, the fur around its broken head hardened into little black spikes – like Dev's hair with all its gel. I giggled. The dog's belly had swollen since we left it, dark and tight. It stinks. The Triff put a hand over her mouth.

'Let's take two legs each,' I suggested.

'And then what?' she said through her fingers.

'Then we throw it in the sea.'

I stooped down and took hold of a front and back paw.

'Come on.' I didn't want to think of the goo and the gore and the feel of the paw pad in my hand.

Black blood, white lime. I can feel it, taste it.

The Triff bent down and took the other front paw, disturbing hundreds of greasy black-green flies. She leapt backwards with a scream.

The sight of my Mum naked, flying through the air with a loud scream, was so funny that all I could do was laugh. She looked at me, looked at the dog and looked down at her own nakedness, then she laughed until she had to hang on to the low white wall that surrounded the porch. We laughed together, Mum shaking and gripping her tummy and crossing her legs until she had to jump over the wall and squat in the sand and I could hear her peeing and laughing.

# Seventeen

It had been a day so beyond his understanding that he could not retain it in his body.

Mr Beaufinn had dragged him out of unconsciousness, heavy and thick as treacle, rattled him till he was awake, and then made him drink a cup of coffee – his first ever, a black wheel spinning round and round as more and more sugar was stirred in, like space, like a hole.

Weld had trudged back to school, his feet heavy like boots caked in clay, his clothes tugging and twisted as if they were on the wrong way. Then people were around him and the warning bell for Evening Studies rang and they were asking him about the Noonatic and he was telling them about the Ferula, and someone asked if he'd cried, and he said he had. It hurt more than anything, he tried to explain as everything began to whirr. Then Linnet said 'so you blubbed', and he said 'only a bit', and Linnet said he was a 'blubber' and Weld thought it was from a whale, a harpooned whale that men would cut, lumps of yellow fat and blood, or was it white and red, men with yellow boots, wellington boots and giant razors on broomsticks walking through gushing blood and stinking fat all spinning around with the bitter black coffee. He felt sick and 'blubber' was chanted at him till he could taste it in his throat and he threw up over everything. He sat on the floor with sick everywhere and then the prefect came and he was taken to the infirmary and the matron undressed him and sponged him with a large and scratchy sponge and put him in pyjamas which were not his and took him to bed and told him that if he was going to vomit he must vomit into the bowl. Did he understand? He went to sleep wondering what vomit was.

In the morning he was hungry but the matron said that boys who vomit everywhere did not eat breakfast. She took his temperature, digging the glass thermometer in under his tongue. He did not dare move it because it was full of mercury which was a deadly poison. Silver, like a liquid pearl, but poison. He went to sleep again and in the afternoon he was allowed some toast and tea in a red plastic mug with lots of milk in it. And although the toast was cold and chewy and without butter, it was good because he was starving and the tea was sweet and cool, but not as sweet as Mr Beaufinn's, and it tasted like tea.

Weld hoped he had not done anything terrible at Mr Beaufinn's. He hardly remembered what had happened, but he felt a horrible dread in the deepest, lowest part of him which made him wonder if he had done something terrible. In the evening he had a shallow bath and some tomato soup and read a comic. The matron said he was better so he would have to go to class the next day. He was sad because he liked the comics and the sound of her footsteps as he fell asleep.

The next morning he lay in bed, listening to the boys thunder this way and that. There was a fluttering in his stomach like a trapped bird as he thought of being separate from everything. He rubbed his face on the stiff white sheets of the infirmary linen, breathing in their clean smell and listening to the chant of Morning Prayers that sounded like magic. He made his own prayer that everyone would forget about him and leave him where he was and maybe, because he was forgotten, he would be allowed to go home. By the time the roar of breakfast was ebbing about him his eyes were closed and he fell into the deepest sleep, woken by the sharp cold grip of the matron tugging at him.

'Come on, up you get. There's nothing wrong with a boy who sleeps so well. No shirking in my infirmary. Toast on the table and I'll bring you some clothes – as we had to wash yours to get the vomit out.'

He got up and ate the toast and drank the tea and then, as the morning bells knelled, he saw with horror the strange uniform the matron had placed on the bed.

'This isn't my uniform,' he said.

'It'll fit.'

'But it's not the right one.'

'Whatever do you mean, you foolish boy?'

'It's a different colour. It looks funny.'

'It's clean and there's nothing wrong with it. There are children all over the world who would give their right hand for a uniform like this one, you spoilt boy, and their left for that matter. Now stop wasting time or you'll be late for class.'

She reached for the button of his pyjama top and he recoiled as if electrocuted.

They were both astonished. She was about to ask him for an explanation but the child swiftly undressed himself and she let the question die in her mind. As matron of St X's, she was far too busy to deal with the abnormal behaviour of small boys.

'You can move quick enough when you want to,' she commented when he was dressed, pointing him towards the bathroom to wash his face and brush his teeth.

When Weld saw the effect of the strange uniform in the bathroom mirror he was horrified. To a casual eye, any differences may have seemed slight, but to Weld they were abhorrent.

The shorts were a heavier, darker grey, and closer to the knee than the modern ones and the sweater had a light blue line around the neck. Weld stood frozen, his mind churning.

The matron opened the door and walked in.

'What an earth do you think you are doing, staring at yourself? The second bell has rung and you should be in class. Go this instant.'

There was no resisting her brisk force as she ushered him through the bathroom door and out of the infirmary.

'Now, straight to class and no more of this shirking.'

Weld walked down the long corridor like one heading to an execution, his skin crawling under the unfamiliar fabric. The corridors empty and hushed with the negative space of boys in silence.

He knocked at the door to his classroom.

'Come in.'

He pushed open the door and felt himself being lanced by twenty-five pairs of eyes.

'Better, Weld?' his teacher asked.

'Yes Miss.' He could smell disinfectant and a familiar sourness in the air.

'We are most relieved. Sit down and catch up.'

He made his way through the glare of his classmates to his desk. As he sat down he saw to his horror the damp stain in front of his desk where the floor had been scrubbed. Underneath the metallic tang of the disinfectant he recognised the sour reek of sick. His sick. His vomit. Everyone could smell his insides. This was his smell.

His life was over.

# Eighteen

Max greeted everyone in the village with an exuberance that was received with casual interest by the oldest inhabitants, indifference by the mature, and derision by those nearest his own age, who dismissed his breezy greeting with the response *'malaka'* – an insult gesturing vaguely towards the detumescence that follows a bout of male self-pleasuring. Tine's father and his bohemian assortment of friends had staggered about for years issuing forth enthusiastic greetings in Greek and other languages after a few gallons of retsina and an ouzo or four, but this had still been soon enough after the liberation of Greece from the Nazis to ensure carte blanche for anyone with a British or American passport.

Max's first stop was Angelika's for yoghurt. Tine had warned him that the old woman could, on occasion, take against strangers and until she understood who he was, her demeanour might seem off-putting. He counted what seemed to be five doorways from the balcony overflowing with bougainvillaea, as instructed, and knocked on a freshly painted door. A voice replied to his knock and he waited, the brown, red and white string bag Tine had thrust into his hand moving slightly in the breeze, like the fishing nets drying by the harbour. When minutes had passed and the door had not opened Max knocked again. This time there was a volley of words, he heard the creaking of stairs and then the door was thrown open with curses so rich in onomatopoeia that Max could almost hear the priests and barnyard animals abusing each other. An odiferous

woman somewhere between fifty and seventy stared bel-
ligerently at him with bloodshot eyes and the swaying
movement of one who has spent too long at sea. She
didn't like what she was seeing and swung the door closed.
Having been coached to expect a degree of resistance, Max
determined not to founder so quickly and stayed the door with
his hand.

'Valentine ... boyfriend. I am Valentine's boyfriend.'

The woman was far from impressed and with a determined
battle cry launched her sharp and bony frame against the
door, but Max blocked it with his foot. The woman wailed,
producing a large and unlikely trident – intended for the
spearing of octopus – and slashed at Max's face. He leapt back,
landing at the feet of a muscled young fisherman who had
been torn by the war cry of his bellicose aunt from a private
moment with an old pornographic magazine, as worn and
creased as a treasure map.

With little self-consciousness, the young man adjusted
himself within his light cotton trousers and communicated
in a colloquial Greek that he would soon be obliged to do
Max some sort of violence. Max attempted to explain the
situation, shrugging with open hands to communicate the
transparency of his position before pointing to the Olympian
weapon the aunt was brandishing. The woman insisted to
her nephew that Max was in the grip of illegal drugs – no
doubt from the mainland – and had burst through her front
door and had intended to rob or more probably molest her.
She concluded that the only solution was a long and merciless
beating.

Although the nuances of the old woman's words were lost
on Max, it was clear to him that Valentine had underplayed
the hag's hostility and he was beginning to suspect that the
young man was planning an attack.

'I am sorry I have offended you Angelika,' he pleaded. 'I'm only here to buy *yaourti*.'

Max held up the empty string bag in front of the fisherman's face. The fisherman decided that this might be a foreign insult of sorts, and raised his fists. As biceps the size of grapefruits swelled in his arms, the harridan issued a cheer from the first-floor balcony, where she had repaired to enjoy the spectacle.

Max began to back away, calling for help.

A neighbour appeared from next door, a magnificently wrinkled octogenarian with fierce eyes, a deep-brown face and hair perfectly coiffed into a marzipan swirl. In her hands was a terracotta pot neatly covered with a piece of white muslin. She stepped between Max and his assailant and handed the pot to him.

Max looked at her with sudden hope. 'Angelika?'

'Ne, ne,' the ancient replied, grasping his arm and propelling him towards her door. She paused by the young fisherman and placed her hand on his stubbly cheek to enquire about his mother's sciatica.

There was a last attempt from the balcony as the old lady demanded her nephew at least poke the foreigner with the trident, but the moment was gone. The fisherman dropped his fists and answered the newcomer's questions about his dozen or so immediate family members. He turned and shrugged at Max as if explaining that there was no bad will and walked back down the narrow lane ignoring the shouts of derision from above.

The real Angelika, for it was definitely her, silenced the troublemaker with a look seasoned by half a century's loathing. As the balcony windows slammed shut she took Max's arm and guided him through her front door, putting her thumb to her mouth pointing back to the balcony.

'Ouzo,' she said shaking her elegant head, 'ouzo, ouzo, ouzo ...'

As soon as Max had stepped into the cool shadows of the house she tugged at his sleeve with a question.

'Valentina?' she said looking about her.

'Fine, good,' Max replied.

'Where?' she demanded.

'Er ... at the house ... not well,' Max replied, checking behind him, still nervous of the trident. 'At the house,' he gestured to the sea, 'resting.'

Angelika did not know what he meant.

'Sick. Unwell. Valentine.' Max held his belly and groaned.

'Valentina sick? Ohhhh.' She snapped a white crochet shawl off the back of a chair and threw it round her shoulders with the purposefulness of a soldier shouldering his gun.

'No. She is not exactly sick ...' Max shook his head. 'Not sick.'

'Sick, not sick?'

'Woman.' Max pointed to his lower abdomen and looked at Angelika, whose face was rucking with disdain at his antics.

'Sick or no sick?' she demanded.

Max tumbled into a confusion and embarrassment exacerbated by the recent threat of violence. He wished he had a dictionary or, better still, that he had kept his mouth shut. He looked around the room, his eyes adjusting to the darkness. He pointed to a calendar on the wall under a gaudy picture of a winged saint, pushed up the paper and then indicated the month beneath.

'Woman sick.'

Angelika considered this and nodded. She looked up at a large silver framed photograph of an old man in a three-piece suit and said a few words. Max had assumed the picture was a popular leader or a rather scruffy king, but now understood that it must be her husband. Angelika, satisfied that she had shared the relevant information with her long-dead spouse, removed a piece of paper from a marble-topped dresser, and tore it into four neat squares. She wrote on one of the squares and replaced the other three in the dresser. Max wondered if he was about to witness some esoteric cure for menstrual pain.

'Go Andromeda. Give Valentina,' she said handing the paper to Max.

'Andromeda?' Max asked.

Angelika pointed to her belly and mimed putting something in her mouth then ushered him out of the door.

Max looked at the paper as the door closed behind him with a heavy thud. The old woman's Hellenic script was neat and small and unintelligible to Max. Of course, he concluded, it was not some strange superstition, it was the name of a medicine. He set off towards the main street hearing echoes of her voice chatting away to the photograph.

By the time Max had bought tomatoes, spinach, honey, wine, matches, feta, olives, candles and soap, the drama outside Angelika's house was shaping itself into a comedy. Max returned to the tiny shop he had passed earlier, where Yannis the butcher, with a cigarette in the centre of his mouth, was now quartering a scrawny yellow chicken, ignoring a barrage of instructions from a crowd of women and conversing with an aged man with no teeth. Children chased each other around the chopping block and out onto the street as Yannis sectioned the bird with decisive chops, relishing, it seemed, the proximity of his cleaver to his bloodied and calloused hands.

Everyone looked at Max and offered courteous *Kali mera*'s before turning back to the drama of the chicken. There was nothing to do but wait, so Max dropped his bags of shopping and seated himself on the stone steps. The sunlight was fierce. Max reached over to open one of the bottles of water but, judging that broaching the plastic film that held them together would make it difficult to carry them, he resolved to wait until he'd arrived at the house.

The women soon bustled past with their pieces of chicken wrapped up in neat parcels and the toothless man wrangled his horde of children in the opposite direction.

Max rose and asked the butcher what was available as there was nothing on display.

Yannis the butcher looked at him blankly – waiting, as everybody waited, for Max to speak in a comprehensible language. He wiped his hands on the rag stuck into his apron, turned and pulled open the wooden panelled door of an antiquated refrigeration unit. An icy mist tumbled out, delicious after the heat, and amidst the yellows, pinks and dirty whites of motionless flesh, Max spotted a leg of lamb. He mimed that he wanted a small piece, enough for two. Yannis nodded, and boned the entire leg with skilful sweeps of his cleaver. Max wondered whether to tell him he wanted much less of the meat as Yannis wrapped the large bundle with paper and a great amount of string but it was clear that the decision had already been made, and having crammed the oozing cushion of meat into his string bag, Max staggered out of the shop.

His last task was to pick up the medicine. He discovered the pharmacy in the street next to the butcher's and handed the paper to a white-coated woman with black hair, a strong nose and large beautiful eyes. She read the note and giggled, calling to a colleague who appeared from the back of the shop.

'What's wrong?' Max asked.

'This you do not purchase from a pharmacy,' the woman said to Max.

'Are you sure? Where do I get it?' 'Max asked.

'Try asking your mother,' the woman suggested.

'Or your wife ... but only if she can cook,' her colleague volunteered, both of them sniggering.

'I don't understand,' Max said, looking at them.

'It says *A honey cake & not one of those stale ones you sold me last month.*' The woman handed him back the square of paper. 'I think you should try the bakery. Down the road, on the left,' she said, stifling a laugh as he departed the shop.

Max's embarrassment melted away in the strong sunlight and by the time he reached the bakery he was chuckling to himself. Angelika was not a woman to disobey, he decided, purchasing a honey cake and hoping it was not one of their stale ones. Whatever its age, it was a dense and weighty ring of sweetness enclosed in a cumbersome cardboard box decorated with pink angels. The package was wrapped with a oversize ribbon whose ends bounced up and down like a pair of pink springs as Max tramped out of the village, struggling to manage his chaotic haul of purchases.

By the time he had reached the turn off from the road, Max was exhausted. The handles of the bags were cutting into his hands and when he stumbled, a bottle of water split from the pack and tumbled down the slope, lodging itself in a thorn thicket below. Although parched with thirst Max did not want to risk freeing another bottle to drink so he struggled on, resting every few hundred yards and imagining the relief of tearing off his clothes and diving into the sea. Halfway down, he stopped at the cliff that overlooked the house. Tine had insisted that he throw a rock – as big a rock as he could manage – into the sea from this very point. This, she had explained, was the Lemonade Rock and on hearing the splash, Tine would be able to prepare for his arrival. It would all become clear when he reached the house, she had said.

He wondered whether to press on but considered that she might be disappointed, or even annoyed – the idea made him pause. Tine seemed to know exactly what she wanted in so many moments of her life, such confidence in the precise nature of how she wanted things to be. He wondered what the difference between this and being controlling was – whatever it was, he could do without it, or with less of it, but then he remembered that he loved her and would soon tell her, so he put down the bags, selected a melon-sized rock and tossed it in with all his might.

He was a little disappointed when he arrived at the camp he'd made for her. He'd been hoping that she might surprise him on the path, or at least be waiting at the new camp, but the only sign of her was a disorder of cushions, the fruit – untouched but for the wasps – and the tea he'd made half drunk. He picked it up to swallow it, pausing as he saw the flies bobbing in the sun-warmed liquid. He shouldered his bags and made for the house, anticipating she might have some sort of surprise waiting; a beautifully prepared lunch in some exotic new spot, the house made more lovely in some peculiarly female way, or perhaps an erotic excitement ... an outfit, the denuding of her pubic hair perhaps. The idea buoyed him up. How would she look shaved, just for him? The idea excited him. He thought of her crouching before a mirror in the bathroom, is that what they did? Looking at herself, becoming turned on as she prepared herself for him and suddenly the memory, that morning, of the string hanging between her legs. Of course, she'd probably not be in the mood for such games. He thought back to a brightly painted wooden clown that used to hang in his childhood bedroom, a red vine trailing between its legs. Its limbs would splay when you pulled the string.

It was unnerving.

As Max neared the house he noticed that the shutters and door were closed and for a second he feared she might not be there. Suddenly he wondered if she had tricked him into going out so she could abandon him. He did not stop to consider the logic of this, because the idea immediately made sense – somewhere in the recesses of his mind there was a voice darkly whispering: *I told you so, I told you so. I told you so, I told you so. I told you so.*

He pushed the door. It was locked. He dropped the bags, boxes and bottles and dashed around the area that, despite the paucity of anything other than scrub, they called the garden. He returned to the terrace and sat on the wall to reason with himself, but his mind was ungovernable, his thoughts like scraps of blown paper.

He stood and shouted her name.

A voice replied from within the house.

He ran up to the door.

'What are you doing?' he asked.

The door creaked open. Her eyes were red and swollen, her hair crazy from the bed.

'Are you OK?'

'Oh God,' she said. She turned and headed back to her nest on the bed.

'What's wrong?'

'Someone was here, creeping about, watching me. I went straight back to the house when you left – your camp was lovely, it was sweet, but I wanted to be in bed ... As I was heading back, I had this feeling that I was being followed and the next thing I was running. I got back to the house and suddenly it all seemed silly so I lay down for a bit and slept. When I got up I felt better and was wandering about doing things. It was so hot I didn't bother with my clothes and then I got cramps again and was trying these stretches that sometimes help. I went to the loo and I came out and ... I'd forgotten about before ... I thought I was on my own ... and

133

then suddenly I knew the bastard was watching me, had been watching the whole time.'

'No, no. It was me,' Max said, sitting on the bed. 'I was looking at you from the cliff. I saw you run back to the house.'

'No. It was close by. I might have heard something, I don't know.'

'Where were you?'

'What do you mean?'

'When you first thought you were being watched, where were you?'

'Outside on the terrace. What difference does it make?'

'Well, what direction were you looking in?'

'I don't know. I wasn't looking in any direction.'

'What were you doing at the time?'

'God, Max, does it matter?'

'I'm just trying to picture it, get a clear idea of what was going on.'

'Someone was watching me OK?'

'Look, I'm just trying to build a picture.'

'A picture. OK.' Valentine sat up and glared at Max. 'I was standing right here with one foot on the chair where you are. I had my back to the house and I was looking down at my crotch because I was shoving a tampon into my vagina. OK Sherlock?'

Max said nothing but stood and went outside, scouring the bushes near the wall.

'Here?' he called.

Tine sighed but did not respond.

'Here?' he shouted, trying another position. 'Could he have been this far?'

'I don't know,' she replied, falling back into her pillows.

Max spent a few minutes looking at the sandy ground, not

sure what he was looking for – wondering how he would be able to read any sign amidst the scrub scratched and crossed with ridges and hollows, and scattered with dead leaves and stones.

He walked back to the house, where Tine was now tidying the kitchen, removing every speck from the two plates they had used the night before and scrubbing everything with peculiar attention.

'I couldn't find anything,' Max said, wiping his sweaty face with the tea towel. 'Did you actually see anyone?'

'I told you, no, but someone *was* there.'

Max tossed the towel onto a chair and then sat down, putting his feet on the counter next to Tine.

'It's difficult to visualise, logically, from what you were saying. I mean, of course it's possible that you were feeling a bit weird from, you know, your period, woozy maybe – did you take painkillers?'

Tine spun round.

'Difficult for you to visualise? Not logical is it? You think that I've gone mental because of my period? Fuck Max, it's not the first time I've had it, it happens every month. But what doesn't happen, Max, is a whole load of weird shit, like someone mysteriously sweeping the house before we get here. Or stealing my swimsuit. Or, if that's not enough logic for you, some creep spying on me as I walk about naked. There's nothing logical or illogical, Max, there's just you not believing me.'

She stormed away but then returned. Max supposed she might be coming back to apologise, but she was furious.

'Just explain to me, Max, how you can be in me, actually in me, fucking me, one day and then not give a shit the next?' She ran off, grabbing her wrap and charging up the nearest hill.

Max remained where he was, staring after her but not seeing anything that made sense, shaking his head slightly with no other thought than the certainty of his blamelessness.

# Nineteen

It did not happen straight away.

A lion will leap on its prey as soon as it has a chance, but hyenas will follow, snap and observe, savouring – sometimes for days – the weakening of their victims before they close in. Weld was able to pass through First Recreation without incident and by the afternoon he was feeling better and the disinfectant stink had assimilated closer into the familiar fug of boys and dust. It was Fr Le Saux who unwittingly condemned Weld during the last class of the day. He enquired about the source of the now faint ammoniac smell that had snaked into his ancient nostrils. Linnet, who was quite popular and the second fastest runner in the class, shouted out.

'It's Smeld, Father.'

Howling and cackling ensued at the introduction of the new name. Fr Le Saux silenced the class with one eyebrow, but it was too late – the wound had been opened. Had it just been the incident of throwing up, Weld might have survived, beating off skirmishes and suffering only minor tears and bruises, but when Linnet produced a nickname and later, in the supper queue, pointed out that Smeld not only 'smelled' and was a 'blubber', but also wore strange clothes and went to 'suck-up' classes with Richard Beaufinn, there was no hope for him, he was quarry.

Life quickly became intolerable; even the precarious sanctuary of visits to Mr Beaufinn had faded into a dream-like memory after that afternoon when he had cried and fallen asleep, a memory that was both comforting and nightmarish. Weld wondered what unfamiliar crime he had committed, damning him in his teacher's estimations as something even worse than a 'poop. Perhaps, Beaufinn could sense, or had heard about, the ignominy of his vomiting in class, and scented on him the reek of the unpopular. Whatever it was, Beaufinn had become cold, stiff and strict; not offering tea, not talking about Fynton the Boar, not asking to be called 'Beau', coldly setting dictation and underlining mistakes instead, as if the kindness and the tea, and especially the hugging, had been done by someone else.

Weld almost understood why he was being picked on at school, but he could not work out why Beaufinn was so different, or why it made him feel so desolate – or why, sometimes, Weld caught his teacher looking at him with horror.

He must be doing *something* wrong.

'You'll have the start I never had son,' Pa had said before Weld left home that first term, pride shining through exhausted eyes. His mother had held him for ages before she broke away, promising, with cracking voice, that everything would be all right, that she would always be there for him. He knew his mother would not lie to him, any more than the Blessed Virgin would sin, so it could only be himself, Weld, who was wrong in some invisible way. As if he had turned his back on God.

His borrowed uniform was the most visible part of the problem, the mark of Cain, the weakness that separated him from the safety of the herd. Linnet worried and tore at him: Why didn't he have a proper jumper? Did he think he was better than everyone? Had he wet himself in his proper clothes like a baby?

Eventually Weld would begin to cry and the animals would howl: Blubber, Blubber, Baby Blubber.

The terrible truth was that he *was* a 'blubber'. He cried more than anyone else, more, even, than they knew – every night, as he longed for home.

He tried to get rid of the strange uniform, running to the infirmary after the first onslaught and begging the matron for his old uniform. She sent him away. There was no point dirtying clean clothes, she snapped, he could have them when everyone else changed their shorts and sweaters – more than a week away.

As he made his way back to class, one arm brushing the hard grey gloss of the wall that divided the refectory from the main corridor, hoping he might wear away the odious jersey, he prayed to the Virgin Mother for help. But as he prayed, a part of him knew that the blue-robed, wan-faced statue at the end of the corridor, with her gold halo radiating lightning bolts of gleaming bronze, even she – real as she was – probably wouldn't help him. Of course, she loved children including him just like his mummy, who, just as real as the Virgin, was also not there and was not likely to turn up with his Pa and tell him the whole thing was an awful mistake and take him home for ever.

He was on his own.

That night at supper it was his table's job to clear the plates. As he took a stack of sloppy crockery into the industrial kitchen and set it by the (normally quite exciting) conveyer belt dishwasher, he saw a huge battered tray of leftover lamb chops swimming in grease on the top of the oven and he had an idea.

Willy the cook was in the next part of the kitchen swigging the bottles of cooking sherry that had ruptured the capillaries in his nose, eased his bad conscience at his culinary negligence, and made him reek like an old barrel. Weld checked no one was looking and pulled the tray on top of himself, slipping to the floor with a deafening clatter.

Willy stumbled in.

'You clumsy bugger.'

Mr Maxwell, the flaxen-haired geography master on duty that night, heard the noise and rushed into the kitchen.

'What the hell's going on here?'

Weld was sitting on the filthy red-tiled floor of the kitchen, fatty chops scattered around him and piled up in his lap as the warm grease sank pleasantly through his clothes.

'I slipped, sir. There was something on the floor and I slipped.'

'Are you hurt?' the master asked.

'No, sir.'

'Well, that's something. Go upstairs, fetch your dressing-gown, leave your clothes in the laundry, have a shower, change straight into your pyjamas, miss evening prayers, read your book in bed, and I'll come and see you with clean clothes from Matron tomorrow. Got it?'

'Yes, sir.'

'Good lad. Are you sure you're not hurt?'

'No sir ... am I getting an MC?'

'No, you silly boy, off you go.' He helped Weld up and almost ruffled his hair as he exited the kitchen.

# Twenty

Max decided to compound his blamelessness and elevate it to martyrdom by tidying the house and scrupulously putting away all the supplies he had bought. When Valentine did not return to find him at work as he hoped, he set off in search of a place in which to sulk. He liked to think that Tine would soon return and, seeing more evidence of his selfless behaviour, realise the injustice she had meted out with such heartless abandon. She would then rush to find him in one of their usual places, and when she could not, she would be overcome with worry and guilt – fearing perhaps that he had taken up his pack and moved on to an environment where kindness and fairness were properly valued.

But instead of a comfortable and shady spot, Max found only thicket after thicket of thorn bushes. Frustrated with his lack of progress, he pushed into the woods, catching and scratching himself until the woods fell away to a low cliff above the sea surrounded by impassable walls of thorn on either side. He was forced to turn back and made his way to the house.

Valentine was still not there. He wondered for a second if something might have happened to her and then the old machinery of his mind lurched into life, bringing the suspicion that she had returned, packed up and left. He no longer felt like punishing her with his disappearance and wished that everything could return to the idyll they had enjoyed only hours before. How could things slip so? One minute they were in a hazy world of connection and passion, and the next, everything was raw and jagged. All he had wanted to do was be recognised for his achievements and then tell her the wonderful news that he loved her.

He wondered if he still did.

He had not eaten all day but was not hungry. An infernal merry-go-round of dark and familiar thoughts was beginning its revolution and the only thing he felt like doing was sitting and smoking cigarette after cigarette until they made him feel sick. Since he had no cigarettes he went inside the house and collapsed onto the bed with an angry sigh. The long walk to the village and back had exhausted him.

Max closed his eyes and forced a few moments of reeling darkness over his thoughts before yanking them open again. Where was she? He leapt up then lay down again. The window before the bed was partially covered by a threadbare blue curtain. Bright lines of light shone through the gaps in the shutters, filtering through the tears and rents in the curtain. The situation felt desperate, yet familiar – he was not sure why. He looked at the curtain and felt a surge of old panic, as tangible as the blue fabric in front of the window, but somehow separate from him, as if it were someone else's memory.

He now knew: Tine had gone because of him.

He lay with his arms crossed, hands on opposite shoulders, his mind spinning with whispers: what he was, what he was not, what he should be, what would be done to him. He dug his fingernails into his skin to stay the barrage, scraped ditches down his sun-darkened arms to halt the march of thoughts. His nails left a trail of white lines smeared with blood where he caught the raw nipple of a mosquito bite. The smarting was a relief to him, the marks proof like the bars of light between the blinds of the window.

He slept.

In a doze he heard her at the window, her shadow breaking the beams of light. He woke, waiting for her to come to him, to stroke his head, encircle him with her arms, to make everything right.

But she did not.

He rose and stumbled through the kitchen, expecting to find her sitting at the table, but she was not at the table, there was no sign of her. He saw a beetle nestled in the folds of a towel discarded on the limewashed floor. Max made for the sea, hurt that Tine must have looked at him through the window and then left, like someone gazing at pets abandoned in a pound and strolling off without another thought.

Tine was there, lazing by the edge, one foot in the water. She opened and closed her eyes.

'Where've you been?' she croaked.

'Me? You were the one who left. Where have you been?'

'I've been here, right here.'

'Doing what?' he asked, not knowing what else to say.

'Sitting, thinking, swimming ... maybe a little sleeping.'

'Me too, but in the house,' Max said, editing out his trek through the woods. 'You were looking at me.'

'What?'

'When I was in bed, through the window. Just now.'

'No, I was here,' Tine replied.

'What? You were here the whole time?'

'Yes. Why?'

Max caught himself. 'No reason.'

'No, tell me ...'

Max had pulled off his T-shirt and was tugging down his

shorts. He stepped out of them, took two steps towards the edge and dived.

'ROCK,' Tine screamed.

He heard her and twisted like a shot bird in the air, coming down hard with a slap on the water.

'Fuck, fuck, fuck, that fucking rock,' he swore through clenched teeth.

Tine reached out to him as he swam back to the edge.

'Are you OK?'

He pulled himself out and sat on the stone, the sting of the water soon ebbing away.

'I'm fine, it was just a belly flop.'

'It was a corker,' she said, smiling. She put her hands on either side of his face and stared into his eyes. 'Max, I'm sorry. I know it's not fair of me to be angry with you, not fair at all. I don't understand it fully ... there's this tension in me, I've never had it before but it's been building up – in the background anyway. All these little things: the house being swept, my swimsuit disappearing, this ... person watching and you not believing ... you wouldn't believe me.'

'I'm sorry, I thought maybe you were ...'

'I hate not being believed. It feels like I'm in a dream trying to scream and not making a sound. It's one of my things ... I don't know, there's more to it, I suppose ... whatever happened here ... things from the past, things that happened here.'

'Like what?' Max said, pulling himself out of the water.

'Nothing. I don't even remember. The important thing is I care for you so much Max. In fact, I love you, I really do.'

It was the button he wanted pressed and he was suddenly drenched in joy, flooded with a sense of completion, every yearning, every gully filled by what she had said. As if her words met all that was missing in him.

They held each other, Max gripping onto Tine until she pulled away and kissed him. Max manoeuvred himself on top of her, resting one leg between hers, kissing and sucking at her neck, pulling her bikini top aside and licking around her nipples, faster and faster like a dog chasing its tail. She wrapped her legs around his waist and rubbed against him. He tugged at one of the bows on the side of her bikini, releasing it. He dragged the material away and placed the palm of his hand between her legs; she moaned but as he leaned into her, she changed her mind, sitting up and pushing his hand away from her.

'Let's go inside,' she said.

'Why?'

But she was already standing, covering her breasts and retying the bow at her hip before dashing into the house, brushing sand off the back of her legs as she walked. Max caught up with her, not bothering to pick up his clothes, grabbing her and pulling her into a run. They kissed again on the porch, laughing, the sand on the soles of their feet rough and delicious on the powdery lime floor. He pushed his hand into the front of her bikini feeling the soft tufts of hair between his fingers, resting them on either side of the split of her. He squeezed the flesh between his fingers, holding her together, excited when he felt her knees give and she hooked her hands over his shoulders and clung, biting the muscles on his shoulder whilst he squeezed between her legs.

He avoided the string of her tampon, letting it hang between his fingers, pushing it to one side with his knuckles, as if it were something that could not be acknowledged.

'In, let's go in – shut the door,' she whispered.

They pushed through the door together, tripping, clumsy.

'Let me get rid of this . . .'

She broke away and disappeared into the lavatory through the kitchen. Max was waiting for her when she came out. He kissed her neck from behind, undid her bikini top and pulled it off. She put both hands to her hips and pulled the bows like pins on a grenade, dragging the unfastened material through her legs, pushing him onto the bed, turning her back and lowering herself onto him.

'Turn round, I want to see your face,' Max said.

'No, please,' Tine insisted, kneeling on the bed and lowering her head onto the bedcovers, exposing herself to Max in a way that was almost violent, 'this way.'

'Valentine . . .'

'Please Max.'

Max spat on his hand and wet his penis. He pushed into her with a grunt, gripping her arms like reins and pulling himself against her with short, hard slaps. Tine's face was on the bed turned to one side, her arms stretched behind her, fists clenching and unclenching, one eye pressed into the bedclothes, the other open, staring at the window like a dead fish. Max was lost in a world of possession, grasping at her, and pushing, wanting somewhere in him to hurt her, but when she screamed and leapt away Max fell back in shock and smashed into the wooden cupboard that sloped towards the door like an old man. He looked down in horror at his penis, bloodied like some dreadful crime.

'Tine . . . what have I done, what have I done,' he whimpered.

She was by the window, the curtain ripped to one side, the shutters open as she craned her head outside.

'He was there,' she whispered.

'For fuck sake,' Max exclaimed, realising what the blood was.

'He was there, at the window.'

'Who ...? Fuck.' Max grabbed Tine's wrap and ran out through the house. When he was on the other side of the wall he shouted through the window.

'There's no one here ... hold on.'

He reappeared and stood in the doorway, the wrap wound round his hips like a miniskirt.

'I saw him – well, something, a shadow,' Tine said quietly. She put on Max's T-shirt.

'I believe you,' Max replied. 'But whoever it was, he's gone now.'

'He? You saw him?' Tine asked, pulling Max's T-shirt down her thighs.

'I don't know, they, him, her ... There were marks in the sand. I didn't find anything else.'

'We should go to the village, find Zeno if he hasn't drunk himself to death.'

'Who's Zeno?'

'The policeman ... part-time, if he's still alive. He was useless anyway.'

'I don't want to go back there today. It's probably just boys from the village.'

'It's not boys from the village.'

'How do you know?'

'It's not the fucking boys from the village,' Tine said, getting up and walking away from him.

Max looked at the close tuck of her buttocks, a streak of blood already dry. Suddenly, he yearned to be between them, stretch them open. He moved towards her, gripping her hips.

'Shall we get back to business?'

'God Max, the moment's passed.' Tine pulled away. 'There's not really room for you anyway.' She took a step apart, revealing the new string between her legs. She gestured to the torn wrapper on the ground.

'Already . . .' Max complained.

'I had to.'

He followed her eyes to the floor where spots of blood marked her passage to the window, like the path of a wounded animal.

Max stood in the bedroom looking at the drops of blood leading to the window. It was not that he minded being watched, nor the blood on him – once he'd worked out what it was – but everything was ruined now. The intruder had stolen something from them, made off with their paradise.

For the rest of the day, they hardly spoke about what had happened, but the interloper's presence lingered like terrible news. Valentine now refused all sexual advances – but it was not only the rejection that bothered him, there was something eating away at their happiness. She said it was menstrual, but he sensed there was something else.

They carried on, though. Swimming, reading, lazing together. They cooked, slowly grilling the butterflied lamb over low embers. Tine ate the honey cake, consuming piece after piece while she listened to the story of its purchase with feigned enthusiasm.

'It's polenta,' she told him, to fill the silence after his tale, taking solace in another moist lump and stuffing it into her mouth, courting a nausea that she would later use as a barrier to intimacy.

They went to bed that night, and for the next few nights, less entangled in embraces and separating further in sleep, as far as the corners of the bed would allow.

Increasingly, they supported each other's reasons to be alone; Valentine would go looking for shells, Max might seek firewood. One morning he walked to the village; they did not need anything but he bought an octopus from a boy in the square.

As he was returning, sliding down the final cliff path, the warm squishiness of the plastic bag bouncing against his leg, he caught sight of something on the path below. He knew it could not be Tine because she had headed off that morning in the other direction. He was wondering whether to conceal himself and surprise the other person when he realised with a shock that the looming presence was now closer to him, observing him from the shade of a thorn bush. The bag dropped from Max's hand as he exclaimed in surprise. The figure approached him, picked up the bag, sniffed it and said something impossible to make out.

The man's hair was long and lank, and his clothes were ripped and filthy, but had it not been for the palsy that pulled one side of his face down, extending the socket of his left eye and distorting his mouth into a leer, he might have been handsome. He mumbled something to Max, the line of freckles under his eyes collapsing on one side like flecks of ash, the words tumbling out of the side of his mouth like a cartoon character making a wisecrack.

'I'm not sure what you're saying.' Max looked past the man and wondered if he could get by him and run. He was not much taller than Max but he looked tough and weathered. He was jabbering at Max, repeating the same sentence, then a single word.

'Acta-pwer,' he said, spitting the last syllable through broken teeth.

'I'm sorry, I don't speak Greek,' Max said, wondering if this was the man who'd been spying on them.

'Inglesss,' the man insisted, 'actapwer.'

'Octopus?' Max ventured.

'*Ne, ne, ne,*' the man said.

It was sometimes hard to remember that *ne* meant yes but there was no question about it in this instance.

'Actapwer,' the man repeated.

He seemed pleased and attempted a smile that collapsed his palsied face in such a failure of happiness that Max felt pity amidst his revulsion.

'Eating,' the man said.

'Yes, that's the plan – lunch,' Max said. 'Anyway, nice to meet you, I must be off.' Max offered his hand in a reflex action but the man did not shake it. Instead he grasped Max's wrist with a three-fingered hand and guided him towards an opening in the bushes. There was something more desperate than threatening about him, so Max followed, determined to find out if he had been the voyeur.

Despite the man's solidity he moved through the bushes, over boulders, and under branches, with agility and surprising speed. He stopped suddenly and scrambled up a rock that rose five or six feet next to a tree. He pulled Max up behind him and pointed to a nest, a neat whorl of twigs snug in amongst the boughs. Max levered himself up over the edge of the nest and saw three green speckled eggs nestling like treasure. Max smiled at the man, who nodded gravely and then tipped the eggs into his hand, taking one and offering the rest to Max.

'I don't think so,' Max said.

The man laughed and dropped the eggs onto the rock, where they crumpled with a quiet crack. He stepped off the rock, landing lightly. Max wavered, wondering whether to jump or slide down.

The man signalled for Max to jump.

Max landed with a hard thud and was rewarded with a slap on the back and a broken-toothed grin. The two of them walked on for a few paces before the man halted at a bush and examined it portentously. It looked the same as any other bush, dry, woody, scraggy, although sprinkled with tiny bright green leaves.

'Rigani,' the man said proudly. He snapped off a crooked stem. 'For Ohcta-pwer,' he offered, trying to imitate Max's pronunciation.

Max rubbed the leaves, smelling woody smells and savoury cooking. He followed the man to the path and was relieved when he saw him dart back into the forest without even a wave. As Max reached the path at the bottom of the cliff, wafting his wand of 'rigani', he caught sight of the tiny ant-like smudge of Valentine lying in their favourite place in the sun. As Max neared he was able to make out the strips of colour of her bikini. Max grinned to himself; he felt like a returning warrior – not because of the octopus and this mountain herb – but because he had untangled the ridiculous set of events that had seemed increasingly sinister – even to Max, who had not revealed his own terror throughout those sleepless, sexless nights.

He had not mentioned his concerns to Valentine because she was already burdened by her own mad theories, but it no longer mattered, all was revealed. Everything would go back to normal. This broken-toothed hobo was the intruder – a harmless bum – maybe a bit soft in the head, but certainly not dangerous. A voyeur at worst. Max was pleased with himself: he'd not only befriended the poor fool, but in some way, he felt he had mastered him, rescued his Valentine from her terror. The way men should.

And the idea came to him that it had not been something he had been doing, or not doing, that had caused Tine to drift away, to close her legs to him, only the exaggerated shadow of this harmless fool. Now he had sorted out the problem, she would be herself again, the self he was in love with.

And everything would be perfect.

# Twenty-one

It had been a solution and, for a few moments, a triumph, but it was of course, only temporary. It took more than a new pelt to camouflage prey once the scent was out. Especially from Linnet, who had found his role as Weld's tormenter to be so full of reward that it lessened the inconvenience of the 'dead arms' his brother in the top year administered to him most days, and even the discomfort and humiliation of the 'wedgies' his brother's friends would give him, sliding their hands as far as they could down the back of his shorts and pulling up his underpants with breathless glee, sometimes carrying him round so that his legs peddled comically in the air whilst the elastic cut into him.

Torment took time, and time, like food, was in short supply at St Xavier's. It had to find its place amidst the hours of classes, of set work, of three meals with grace before and grace after, of the queues in and the queues out, the daily assemblies, the emergency assemblies, the waiting for tea and three biscuits (chocolate ones every other Friday), the hours of trudging after rugby balls on rain-blasted fields cratered with mud, the cross-country runs – up, down, along and back and another circuit for dawdling – the drizzly not-quite-hot showers over-seen by the matron or some bored member of staff, hair washing on a Thursday, with an iridescent puddle of shampoo from a great green bottle achingly labelled 'Family Shampoo'. Toothbrushing, morning and night; sheet changing, every other Wednesday; socks and pants, every other day; shirts, once a week; shorts and sweaters, every two. Prayers: morning mass, morning prayers and every night before bed, benediction on Saturday and high mass on Sunday, not to mention the litany of Ascensions, Assumptions, Epiphanies and Transfigurations and an army of saints and martyrs that needed attending to. Then, and only then, there might be time for Torment.

At first Weld stumbled into every trap on offer, straying too far from the teacher's sight in the playground, arriving early for class, arriving late for class, using the lavatories without checking, getting things right in class, getting things wrong in class and – most damning of all – despite it being the goal and consummation of all Torment, tears.

Weld soon became more skilled at avoiding situations or even states of mind that might make him vulnerable, as an animal avoids places without cover or sites of recent ambush. Sometimes he succeeded, but his most disastrous maulings came because he was desperate to please Linnet and so fell for the apparent changes of heart in his tormentor.

The first was at supper one night. They had frankfurters and baked beans – Weld liked baked beans, at least he thought he did when he had them at home, but these were not the same as at home. Weld had supposed baked beans could be relied upon, like oranges or Mars bars, but these beans were horrible – hard and in a transparent red sauce – and the frankfurters, they came in a big can with grey water, he'd seen the can out in the rubbish, and they were cooked in the murky water. Brown on the outside and spongy pink within.

He ate them though. Father Demain had told the boys they were lucky to have food when people were starving in the Missions.

Linnet hung two frankfurters from his mouth and pretended to be Dracula. Everyone laughed because two wobbly sausages coming out of his mouth did look funny. Weld said, without thinking, that Linnet looked more like a walrus than a vampire. The table fell silent and Weld wished he could make time go backwards, like a tape recorder or Superman going round the world the wrong way, but Linnet just smiled and asked him what a walrus was. Weld rushed in to fill the gap, saying that walruses were very rare, and he only knew about them because he'd seen them on the back of a Shreddies packet at home.

'Well, what exactly *is* a walrus then Smeld?' Linnet demanded.

Weld ignored his nickname. He looked around and wondered if he should risk an answer or was this a trick, but Linnet seemed interested, and even friendly, so Weld explained that walruses were fat seals covered in thick leather, as big as buses and with two fangs as long as his arms. He knew that the Latin name was Rosmarus because he played an animal game with his Pa on Sundays when he was at home, but thought it better not to say.

'That's very interesting,' Linnet said, looking down at his plate and flopping the sausage up and down. 'Maybe you can help me with another thing I don't know?'

Weld was more than ready, desperate to share his knowledge and win favour. He nodded excitedly.

'It's a word … *erection* … do you know what it is?'

Weld had been hoping he'd know the word – maybe if he did, Linnet might stop tormenting him, or even be his friend – but although the word sounded familiar, so many words did and he couldn't place this one.

'Sorry Linnet, I don't know that one.'

'Oh,' said Linnet, seeming disappointed. Stellmark, who was the tallest in the class, started sniggering, but Linnet rounded on him.

'Shut up Stickman.'

Stellmark withdrew like a threatened snail.

'It's such a shame as I really, really, wanted to know what that word meant. Do you think Fr Demain might know?' Linnet looked straight at Weld and smiled.

'Of course he would. He knows almost everything,' Weld replied.

'Ask him,' Linnet said, throwing down the gauntlet, 'I dare you.'

It was frightening to ask the Father something, and Weld did not even know if it was allowed, but from the first day at St X's, boys had been indoctrinated with stories of saints and soldiers bravely martyring themselves, blessed by fate with an opportunity for selfless, suicidal courage. It might be fighting a Philistine giant, facing down Nazis, refusing to swear allegiance to the Protestants, refusing to betray the Catholic queen, but in general it involved striding happily towards one's execution – ideally after a prolonged and barbaric session of torture.

Weld had been fantasising about laying down his life for his country, or for God, or for his classmates – he was not sure which, but the important thing was that he would die a hero. There'd be a short and dignified speech from the scaffold, during which everyone would realise Weld's extraordinary courage and feel terrible for ever thinking he was a blubber. Then there'd be tears all round, the execution and everlasting glory.

The silence bell rang and the noise of the large room gradually extinguished like bush fires hissing under wet blankets. Linnet nudged Weld. He took a deep breath and pushed himself off the oak bench towards the towering black-robed figure that was Fr Demain.

'Please, Father.'

The priest did not ignore him – he did not hear him; he did

not expect to hear a sound from so close to the floor. Weld's table watched with horrified delight. Weld considered abandoning the mission and scurrying back to his table but Fr Demain had become aware that the table of older boys were all staring at something behind him. He swung slowly round like the turret of a tank. His gaze found a small boy struggling to keep his composure.

'You are a small boy who should be seated at his table.'

'Sorry, Father. May I ... I wanted to ask you a question.'

'Name?'

'Weld, Father.'

'Weld ... Is your papa Giles Weld?'

'No, Father.'

'Elder brother, Luke, a handy Wing-Forward? And the older one, Julian I think it was, one of our best ever Centre-Halves ...'

'No, Father.'

'I thought not. Now tell me, young Weld, of no obvious relations, is it your prerogative to simply ask questions whenever one should float into your enquiring little mind?'

'Father?'

'Never mind.' He sighed. 'Pray continue, what is this question?'

'A word Father, it's a word. I don't know what it means.'

'A word?'

'Yes, Father.'

'Go on then.'

'Erection, Father.'

'Again?'

'Erection.'

'What ... Did ... You ... Say?' Fr Demain extended each monosyllable, as if offering in each pause an opportunity for penance.

With a gathering sense of alarm Weld realised that something was very wrong. He supposed asking the Fathers questions after the silence bell must be strictly against School Rules.

'Sorry, Father, it doesn't matter.'

'I asked you a question, you impertinent child. Now answer me. What did you say?'

Whatever crime Weld had committed, the deed had been done, so he thought he had better do as he was told.

'Erection, Father.'

'Where did you hear this word?'

'Linnet asked me, Father, he wanted ...' Weld had not wished to condemn Linnet but it was too late.

'LINNET MINOR come HERE.'

Linnet arrived with an expression of utter innocence.

'Linnet, if your brother were not such a good Prop Forward and you were both not Mites in your first term, I would send you to Brother Noonan and by the time he'd finished with you, you wouldn't be able to tie your own laces for a *week*. How *dare* you play the fool with me! As you are Mites, I will give you two MCs each so count yourself lucky. Books!'

He snatched the plastic folders from their hands and signed demerits for them both. As they were heading back to their table Linnet hissed.

'Smeld snitched on me. He's a snitch.'

# Twenty-two

'You did what?' Tine had snapped from torpor to attention as Max told his tale.

Max grinned. He felt as if he were holding a magnificent hand of poker that he could lay down whenever he liked.

'I met him. Our intruder, our voyeur. I spoke to him, tamed the beast, so to speak.'

'Are you sure it was him?'

'Pretty much,' Max replied.

'Stocky, muscular, looks like he sleeps in a bush ... rugged face, thinks he's handsome?'

'You seem to know him pretty well,' Max ventured. 'Anyway, that's him – but not handsome, not even to a girl. Maybe once upon a time, but now his teeth are broken and half his face is sort of limp. Paralysed.'

'I heard about that ... wish all of him was ...'

Max had not been expecting this – her expression so hard, without compassion, maybe even malevolent. He had not seen this side of her before, perhaps he had been blind to it.

'He seemed OK to me, poor fellow, harmless anyway.'

'He isn't harmless.'

'You actually know him?'

'I should have told you ... He hung around here when I last came with Mum. They were ... I don't know, sort of friends ... she took a shine to him, I suppose he was young, and handsome.'

'Well he's not handsome now. What happened to him?'

'It was after I left. Bell's palsy or something. The villagers
... sleeping outside in winter ... I don't know.'

'He's definitely not all there. He was lurking round looking
for company, I'll bet. He's probably lonely.'

'He deserves to be.'

'That's a bit cruel. At least we know who it was and he
won't come snooping any more.'

'What makes you so sure? Did you talk to him?'

'We communicated. We understood each other. He showed
me things, a jay's nest I think, and look, he gave me this special
herb for the octopus.' Max waved the green-leafed switch
towards her.

'That special herb?' She laughed at him. 'It's oregano.'

'So?'

'So stay away from him. I don't want him near the house
again.'

'He's harmless, we explored a bit, he found me the
oregano ...'

'It's everywhere, Max, half the fucking bushes here are
oregano.'

'What's up with you?"

'I don't want you to fall for his wildman-of-the-woods act.
Just leave him alone.'

'I don't understand.'

'God, what is it with you Max? Why can't you leave it? OK,
his name's Khalib. He used to lurk around us, around my
mother and me. She lapped up his Man of Nature bullshit
too – it was the worst summer of my life. Anyway, this was
years ago, he probably still lives in a disgusting shack in the
woods. The villagers won't even let him in the village because
he's such an animal. Is that enough?'

Max turned and walked towards the house, shaking his head

at Valentine's collapse from the pedestal he had so exhaustingly built for her. When he reached the kitchen he wrenched open the kerosene fridge, tossed in the warm sack of octopus, twisted round to shut the door. Tine had appeared on the other side of the door, ploughing a fingernail along the old seal of the refrigerator.

'Look Max, this ... fury ... it's not me. I mean, it's *new* to me. It has something to do with Khalib and being here, I suppose. I'm sorry, I really am ... and I should have told you the whole story. I suppose I'd stopped thinking about it and didn't want to begin again. My parents split up that summer but they didn't bother to tell me, didn't think I would even notice ... I hate talking about him – them I mean – all that. It's so negative.' She paused and examined the muck she had scraped from the grooves in the rubber seal. 'It's just that I kind of had to put up with Khalib as a child ... feeling sorry for him but then not wanting him around ... and now he's here again. He's a creep.'

She moved her lips to Max and they kissed. He took her head in his hands and brought his thumbs round into her mouth.

Tine backed away and squealed.

'Yuk. You stink. You touched the octopus, didn't you, and now it's on your fingers.' She crossed the kitchen to pick up an earthenware bowl. 'The locals say the smell's harder to remove than the sin of a harlot from an archbishop's soul. Let's eat him – I'll show you how it's done.'

Valentine hooked the bag out of the fridge with one finger and tossed it in the sink. She slit the bag open and dragged the slimy bundle out with the tip of a knife. 'Now for the fun part.' Without touching it, she manoeuvred the creature into the bowl and headed outside to the shore, a few metres from their usual spot.

'This was always the octopus rock,' she said to Max who followed behind.

Valentine slipped into the sea, tipped the octopus out and rinsed it in the brine, swirling it around like a rag. It seemed to come to life, its head filling, its tentacles making graceful arabesques in the clear blue water. With her hand inside the head like a mitten, Tine pulled it out of the water and slapped its eight legs against a rock in front of her.

'Do you want a go?' she called to Max.

Like a sulking child his sullenness had thawed as he watched her well-practised technique and enjoyed the slap of the gelatinous body against the rock. He slid into the water and took his turn beating the octopus.

'The best thing for tenderising it is freezing,' she said, 'for at least three weeks, then it gets soft and easier to cut. But beating it, this is the old way.'

Max slapped the limp beast, dipping it back into the sea to wash off the grains of rock, marvelling at the way the crenellated edges of the creature opened in the water like anemones, then ripping it out again and focusing all his strength on battering it anew. After ten minutes, he was slapping it harder and harder against the rock, grunting with the effort until the head split and the octopus arced through the air and snagged in a thorn bush.

'Easy there Rambo,' Tine said, both of them laughing at the octopus caught in the bush like laundry scattered in the wind. It took them twenty minutes to unhook the tentacles from the thorns. Tine boiled it for half an hour with the remnants of the retsina and half a head of garlic. Later Max watched her crouch over the pit they had dug in the sand, grilling the tentacles over the embers, like some bikini-clad stone age princess.

Valentine made no more mention of Khalib or her parents,

so neither did Max. He did not give a thought to the man in the woods, he just wanted everything to be good again, to be allowed back into paradise, back into her.

Max lay balanced on the low wall that surrounded the porch, imagining Tine naked, legs astride his lap, facing him, how her mouth and eyes might look as he pushed into her. He thought of lying face to face, or pressing down on top of her, his weight on her legs, stretching them back over her head, opening her, her smiling, or gasping, or closing her eyes, or widening them, or ... it didn't matter what he thought, she would only have sex in one way: away from him, her head down, buried. He would have liked to look into her eyes – weren't you supposed to do that? – but it was not an option, even when she was letting him have her, which she wasn't.

Later they sat together on the rough, uncomfortable bench outside the house. Max opened a small and dangerous looking bottle of retsina with a top like a beer bottle that he had stashed in the coldest part of the kerosene fridge, along with a couple of glasses which had become cloudy with condensation. The table top was creased with cracks and a scattering of crumbs and peach pits. Max was trying to woo her again; sit close, tell her how lovely she was, try to reclaim that happiness that had been stolen, that he needed.

He sloshed the preciously cool wine into the tumblers as Valentine jumped up from the bench. She returned a few moments later with a broom and hovered over the table.

'Grab everything for a sec.'

Max took a glass in each hand, put his mouth over the bottle and picked it up in his mouth, shouting 'da-dah' through his teeth. Valentine ignored him and swept the detritus off the table and onto the limewashed floor. Then she brushed the crumbs and rubbish off the porch and into the sand.

'Come and sit down,' Max said.

She did.

'My father made this bench . . . did I tell you that?'

'Yes, it took him all day . . . cheers Valentine.' Max held up his glass.

'Hold on, it's getting cooler.' Valentine stood up again. 'I'm going to grab my top.' She dashed into the house.

The sun was setting, the light roseate. Max was delaying the pleasure of taking a sip until she returned.

He sat for a while and then called her.

'I'm making the dressing for the octopus,' she shouted from the kitchen.

He waited again, the light deepening, concentrating from pink to orange, to a cordial red.

'Come on, Tine, you're missing it.'

'Just a sec.'

She did not come. The sunset ebbed, darkening from the centre.

Max picked up his glass and took a swig of the wine – it lacked the ambrosial chill he had been anticipating. He took another sip; it was sharp and rough.

'Come on Tine. I want to say something to you.'

She appeared at the door, yellow washing-up gloves on.

'Yes?'

'I wanted to say . . . come and sit down.'

She perched on the bench away from Max. He handed a glass to her and they clinked.

'Go on then,' Tine said before sipping, holding the glass, yellow gloves still on.

'I don't know . . . maybe the moment's passed . . .' He forced himself. 'I just wanted to say you're special, I think you're special.'

'I think you're special too,' Tine said taking a gulp of

wine. 'Jeepers, this new stuff, it's evil. You could burn tumours off with it. Give me some more before I realise what I'm doing.'

Max refilled her glass and Tine took a sip and stood.

'I'll get the octopus. I'm quite literally dying of hunger. Stay where you are.'

Max stared down at the table. He swiped his hand hard over the surface and splinters rammed into his hand like pikes. Max cursed and tried to pinch them out, worrying at the points until Tine reappeared with the grilled octopus and a plate of spinach.

'I'm in agony here, can you help me?' Max asked.

'Just a sec, I'm starving.'

'Right.' Max looked at her angrily and put his hand under the table. 'Well let me know when you're ready. I'm not that hungry.'

Valentine ignored him and began eating.

Max swallowed his wine, refilled it and swallowed again.

Unable to ignore his sighs Valentine proffered him a tentacle. 'Try, some, it's delicious.'

He leaned over and bit off the end; it was chewy and charcoal bitter with a slight sweet taste of the sea. He took one of the fatter pieces lying slightly curled on the plate. The outside was mottled pink with lines of black from the grill. He bit into the thickest part and chewed the sweet white meat in the middle. It was unimaginably good, juicy, coated in olive oil, flecked with the pungent green leaves of the wild oregano, and sharpened with lemon juice. Delicious enough to make him forget about Tine's coldness.

He joined her and they ate with appreciative sighs, even the spinach: the dark green *horta* grown in every vegetable patch in the village was delicious and bitter, glistening with olive oil.

By the end of the meal the plates were empty as was the bottle of retsina. Max's glass was smeared with grease from his mouth and hands, a few oregano leaves and flecks of carbon floating in the last puddle of wine. Valentine's glass was clear and hardly touched, amber in the candlelight.

Max picked up a tea towel and wiped his mouth and hands before reaching to kiss Valentine.

She recoiled from him, frowning at the cloth hanging half off the table with its fresh smear of oil.

'I wish you wouldn't do that, it's just been washed.'

'What's it for then?' Max said, bristling, 'I mean if not to wipe my mouth.'

'There's a sink, a hose ...'

'What's up with you?' Max demanded.

She stood up from the bench.

'Nothing's up, nothing at all, you just dirty everything.'

'Dirty everything?' Max got up too and strode off towards the sea.

Max stomped to the water, feeling a tightening in his chest somewhere between desperation and rage. All he really wanted was justice but he could have so easily been soothed with a few caresses and words of comfort. It would be enough to rest his head on Tine's breast and have her stroke his hair and tell him everything would be all right. Yet he could see her growing more distant with every moment. He'd known it was true for a while but he had been making excuses to himself. Now he submitted to the reality. She was going.

She'd already gone.

She'd said he was a child. How fucking dare she. He was feeling like a child and he hated that feeling, despised yearning for comfort, like some weak defenceless little boy. It was disgusting.

'Fuck you,' he whispered to himself, snapping off a branch. 'Fuck you, fuck you, fuck you.' He sank to his haunches and rested his chin on his hands. The ground lurched to one side like an old ship and he stretched his hands onto the sand to steady himself.

He was drunk.

He needed to swim, that would clear his mind, stop the ringing, the revving reel of thoughts. He tugged off his clothes and clambered into the water. The warm night sea enveloped him, supporting his body. He pulled himself through the water, enjoying the freshness of its fingers, especially between his toes and fingers, in his armpits, the snaking coolness between his legs. Each stroke made him feel better but then something smashed into him, something sharp and unyielding. For a moment he was engulfed with panic – and then he remembered Valentine's Rock, this underwater cliff lurking like a half-forgotten memory. He clung onto it for a moment, panting, hanging onto it like a tick, a shell-less mollusc, and then swam back to the shore.

Max found Tine sitting on the low wall of the house, twisting her hair into plaits and threading a shell onto each strand, lost in the action like a child. He approached stealthily, feeling the sand push up between his toes. Her head was tilted, the line of her neck so vulnerable. He was near enough her to smell the fake apple scent of her shampoo. He grazed her neck with his lips, causing her to leap off the wall screaming.

'You stupid fuck!'

Max backed away.

'You scared the life out of me,' she stammered. 'I'm sorry ... don't ever do that again ... creep up on me.'

She went to bed and Max paced, picking up things and putting them down again, trying to read the end of

*Gormenghast* by the flickering light of the remaining candle, looking for a drink, desperate to feel different. Unable to sleep.

# Twenty-three

Survival might have been impossible had there been no respite, no coppery seam in the slate grey clouds of every day. Like many at St Xavier's, Weld learned to mentally structure his week so that there was always something to look forward to. On Monday it was Double Art – which he enjoyed because it did not feature Trench-Foot, or numbers, or letters, and the colour in the bottles of paint was so intense, it was magical. Most of all he liked Art because he was allowed to cover a great space of paper with expressions of himself and these were accepted without complaint by the Art master, and sometimes even with compliment.

Tuesday was the worst day of the week. Not only did it feature Double Maths and a spelling test (he would always be second last, beating only Samual Ibwe, the Nigerian boy who was a novice to written English), but it was also too distant from the weekend to give him an end to look forward to. To alleviate the featureless gloom, he might try and save a treat for the afternoon, like a sugary remnant from his tuck box, or a letter from home. Tuesday night, after lights-out, could, to an extent, be savoured simply because another awful Tuesday had been crossed off a term – but this in itself was not a pleasure rich enough to be looked forward to.

Wednesday had few real qualities and was sometimes blighted by an alleged Cornish pasty at lunch. These were damp sacks, swollen with gristle and nameless lumps of horror that required gulps of water to swallow down. Nevertheless, there followed rugby practice all afternoon – which, although uncomfortable, boring and more often than not injurious, was better than being in class with Trench-Foot.

Thursday was blessed. Other than Religious Doctrine with Fr Le Saux, which was a delight, and the possibility of chocolate pudding at lunch – which was clearly a good thing – there was nothing obviously great about the day. It was just mysteriously good.

Friday marked the beginning of hope: there were fish and chips for lunch, and the weekend was near. Saturday began with the extraordinary treat of cornflakes instead of porridge – which was a bit like home – then there were classes as usual but by the time First Rec was over there were only two more until Monday. After lunch, if there was a rugby match against another school, you could support rather than go to practice. This involved standing on the touch line, blowing smoke rings in the cold air with your breath and sloshing through puddles in wellington boots. After showers, the sweet shop was open and then there was an hour of completely free time. That evening, during Studies, a prefect went round shouting 'Confessions, Confessions' and if you had committed any sins against God – which mostly everyone had – you could go to Confession. If you did not go to Confession and you had recently committed a proper sin, you could not take communion the next day at mass.

Unless Fr Le Saux was taking Confession, Weld would make up his sins: not sharing his sweets, not praying properly, telling the odd fib. He would gaze at the carved wood of the confessional and the silhouette of the priest through the grille, longing for the courage to mention something truly evil, something so bad that God would sit up and notice. A proper MORTAL sin so weighty that the Father would be dying to tell the other Fathers, but he couldn't, not even a hint, even if you had broken the worst school rule or stabbed someone with a dagger. Breaking the secret of Confession was the biggest sin a priest could do – as bad as murdering your own mother.

It was strange, but even if they had been shouting at you, or beating you, or making you wish you were dead, the Fathers were nice in the confessional – maybe because God was listening and they had to be on their best behaviour – except Fr Le Saux, he was kind everywhere, but it was the one place you might not want to find him, because if he was taking your Confession you did not feel you could make anything up. You *had* to tell the truth; search inside yourself and admit if you had been mean to someone, or copied the answer to a sum, or said a swear word, or wished someone did badly in the tests. It was hard, but after you had said the three Hail Mary's and a Glory Be he set for penance, you felt quiet and good – not only because he hadn't been shocked at your sins but because God Himself had forgiven you. That was Confession and it was not too bad. You'd miss fifteen minutes of Studies, in return for which, if you died in your sleep that night, you would go straight to Heaven and not be tortured in Hell for all eternity, or even in Purgatory for ten or twenty million years.

On Sunday there was no real work. You got up half an hour later which was quite boring and then had to wear full uniform for mass. Then there was letter writing and when you had finished your letter you had to show it to the master in charge. He would check for spelling mistakes – although everyone knew he was making sure no one was telling their mummies and daddies about the hairs they had found in a Cornish pasty or that a teacher had hit them for no reason.

Mass was boring, the most boring thing in church because it was so long. Along with Confession it was probably the Fathers' favourite part of the week; 'the coming together of our scholastic community in the celebration of the Holy

Eucharist,' they said. The Fathers wore old-fashioned costumes called Alb, Stole and Chasuble. They would wear different colours depending on the date in the Holy Calendar. Green was for a normal day, red was for martyrs (because of the blood of the tortured), purple for penance – which was saying sorry to God for all your sins – and white and gold for special feasts. You couldn't wear blue, ever. Except in South America where the Pope allowed blue as a special favour. There were three hymns, except on feast days when there were four. Everyone sang a few of the hymns really loud, like 'Immortal Invisible' or 'Guide Me Oh Thou Great Redeemer', but most were quite sad and boring, except for the one which went: *By the light of burning martyrs, Christ, Thy bleeding feet we track.* It meant that the Romans were using Christians instead of light bulbs, setting them on fire and then reading their books by them.

If you did not take communion, it meant you had not been to Confession, or you had eaten something an hour before mass – even one peanut was not allowed because you were eating God's Holy Body, and it was not right that He should arrive in your belly and find something like a Mars bar there.

The best words in the mass were: *The mass is ended. Go in peace.* Everyone would say: *Thanks Be to God.* But some people, including Weld, whispered: 'Thank God.' But saying this, even thinking it, was a sin, and one God could hear loud and clear because He was everywhere.

After mass was lunch, which was called Sunday Lunch to make it sound like the one people have at home with their family. But this one was not like that, except that there was Orange Squash instead of water, and roast potatoes which were soggy, although sometimes you got a crispy one. After that you would change into home clothes and have free time in the woods.

Although the woods were full of hiding places and might have seemed like a perfect place for Torment, they were no worse than anywhere else. There were so many better, more pleasurable things than Torment for everyone, even Linnet, to do. Spears and swords to be made, camps to be built, streams to be forded, battles to be waged, lions to be stalked, leaps to be leapt. No one would mind if Weld quietly joined a bear hunting party, or jumped the Big Stream on the rope when it was his turn. Of course if he were on his own and stumbled across Linnet and his gang when they were wondering what to do next, they might shout 'get him' and then he would have to run for his life, sprinting along deer paths and ducking under boughs. They would hardly ever catch him because his fear was bigger than their desire for Torment, and also he was becoming an expert at hiding. Sometimes he would deliberately make them chase him and then enjoy the relief as he lay panting, face down in the gold-flecked leaf mould.

Once, after running further than he had ever dared go, probably even out-of-bounds, he discovered a proper camp, a grown-up camp, completely hidden from everything. It was surrounded by thick brambles and a holly tree next to which was a hole to crawl through. There was a place where someone had made a fire and even a sort of oven made of stones and empty cans. It was frightening and thrilling. A proper adult had slept there and drank bottles of whisky – a dangerous person for sure: a convict or a madman. Despite the currency afforded by such a discovery, Weld told no one, visiting it on his own, hoarding his secret, knowing that whatever happened, he could always hide there, protected by the depth and darkness of the wood, by thorns and secrecy.

In the showers, after playing in the woods, he might get flicked by a towel but mostly people were hurrying so they could save a place for The Film. This was the high point of

Sunday, the pinnacle of what was looked forward to, the jewel of the scholastic week. A queue would stretch all around the playroom and then in a breathless moment, the doors would open and everyone would rush in and sit down. If you were in the lower two years, *Elements*, you would sit on the floor in front of the screen, third and fourth years, *Figures*, could sit on benches and the top year, *Rudiments*, had chairs. The Head Boy had a special armchair that was carried from the Staff Common room by two boys in the year above Weld's. Favoured Mites could sit by his feet. Linnet was often there but even if not, he would always get a good position without even having to queue because he would suck up to someone near the front and they would let him in. There was a lot of pushing and squeezing and begging of sweets from people who still had them from Saturday but once the film started no one said a word.

Sometimes the films were good, and sometimes they were boring. Weld's favourites were about other worlds and lost civilisations. One was about a man and his friend who found a hidden land on the other side of a snowy mountain and they made him king and he had everything – a palace and jewels and a princess for a wife, but he was homesick and he knew that if he tried to leave, which was impossible anyway, the natives would kill him. Another Sunday there was a film about cave men wearing skins and hunting mammoths. The teacher said it was inappropriate because this woman appeared wearing a bikini made of rabbit fur and the camera kept focusing on her huge big bazongas and the older boys shouted and the teacher made the focus go funny because it was most probably sinful. To Weld the sinful thing was that they were focusing on her bazongas when there were savage mammoths to see and, later on, a sabretooth tiger – which was like a see tiger but five times bigger.

Everyone else said the film the week before was boring. It went on for ages and most people left – but Weld watched it to the end. It was about a man on a spaceship, all alone except for robots. There were domes on the spaceship made of glass, each one the size of ten rugby pitches and full of every single plant in the world, complete jungles and flowers and trees. The man loved them as if they were his friends because he was alone with no one to talk to – which was quite boring, but Weld thought about the film for ages afterwards. He wished that he could be there with the gardens – but maybe on his way home to see his parents, who'd be happy to see him and keep him with them for ever – or at least until he was grown up.

When The Film ended it was like the big sign at the gates of Hell painted by the Devil that said: *Abandon hope all ye who enter here.* Although it was still officially Sunday, there was nothing to hope for, nothing to do after the film but dread the coming week: the opportunities for MCs, the hours of boredom, the spelling tests, Wednesday's Cornish pasty, the cross country. After The Film was also prime Torment time and Weld would usually try to hide somewhere rather than play in the open.

Hell is terrible. The very worst thing times ten million. People went there if they were not Roman Catholic, or even if they were, and had died having committed a Mortal Sin without making Confession. If they had committed Venal Sins, like missing mass on a Sunday or fibbing about something, then they would not go to Hell, but to Purgatory which was like Hell, but not so Eternal. Eventually, when they had suffered enough torture, they could go to Heaven.

Satan, which was the Devil's proper name, was in charge of Hell and he was the worst and scariest thing in the universe as well as being almost, but not quite, omnipotent – which meant he could do everything God could, but less – in the same way that Linnet was almost, but not quite, as fast a runner as Davies.

Some of the Torments regularly used in Hell:

1. Dropping water on your head until it drills a hole through your brain and you die.

2. Pushing strips of bamboo under your fingernails and setting them on fire.

3. Making you eat a thousand green apples and strawberries and other fruits and then locking you in an Iron Maiden from a castle until you suffocate on your own diarrhoea (probably Satan's favourite).

Weld's father did not believe in Hell, or in the Holy Trinity, or even the Blessed Virgin Mary. He didn't go to church because he was Jewish. He did not even go to Jewish church because he said he could not believe in his God after what had happened with the Nazis. Weld asked him what had happened but he wouldn't reply.

Weld asked him what he did believe in and his father said *education*.

Weld would lie awake on Sunday nights and wish he was at home and pray to God not to torture his Pa in Hell for being Jewish. He also prayed that God would make everyone understand that he hadn't meant to be a snitch.

# Twenty-four

We moved it eventually.

We managed, grimacing, giggling with horror, made braver by laughter, to carry the dead dog to the sea. By the time we'd one-two-three'd it into the water, we both felt sad for the poor thing. We saw it floating away, taking a few moments, quiet like pirates watching a dead cabin boy sink into the sea. Sad and relieved to see it disappear. I was even saying a little prayer to whoever looks after the hurt, unloved creatures of the world when the Triff put her hand to her mouth and shrieked:

'Oh God, Jojo.'

We ran back to the house but he was fine. He had crawled off the wrap and was having fun in the sand, making mountains and flattening them with his hand, not even noticing that we had left him. The Triff swooped down like a carnivorous plant and almost suffocated him with kisses. He would have been much happier left on his own. The sun was getting hot and none of us had eaten a crumb of breakfast, let alone the minimum three cups of strong coffee the Triff needed to fertilise her roots.

We crossed the terrace into the house and Triff warned me not to look – but I couldn't resist a peek at the dark sticky stain. It was thick with blue-green flies, browny red against the white of the terrace.

I wished I hadn't.

We had our breakfast in the house, like we had once before when it had rained and thundered all morning and Dad had taken off all his clothes and danced outside like a witch doctor from Africa. But it was sunny and hot so it was strange to be inside. I sat on the floor with Jojo who crawled about, opening the kitchen cupboards and getting stroppy when I took a bottle of bleach then a screwdriver off him. I looked at my yoghurt while the Triff scrubbed Jojo's handprints off the wall. No matter how much honey I poured on it, or how I tried to stop myself, I couldn't help thinking about the dog brains and wondering how they would feel in my mouth. The Triff might have been thinking something similar because she didn't drink her coffee or have anything else. She threw down her cloth and announced that there was one thing, and only one thing, to do:

'*Asbesti.*'

In a strange way, *Asbesti* is one of the things Mum and I like most about Ithica.

Dad doesn't.

He used to look at me when Mama said that word and then look at the sky as if only God understood what he had to suffer. I don't know why though; he hardly did anything to help and when he did, the Triff would usually complain that he was not sweeping properly, or was mixing it wrong, or adding too much lemon and he would stomp off or have to call l'Agent *urgently* – or he'd make up some other fib.

The Triff is very serious about the *Asbesti*. She says that it's an Art – at least, getting it right is.

First. Check the weather: it must be sunny (which is not difficult), and windless (easy).

Then. Sweep every speck of dust from the terrace, not just here and there like Cinderella with her broom on party night, but EVERYWHERE – *the Full Forensic* Triff calls it, like those policemen who catch the serial killer with one fleck of dandruff, and she's right, even one little dust atom spoils the whole effect.

'Spotless, darling, it has to be spotless – one speck and it's like a boil on a supermodel's nose.'

She hasn't mentioned spots this summer, for obvious reasons.

On the rare occasions Dad might help, he'd tiptoe about like a goblin in a cartoon, leaping on a speck of dust and shrieking *yet here's a spot* in his demented Scottish old woman voice – which was funny and made us laugh every time, well, me more than Mum, now I think about it.

Once the 'Full Forensic' is finished, it's time for one of my favourite parts.

You need:

*Asbesti* powder (a lot).

Lemons (five or more).

Water (of course).

Dad calls the powder *lime*, but not the sort that goes in drinks. The lemons are, though. You have to stir the whole lot for ages with a big paddle and the Triff will watch it like mad, saying 'more *Asbesti*, more lemon, stir stir!' and Dad will shriek 'Yet here's a spot' and the Triff will tell him to shut up. It's not ready until it's all white and thick – but not too thick – and most of all, silky. Then, when it's perfect, with bare feet and big mops we paint it on everywhere. When the painting is finished it looks terrible: a criss-crossing mess of wet stripes, like a badly mown cloud.

Finally (almost). We jump into the sea to wash off all the *Asbesti* which is all over our feet and hands then we walk up to the village and have a very slow lunch at the taverna with Captain Maris. We have to be gone at least three hours in order for the *Asbesti* to dry properly, so going to the village or town is the best way. We tried being patient and waiting outside the house once, but it didn't work. Someone always has a reason to step on the drying *Asbesti* – like they are bursting for the loo or can't live without their book, or more often MUST have a glass of retsina. Then there are footprints and the whole thing is ruined and must be done all over again.

In order to make lunch slow enough we have loads of courses: tzatziki, which is yoghurt with things in it, and tara-masalata, which is fish eggs but not disgusting like sea urchins – pink as sunburn and delicious, then a tomato stuffed with rice, then a fish and I get to eat the cheek like Captain Maris taught me. Dad would always dare me to eat the eye – because that is what a Real Greek Girl would do, and Captain Maris would nod and say that it was true, a Real Greek Girl would eat the eye of a fish. Dad would make chicken noises like a hen that had lost its friends and was walking around looking for them, and they'd get louder and louder until I'd tell him to *shush* because he was teasing me for being scared. Mum would tell him to *shut up* but he would get up, moving his head forwards and backwards and then I'd get upset and Captain Maris would change his mind and say that you could still be a Real Greek Girl and not eat a fish's eye, and Dad would cluck louder and start circling round our table, pecking at everything. If there were other children in the restaurant, they would be laughing, but the Greek families, they would just look at him and think he was silly. After the fish, I used to have ice cream, but I don't any more because it's not good for spots – although I do have lemon ice cream occasionally, or sometimes chocolate chip.

But once, when I was nine, this was all going on as usual, the clucking from Dad, the shushing from the Triff, and me feeling upset – but almost grown out of feeling upset – and I reach over to the great deadness of the fish with all its bones, like a zombie's comb full of rotting flesh and I scoop the eye out with my finger and put it in my mouth and swallow it down with a whole glass of water and Captain Maris shouts 'Bravo' and kisses me and says I'm a Real Greek Girl and one day I'll be a Real Greek Woman 'and beautiful too' he says emptying his glass – but I don't care, all I care about is Dad, and I turn the remains of the fish over and scoop out the other eye with Mum's coffee spoon and hold it out and say:

'Your turn, sucker.'

Mum, the Captain and Diogenes, who owns the taverna, demanded he eat the eye. I could see him look at it and maybe he was thinking the eye was looking at him and I could see he was scared because, more than anything, he *hates* gross things, but everyone's shouting, especially the Triff:

'Eye the eye, eat up the eye, eye the eye, eat up the eye.'

And it's getting mean like at school when some girls were teasing me for being so skinny and all the other stupid things that I don't care about anyway, and Dad takes the spoon up to his mouth and maybe he's about to eat it and maybe he never was, but he drops the spoon and makes a loud chicken noise and runs out of the taverna clucking madly and zigzagging all the way down the street. And he doesn't come back and we find him in the hotel bar on the way home singing and drinking so many ouzos he can't even walk properly and Mum gives him one of her death looks, tells him not to bother coming home till he is sober.

Normally after *Asbesti* we'd walk home from the taverna, or if enough time had passed, jump in Captain Maris's boat, which only takes ten minutes rather than forty on foot, because we just have to go round a few cliffs rather than all the way up and all the way down. When we get home there is nothing left to do with the *Asbesti*, so it shouldn't really be described, but I still think of it as a moment on its own because it's my absolute favourite.

If you have done everything right – the sweeping, the sun, the mix, the mopping, and the three hours waiting – something happens that is like magic and all you have to do is look and enjoy it. The entire surface sets into gleaming white. There is no stain, no anything, except wonderful cloudy whiteness. Lovely perfection. It's as if the entire building has been blessed by fairies, smooth and perfect. It's a chance to begin again, a new page. Everything's as innocent and fresh as a brand new pair of trainers, or a thick fall of snow, and it's impossible not to feel happy about the future.

At least that's the way it was for me.

So Mum and I swept like demented beings. I couldn't watch when Mum scraped off the bits of crusted gore, but otherwise we were an Olympic team: sweeping, scrubbing, passing, scooping, brushing, then mixing, squeezing lemons, mixing and painting. We did not speak, we did not need to speak, because we knew what to do.

When we had finished we went for a walk with Jojo and then swam and slept a bit under the olive tree with the face of the sad boy in its trunk. When we returned to the house, it was late afternoon and the *Asbesti* was dry and there was nothing more to do but glory in the whiteness.

# Twenty-five

'Where's Davies, Lao?'

Lao was Hong Kong Chinese. When he did speak, it was usually to Weld.

Lao turned round without answering and began changing into his pyjamas.

'Meow Lao, cat got your tongue?'

He looked back at Weld with imploring eyes and shook his head.

'What's wrong?'

Lao mimed a zip going across his mouth and shrugged before turning away again, folding his sweater in a precise way that Weld had never thought anyone but an adult might do.

Weld progressed down the dormitory, avoiding Stellmark's cubicle, and poking his head into the next room where Eliot lay on his bed eating a toffee. Seeing Weld, Eliot leapt up, Weld thought to whisper something to him but instead he pulled the curtain closed. Weld tried two more boys, with similar results.

Finally he returned to Lao.

'Lao, please, no one will talk to me. What's going on?'

Lao shrugged again, his large head sinking down on his slight body and his frail violin-playing fingers pointing up in the air.

'Lao, please, just tell me.'

Lao leaned out of his cubicle and looked in both directions before pulling Weld in and closing the curtain. He approached Weld's ear, cupping his hand around to prevent any sound from escaping.

'*Coh-venn-tree*,' he whispered, as softly as it was possible to whisper.

'What?'

Lao looked terrified and shushed him with a twig-like finger squashed against his lips. He put his mouth even closer to Weld's ear.

'*Coventry*. You sent *Coventry*.'

'Why?' Weld could smell Chinese sweets on Lao's breath. They were strange. Lao had given him one the week before and they were salty and sweet, and a bit sour.

'Sneaking on Linnet,' Lao whispered. Footsteps were approaching so he pushed Weld towards the curtain. Weld leapt out, almost crashing into Stellmark, who danced round him with his hand over his mouth, snorting like a chimpanzee.

By breakfast the next day Weld was becoming desperate. No one, even people he had thought of as allies, would talk to him. He longed to explain himself. He was sure that if he could just tell everyone what had happened, they would realise he was innocent. No one said a word to him at breakfast, even Davies wouldn't talk to him – although Davies had decided that if he was not allowed to speak to Weld he wouldn't speak to anyone, especially Linnet and Stellmark. He gave Weld a friendly smile and a shrug of sympathy and made sure to pass him whatever he needed.

The day was mired with silent torment, particularly the twenty minutes Weld spent in the playground sitting in the bough of his tree, pretending he didn't mind being excluded from what looked like the best game of Stingers he'd ever seen.

Stingers was his favourite game in the whole world. People would form teams then hunt each other with a tennis ball. Weld was probably the fifth or sixth best at it in the class.

By lunch break Weld had retreated to the classroom with the idea that he would create a notice for the board. It would explain that he was sorry Linnet had got two MCs but it had all been a mistake. He would pin it to the classroom board for everyone to see and then everyone would understand.

As he was rewriting the first line Lao shuffled into the classroom. Weld smiled at him. Lao looked even more miserable than usual.

'Stellmark told Linnet I spoke to you. I'm Coventry too now,' Lao said, his mouth turned down.

Weld rushed up to him.

'That's great. Now we can be in it together and talk.'

Lao shook his head.

'Not great. I'm Coventry,' he said, turning away from Weld. He opened his desk and pulled out a Chinese puzzle book with a picture of a rabbit space robot in a gleaming chrome suit.

'In Coventry you mean.'

'Yeah, OK. Big difference.'

'I'm sorry, Lao. I didn't mean to get you in trouble.'

Lao said nothing, but concentrated on colouring in a space-suited mouse.

Weld went back to his notice and read through the few words he had not crossed out.

'Don't worry, Lao. I'm writing this notice and it will help us both. I am going to put it on the board. It explains how I didn't sneak at all – well, not on purpose.'

Weld went back to work, trying to force the letters to stand straight. There was no sound from his neighbour until his large head appeared in front of Weld's desk.

'This is a Bad Idea,' Lao stated.

Weld carried on writing.

'Stop,' Lao said, taking the paper. 'It's stupid.'

'Give it back,' Weld shouted, his voice cracking.

'No.'

Lao, usually no more aggressive than the tiniest ladybird, scrunched up the paper.

'Give it back Lao,' Weld said, his words compressing into a shriek.

'Stupid, stupid,' Lao said throwing it back. 'You make it worse ... Linnet, he told everyone that it was *you* who give him the bad word in the refectory. He says you sneaked on him to get him back for all the Torment he gives you.'

'It's not true,' Weld whispered in shock, 'he told me that word.'

'True doesn't matter, stupid. No one believes you now. Don't you see, he tricked you? He knows what this word means. His brother tells him all these bad words: cock, blows-job, erection, pussy-hair, fucking. I hear him say them. He knows what the word means and he tricked you for Torment.'

'Leave me alone, you ... *Chinky*,' Weld shouted, trying to smooth out the crumpled notice.

Lao walked out of the classroom, leaving the weight of this racial slur with Weld, who could not hinder his tears as he tore up the unfinished notice.

Later that afternoon Linnet passed Lao in the tea queue and stepped in front of him.

'You saved me a place, right Lao?'

'I Coventry,' Lao replied, not looking up from his shoes.

'In Coventry stupid. Anyway, not any more. You are "out Coventry" now.' Linnet snorted with pleasure at the potency of his mercy.

Lao looked up from his highly polished shoes and shrugged his deep shrug, but it was official, the sentence had been lifted.

Linnet had come to understand that by putting two people in Coventry it lessened the effect, and so with the natural skills of a viceroy in training, he repaired his error. Also, by being seen to be a good sport towards Lao it endowed Linnet with a certain virtue, which somehow allowed him more credit to continue his torment of Weld. He did not know why, but he felt compelled to make Weld suffer, duty bound, like a zealous missionary who decides he must drive the Devil out of the natives.

During the ten-minute break before Evening Studies, Weld sat on his own in the bough of his tree and waited for each agonising minute to pass so he could go back into class and feel normal again – at least in class, no one was allowed to speak.

Amidst the scrum milling back into the classroom Linnet manoeuvred himself in front of Weld.

'Hey Smeld. You're out of Coventry – but sneak again and no one will ever talk to you in all your miserable Smeld life.'

Weld had planned this moment for hours, thinking he might refuse to talk ever again after a brave speech revealing Linnet's conniving nature and contrasting it with his own heroic virtues, but when the time came he could not say anything. The enforced silence had been so painful that he had become confused and desperate, and was beginning to suspect that he was guilty, that he had been the cause of all the trouble and Linnet had been right all along. So Weld filed into class with his head down, restraining his relief, not even hearing the friendly question someone asked him, just for the novelty of talking to him once more.

# Twenty-six

Valentine was asleep, or pretending to be, when Max slipped out of bed in the early morning and walked down to the sea. The sun was glaring, already too intense for comfort, and the water blazing where the sun smacked against it. Max eased himself into the water, feeling it cool and close over his head. He swam to where the outcrop of stone shimmered under the water, so much less threatening in the day but impressive in its dark way, its mass almost invisible until he was over it.

He swam back, pulled himself out of the water and walked to the house, stopping at the fig tree outside their bedroom to see if any more fruits were ripe. He made tea and took in a cup to Valentine. She turned away from him and mumbled. He left the tea by her and went outside.

Max spooned yoghurt into a bowl and threw in a handful of nuts, then took the bowl and his tea to the terrace. He watched a hummingbird draw nectar from the hibiscus bush that drooped from the roof. Although he had slept he felt exhausted. Valentine had seemed to be unconscious when he had finally slipped into bed, but she had recoiled when he tried to touch her. He told himself at the time that she was too hot or dreaming, but her rejection murmured to an anxiety he replayed throughout the night. A single line repeated over and over by grotesque versions of himself.

He recognised now, as the hummingbird moved with archi-tectural precision between the red flowers, that there was a relief to being alone. The combination of Valentine's physical proximity and emotional distance was debilitating. *She* was the problem, he decided. Not him. He rose from the table, grabbed a towel and walked down the path. He would take a stroll, see where it took him, meander about without aim or judgement. Put some physical distance between them and work out how to set her right.

He broke into a run, not looking at anything but the path ahead, his most pressing concern to get away. Within twenty minutes he had passed the village path that wound up the cliff. His shirt was dark with sweat and he slowed, allowing his palm to graze the surface of a dry stone wall, each rock a shade of dirty white. He pulled at a strand of green wall vine that crept out between the stones. A long tendril unlatched and he dragged it behind him like a tail, until he let it drop. A smudge of colour caught his eye amidst the dust and dull browns of the thorn bushes. He stopped and crouched down, poking through the bush with a stick, scraping his forearm in the process. It was plastic, a shotgun cartridge, purple, its metal cap corroded by the sea air. Max tossed it into the bush and walked on, enjoying the freedom, promising himself the treat of plunging into the sea as soon as he found it. The path wound on, neither taking him up a cliff, nor to the sea as he was hoping.

The ground was now blanketed with brown needles from conifers and spotted with fallen olives, scorched black by the sun and still attached to pairs of tough and slender leaves. He paused at an enormous olive tree blocking his route which was almost as broad as Max was tall. It looked as if it was a melding of four smaller trees, grown together into one great stump. As Max stared at the shapes and contortions of the wood, he imagined its dark twists and knots as a violent chaos of scrawny bodies caught in erotic struggle.

He was startled by a shivering of bushes as Khalib appeared, his long hair wet and a plastic bag in one hand.

'Kalimera,' he said, displaying his broken teeth.

'Oh,' said Max, tensing.

Khalib opened the bag and reached into it, pulling out the lank slime of a large octopus.

'Actapwer?' Max ventured.

'Ne, ne. You take?' Khalib answered with his half-cocked smile. He replaced the creature in the bag and held it out towards Max.

Max shook his head, imagining Valentine's reaction.

Khalib frowned and opened up the bag again, showing Max the mass of grey pink within, still twitching and contracting in the reeking plastic.

'Thank you, it's kind, but we had one the other day ... and anyway,' Max patted his pockets, 'I don't have any money.'

'Not buy,' Khalib insisted, 'give.' He thrust the bag towards Max.

Max took the mucousy package. Khalib turned and hurried off into the woods.

'Hold on,' Max shouted.

Khalib stopped and turned back.

'You're Khalib, aren't you? Thank you ... for the octopus.' Max held out his hand.

Khalib took it but it was hard for Max to read whether his expression was pleasure or disdain. It was difficult to read one half of a face.

'Perhaps you know a good swimming place near here ... Swim?' Max made the appropriate gestures.

Khalib motioned for Max to follow him and marched away. After a few hundred yards he turned off the path, ducked under a branch and came to the edge of the tree line. A steep drop no more than their body length led to the shore, where a flat outcrop of stone reached narrow fingers into the water.

It was a perfect bathing spot. The water between the spits was turquoise, becoming deep blue, and then blackening as the water deepened. Max scrabbled down the slope and hesitated at the tip of one of the fingers. He was wearing nothing under his trousers and wondered if he should strip off, if it was acceptable for men to be naked. He looked over his shoulder. Khalib was looking at him, urging him on. Max dropped the octopus into a strip of shade, then pulled off his T-shirt, kicked away his shoes and unhooked his trousers. Damp with sweat they snagged on his thighs. He tugged them down and they bunched at his feet. He pulled one leg up and lost his balance, hopping onto a sharp edge with a boyish yelp. He collapsed sideways, grazing his backside on a rock. He yanked off the trousers in a fluster, threw them behind him, and jumped into the water.

The sea was cool after the blazing heat and stung where he had scraped himself, but at least he was safe, no longer so naked, so nude. He looked back at the tree line. Khalib was there, staring at him, not laughing, not even reacting, just there. Looking.

Max swam away from him, savouring the chill of the deeper water, relieved to distance himself from Khalib's bullying eyes. As he swam, the idea that Khalib might be planning some prank – like stealing his clothes – bubbled to the surface. As he looked back, he saw that Khalib was indeed approaching the clothes, but he did not pick them up. Instead he kicked off his shoes and dived into the water, fully clothed.

Max's moment of relief soon flashed into anxiety as he realised that Khalib was making his way towards him, cutting through the water like a bull hippo. Max swam in another direction, feeling vulnerable, not wanting him so close. Khalib veered towards Max, closing in on him, his swimming efficient, somehow familiar. Max turned again, swimming as hard as he could for the nearest outcrop of land, splashing through the water with increasingly clumsy strokes.

Khalib's strokes were powerful, almost predatory. Max slapped his way to the nearest point of the shore with an urgency that was close to panic. He scrambled out of the water, his arms scraping on the barnacled edges. He looked over to where his pile of clothes lay untouched – fifty yards across jagged rocks. Max scrambled towards them, embarrassed and naked. As he was pulling on his trousers Khalib surfaced in front of him like a sea creature. Max stared down at Khalib, emboldened by his clothes.

'What? What is it?' Max demanded.

Khalib disappeared, sank under the water, surfacing by a narrow gully where the sea had cut a channel into the rock. As Max finished dressing, he realised that Valentine must have learned her stroke from him: it had the same reaching power.

Khalib was now staring intently into the gully. Max walked over and peered down the fissure where the sea flowed and ebbed with slow, wet breaths. Anchored on the sides of the rock was a cluster of iridescent molluscs, fine and elegantly long, and amidst them a rainbow of sea anemones moving to and fro like the arms of a corps de ballet.

Max felt he should say something, suddenly ashamed of the fantasy he'd caught himself in.

'Can you eat them?' he asked, swinging the plastic bag with the dead wet weight of the octopus.

Khalib ignored him, and continued to peer. Max backed away, climbed the steep bank, and made his way towards the house.

# Twenty-seven

Had any of the staff discussed Weld's nightmares they might have concluded that these were the result of his teddy bear's massacre. Weld would not have agreed, had anyone asked him, which they did not. Of course, he was upset about what happened to Heavy, that was certainly true, but the source of his nightmares was not the annihilation of his beloved bear. Weld never questioned his dreams. They arrived like fierce winds and left, leaving no physical marks but eliciting screams so extraordinary in their ferocity that no one in the staff dared mention them. Even Linnet and his gang ignored the shrieks for the days after they had detonated through the old building; the noise was too frightening, repellent as a withered arm, or a terrible burn.

He did love his bear though.

Beaufinn's study boasted a few bears, old-fashioned text-book teddies with rheumy eyes, all huddled in a corner like a family of refugees. Weld had caught sight of them on one of the days Beaufinn was being icily formal, so he dared not mention them. He longed for the warmth he had once found with his tutor, but Beaufinn was impossible to influence. Sometimes he would be kind and funny, roaring like Fynton the Boar and showing him inventions and coloured pictures, and sometimes he would be cold like Miss Trench, setting dictation and pointing out mistakes with one thick finger. On such occasions Weld would try even harder to please his mentor, attempting to spell the way everyone else did, disciplining the shaking letters into orderly shapes, and, above all, not doing anything that might damn him as a 'poop. But Weld was invariably unsuccessful, never understanding what he had done to disappoint the charismatic teacher, suspecting by default that the failing must lie within himself.

Sometimes Beaufinn would give Weld cup after cup of sweet tea and they might take apart a tape recorder, or make inventions out of electronics – like a light with a proper switch and batteries. Weld's spirits would soar and Beaufinn would read him a story and then everything would always become too much and the world would blur and spin and he would fall asleep in the armchair. Later Beaufinn would wake him with sweet coffee and Weld would stumble back to school and try not to feel sick and queer from the coffee.

As for Heavy the Bear, RIP.

Nearly every Mite had a teddy bear, potent totems of home propped up on the pillows of each tightly made bed. Like mothers, bears were a subject too significant, too incongruous, too fragile, to be openly discussed at St Xavier's. Linnet's teddy was a stripy stuffed snake with a red forked tongue made of felt. Stellmark had a tiny little Paddington Bear, which was curious because Stellmark was so big. It had a plastic mackintosh with a little label saying *please look after this bear*. Long after lights out, in the camouflage of the night, Stellmark would hold the little bear to his cheek and wish he was the one who was so small and being held.

Lao had nothing in the way of bears. When Weld had asked him why, he replied that boys did not have dolls in Hong Kong. Later he added proudly that in the People's Republic of China they had real live bears called Pandas and a Panda could eat a million bamboo shoots in a single day.

Weld shared this zoological fact with Linnet while they were both sitting on the long padded bench outside the infirmary, pretending to have a sore throat on the matron's day off. Weld had ventured this new fact to reciprocate the latest wave of strategic friendliness Linnet had initiated.

'Don't be a dur-brain Smeld,' Linnet answered, unable to restrain his derision, 'a million bamboos would take up a whole school.'

The bumbling assistant matron arrived and hearing their tales of a 'really sore throat miss' gave them both a camphoric yellow sweet and sent them on their way.

Later, the new camaraderie in full flow, Linnet showed Weld a place just off the playground where it was possible to see the vehicles on the motorway zooming along like racing cars. He revealed to him the school's most terrible legend: a secret and perilous dare that involved scrambling under the fence and running across the motorway and back.

'How d'you get back?' Weld asked.

'No one ever gets back,' Linnet replied.

Weld had heard rumours about the ultimate dare, a mission so dangerous it had never been achieved. It was the same sort of thing, they agreed, as swimming in a lake of piranhas with blood pouring out of your ears, tightrope-walking in a hurricane with toes dipped in slime, or sleeping in a coffin filled to the brim with Black Mambas, Taipans and, Weld added, a Deathstalker scorpion – the most poisonous one there was.

Linnet may have been impressed by the scorpion but he soon topped it by whispering that his big brother had told him that someone in the top year had once attempted the dare, but he'd been caught before he'd even got past the fence. Probably they had electronic sensors or something. The boy had been dragged to the headmaster by his hair and been beaten so hard that the Ferula broke into ten pieces and both the boy's hands were smashed into useless claws. The boy's parents tried to take the school to court, Linnet added, for a million pounds but they couldn't because ... because ... the school said they'd tell the whole world that the boy had a dirty magazine under his bed.

'Really?' Weld asked.

'Yeah. Would you ever do it, Stell?' Linnet asked the fidgeting figure who'd rushed up to see what was going on.

Stellmark shook his head.

'How 'bout you Smeld?'

'No fear.'

A conversation followed about whether the bravest man in the world might do the dare and Linnet said he knew someone personally – actually his Dad's best friend – who was one of the bravest people in the world, or England anyway.

'How do you know?' Weld asked.

'What, that he's brave? That's easy, stupid, he's in the army and he won a Victoria Cross and other medals too, and the VC is the medal for the most brave thing anyone can do.'

'The GC is even higher,' Stellmark ventured.

'NO Stickman. Maybe it's higher for a Stickman who is so tall his head is in the clouds,' Linnet paused to allow the wave of laughter to break over them, 'but for everyone else in the planet, the Victoria Cross is the highest and the George Cross is the second highest.'

'I thought the Victoria Cross was the highest for the armed forces and the George Cross is only awarded to civilians,' Weld said.

'Yeah,' said Stellmark, risking a shaky counter-attack, 'and a civilian could easily do a braver thing than someone in the army.'

'Braver than the army? Shut up Stickman,' Linnet retorted.

'Anyway, even my Dad's best friend probably wouldn't even

do the motorway dare not unless it was to save Queen and Country, of course.'

'Of course,' everyone agreed.

'What did he get the VC for?' Weld asked.

But Linnet ignored him and ran off, Stellmark following. Weld stayed at the edge, wishing he knew as many interesting things as Linnet. He watched the cars and lorries chopping past his gaze like a guillotine, yearning to slip into those spaces where there was nothing.

# Twenty-eight

We didn't see Khalib for a while after the dog, which suited me just fine. The Triff grew an extra stalk that wrapped round me cosy and tight with the green shade of a lovely leaf for protection. We went round as a three – or a two and a half because Jojo isn't really a full anything, although the truth is, we can both see parts of Dad in him, the way his lip catches when he smiles and crosses his fingers sometimes when he concentrates.

Funny how things get passed on.

I asked the Triff if I would look like her one day, and she said:

'You never can tell . . . maybe when you're older.'

'Much, much older,' I told her.

'Ha ha ha,' she said.

I wouldn't mind looking like the Triff because she is beautiful. I told her too.

'Am I?' she said, sprouting fifteen new flowers.

'Yes,' I said.

'How?' she said.

I wish I'd told her the truth.

How is honey sweet?

How is Dev so fit?

The truth is I DON'T KNOW.

My granny was right, when she'd go on and on about *honesty being the best policy*, stuffing Maltesers in her mouth like the mad old Gran she is. But of course I had to go and say something I thought sounded like the person I wanted to be, rather than the one I am, and now I wonder who the real me is. Maybe it was abducted by aliens while I was sleeping in class, sucked out, and then I was implanted with their demon seed.

This is what I said: 'You have a rugged and calloused beauty ... like a ballet dancer's foot.'

'Thanks,' she said, '... wrinkled, cracked and tough. Why can't you just be nice?' And she stormed off into the house.

I don't know who I am sometimes, but I did not mean to be nasty. It sounded fine to me but I'd never seen a ballet dancer's foot. Shouldn't it be the end of something beautiful, like the end of a poet's pen? Sometimes when I am actually trying to say something awful to the Triff, she just laughs. It's all to do with my age, she says.

Nothing to do with the fact that I have a predatory plant for a mother.

The Triff did not sulk for long. She came out of the house with that look, so I went in and poured her a glass of retsina.

'The roots must be watered,' I said, offering peace.

'Yes they must,' she said, accepting. Then she grabbed me, wrapped her planty arms around me and kissed me on the top of the head and we lay down together on the cushions and she told me that although I was growing up so quick and would soon become a young woman, I would always be her baby girl. And for once, I didn't mind, I just lay there, pretending I was a soft diaphanous creature with wings and a kind heart as she stroked my back with the tips of her fingers as a Triff might do when feeling motherly.

As I lay curled with my maternal plant, I found myself thinking about my own body, which generally, I prefer not to do.

I don't like it, not much, but who does? I certainly don't

want my mother's. She says my bottom comes straight out of my back like a boy, but one day it will surely drop, creating . . . a Waist . . . and making me . . . a Woman.

Another mad Triff idea, but obviously it's true, and it's not like I don't know what's coming. The fact is, almost every day my championship cups expand out a tiny bit, less than everyone else, as if they were pillows being inflated by a pair of asthmatic ladybirds. Not like Leah in my class, she's the opposite. She tugs her T-shirt down every time she runs, one arm moving backwards and forwards and the other holding her shirt, trying to stop the tremendous jiggling of her massive breasts. No one wants to be like that . . . but it's good I suppose that mine are doing something. Not that I even want them, well I do, sort of. I want to be part of everything, without it all changing.

Most people who see me say I've developed, even if it's only been a month or two since I last saw them. 'Gosh, you've changed,' they say, looking me over like I'm some sort of freak. The Triff 's changing too, creeping around the house all day muttering that everything is falling.

Are my tits falling? They are aren't they?

It's clear to me that at a certain point everyone stops going up . . . and then everything begins to fall, bum and all, and then of course it's down, down, down until death. I'd rather be down, going up, than up, going down. Jojo is very far down so he doesn't have far to fall, just a low tumble now and then. A baby is almost flat, with nowhere to go. Its whole life is a struggle against, I don't know . . . gravity? Ours too. Adam and Eve fell, Rome fell. If you just lie down and gurgle like a baby, there's no struggle. No fall.

I wish, I wish, I wish, I wish Dad were here. I could tell him this.

When he was here there were lunches and people and

laughing and drama – every single day. Now it seems to be just me and the Triff and Jojo. The Triff reads and sketches ideas for fabrics, Jojo stays close to the ground, and I arrange shells in different boxes and imagine I am a world famous jewellery designer. Or I think about Dev's nice eyes and the way his lips are big like a girl's, but not like a girl at all. Or I go snorkelling for hours imagining the underwater cliff is a whole mountain world populated by the tiny fish that dart in and out of its cracks. I like this time, it's cosy and sometimes I sleep with Jojo and sometimes Mum does, and sometimes we all sleep together and days pass and we don't really notice. Most of the time we are all close to the ground.

That's why it's so good.

Really it is.

I don't want it to change.

# Twenty-nine

Linnet maintained a low-level assault of friendliness. Not like sharing his sweets or choosing Weld for a team, but ceasing Torment, acknowledging Weld's presence and sometimes even telling him things. One Thursday lunch, after the Silence bell, Weld was passed a note instructing him to visit Linnet's cubicle during Rest. 'Dam' Jackson took Rest on a Thursday which meant they could secretly move about and talk to each other as long as they were back in their cubicles by 1.36 p.m., which was when the horse racing finished on the radio and Dam did his last patrol to ensure no one was talking.

Only Linnet's closest circle was allowed into his cubicle. The rumour was that he had a store of contraband from his brother – at least so Lao said. Lao also suspected he might even have a dirty picture as well.

A few minutes after the bell rang, Weld tiptoed over to Linnet's cubicle. Linnet was sitting sideways on his bed, leaning against the wall.

'Dam's an idiot. Don't you think?'

'Yes,' agreed Weld.

'His is the best Rest though.'

'Yeah. Cos he's so lazy.'

'D'you think he knows we all just chat till he comes?'

'Dunno,' Weld said, shrugging in a way he'd picked up from Lao.

'I bet he does and I bet he's got a plan to wait, and wait,

and then catch as many of us as he can and give us all MCs, cos he's such an idiot, a bastard idiot.'

'Yeah.'

'Why are you standing there? I don't bite.' Linnet pointed to the place next to him on the bed.

'OK.'

'D'you like the pink sponge and custard we had at lunch?'

'No,' Weld said, 'it's my third worst.'

'What's first and second?'

'Second worst: semolina with jam in it. Worst: semolina without jam in it.'

Linnet guffawed. 'Really?'

'No. Joke,' Weld replied, pleased with himself. 'First is semolina, second is rice pudding with skin.'

'I don't mind it,' Linnet replied.

'Even with skin?'

'Yeah.'

'Oh,' Weld said, disappointed.

'My brother saw Billy the cook sneeze into the semolina once,' Linnet said. 'A green splash of snot came out of his nose and he just stirred it in.'

Weld rummaged in his pockets, thinking of something to say.

'D'you like the chocolate sponge?' he offered.

'Course.'

'Me too.'

'D'you want to see something?' Linnet whispered.

'Yeah.'

'First you've got to swear you won't tell.'

'I swear.'

'On your mother.'

Weld paused. 'OK.'

'Say it.'

'I swear on my mother.'

Linnet opened his bottom drawer and delved under the socks, pulling out a battered cigar box embossed with gold designs and pictures of men from hundreds of years ago each framed by laurel leaves in gold.

'It's beautiful,' Weld said.

'Not that dur-brain. That's just a box from the cigars my Pa smokes at Christmas. Look inside.'

Weld pulled open the lid, which was secured with a miniscule pin. The box was impregnated with the dark pungency of tobacco, and was empty but for a few pencils and a broken sharpener.

'Notice anything?' Linnet asked.

Weld was thinking of the red velvet jacket his own father wore every Christmas dinner, a stain from the gravy on his Christmas cravat, and the red crown from a cracker perched on the back of his head like the skullcap he wore once a year to commemorate those who had died . . . laughing because he was tipsy and puffing on a big cigar like Linnet's Dad.

'I can't believe you let him smoke those things,' his aunty would snipe at his Ma.

'I adore the smell,' she'd say.

'Come on, Smeld – what's in it?' Linnet demanded.

'I adore the smell,' Weld said, gazing into the box.

'*I adore the smell* . . . Don't be a freak Smeld. It's just cigar-stink. What do you see inside?'

'Pencils and a sharpener?'

'Fooled you,' Linnet announced triumphantly. He took his comb out of his pocket and bending one of the plastic teeth slipped it into the edge of the box and manoeuvred up the base which was a false bottom. Underneath was a tightly packed treasure trove of confectionery: four Mars bars packed like sardines, a couple of Curley Wurleys concertinaed into blocks, half a dozen or more bubblegums filling the spaces and, sure enough, a magazine page, creased and folded.

'It's a dirty picture – d'you want to see it?'

'Can I have a bubblegum instead?' Weld asked.

'It's up to you,' Linnet replied.

'Wow, do you mean it?' Weld's eyes were wide with excitement. Bubblegum was among the best things ever, a real treat, but also like something from *Charlie and the Chocolate Factory* because it kept its flavour for ages, and then it could be kept stuck in a hiding place and even if it had lost its flavour, a bit came back if you chewed it.

Also it was the most illegal thing you could have.

'Of course you can have one,' Linnet said, 'but only if you're in my gang and you're not, are you?'

Weld did not answer.

'You could be. If you wanted to,' Linnet said.

'I could?' Weld breathed.

It was the first time in his life he'd been asked to be in a gang.

'If you pass the test you can. We're the Aces. Each Ace has to pass the test to show he's brave enough. It's not for little babies.'

'I'm not a little baby. What do I have to do?' Weld asked.

'I'm Ace of Spades cos that's the top, Stelly's Diamonds, Wilson's a Club – or maybe Ibwe is, we're still deciding, we'll say they're both Jacks or something, anyway, we've got no Heart.' Linnet pulled out the drawer beside his bed.

'Want to be the Heart?' He took out a penknife from the space behind the drawer and opened the blade.

'What do I have to do?' Weld asked, looking at the blade.

Linnet rested its point against the pad of a finger. 'You've got a teddy right?'

'Everyone does ... don't they?' Weld answered.

'Teddies are for babies.'

'Grown ups have them too. Mr Beaufinn has three.'

'Yeah, and you're his suck.'

'No I'm not. I have to go, for extra lessons.'

'Don't go mental, just joking. Do you love your teddy?'

Weld shrugged.

'You do love him, don't you? What's his name?' Linnet pushed the point against his finger.

'My Mummy packed him, I didn't ask her to. She just packed him. It doesn't mean anything.'

'Your Mummy did, did she? Mummies pack teddies for their babies. It stops them blubbing. Are you a baby?'

'No,' Weld answered, feeling a bit sick.

'Aces don't have 'em. Think about that. Then you can be in the gang.' He passed the penknife to Weld. 'You can borrow this, now scram. Someone's coming.'

Weld put the penknife in his pocket and darted into his cubicle just before the crepe soles of Rufus 'Dam' Jackson squeaked their way along the old wooden floor.

That night in his cubicle Weld picked up Heavy and held the bear in front of him. He examined the two crossed black stitches that were his eyes and the 'U' that was his mouth and what stared back was something that yearned for love. Whatever Weld did or didn't do, whatever happened, Heavy was always there, ready to be loved, never turning away, always needing him. Weld buried his face into the bear, swearing tearfully to keep him safe as long as he had breath in his body. As he crushed his nose into the brown material he detected the faintest scent of his mother's perfume in the thick sponge and for a strange moment, it was his perfume and the baby was him, and he vowed with his whole heart to love him for ever.

The next morning after the bell had shocked him awake he

shuffled his way to the washrooms. Finding an empty sink he brushed his teeth, sawing the brush back and forth, back and forth until the watchful prefect and the ghost of his mother were appeased. Linnet barged in next to him and snatched the tube, smothering his Action Man toothbrush with a fat worm of toothpaste.

'Done it yet?' he menaced through a mouthful of toothpaste.

'Not yet,' Weld answered, rinsing his toothbrush carefully.

White foam bubbled out of Linnet's mouth and down his chin. He spat into the sink, some of it spraying over Weld's hand and toothbrush.

'Oops,' he said unconvincingly, wiping his mouth on his sleeve and walking away.

The next day there was a school cross country run, which was one of the worst things that could happen. The run itself was muddy and uphill and then there were the showers afterwards. On cross country days you showered with everyone else in the school and that meant, not only would Weld be one of the last in the showers with an almost cold drizzle of water, but boys from different years might be there too and Weld did not like being near the boys in the top years when everyone was naked. Some of them had hair down there, and were practically grown-up, and it made him feel a bit sick.

When he had scrubbed off the mud under the trickling water, he put on his dressing gown and climbed the spiral stairs to his dormitory. Above him he could hear shouts and hyena shrieks of laughter. At the top of the stairs was an open space with three doors surrounding it. One door led to the Science Lab, one to the lavatory that you could use only at night and the big one in the middle led to their dormitory. Linnet was there, waiting with Stellmark and Wilson, who was a bit fat and not good at very much but he could burp on demand. Ibwe and O'Sullivan, who was Stellmark's best friend, stood on the other side. They'd showered early and set up an ambush, so that anyone who wanted to pass would get whipped by the towels they had twisted into rat tails and dipped in lavatory water. Mackenzie was in front of Weld and he made a dash for it, managing to dodge Linnet and Stellmark's flicks but there was a terrible crack as Ibwe's towel found its mark. Mackenzie crumpled and grasped his calf, his face contorted in pain.

'Ten seconds of quarter, Mackenzie, and then we attack again,' Stellmark announced. 'Ten, nine, eight, seven ...' the rest of them chanted over the gasping boy, lazily whirring their towels, ' ... six ... five ... four ... three ...'

Mackenzie struggled to his feet, his face red, tears bulging but held back. He limped away before the quarter was up, a purple welt blooming on the white skin of his leg.

'Come on, Smeld,' Stellmark said. 'You're next, don't be wet.'

There was a whirring sound as their towels were twisted.

Weld could see there was a peculiar focus to Stellmark and he understood that if any towel found its mark it would be his, but he knew he would not be able to hold back the tears as Mackenzie had. He turned back, ready to run back down the stairs, but Stellmark stepped behind him, twisting his towel until the end spun like a dog chasing its tail.

'Five seconds till certain death.' Stellmark grinned, targeting a strip of pale calf beneath Weld's towelling robe.

'Who said you were in charge?' Linnet's voice burst from behind. 'Weld's in our gang – well almost, he gets full quarter, for now anyway. Isn't that right Weldy?'

'Since when?' Stellmark complained.

'Since I said. Since it's my sweets you eat. Since you're a stupid Stickman. But even though you are a stupid Stickman,' Linnet twirled his towel in unhurried circles, tightening it like a braided rope, 'you're in the Aces, so you get quarter, just like Weld, don't you Stickman?' As he said this, Linnet flicked out his wrist, launching the tip of the wet towel between Stellmark's open legs with a terrible crack. Stellmark leapt backwards, crashing into the door as it was opened by the towering obsidian form of Brother Noonan.

'What are you boys doing here, still not changed and messing about?'

Linnet's gang fell immediately into poses of exaggerated innocence. Stellmark dropped his towel onto the floor and pretended to pick it up, Ibwe turned away and was examining a crack in the wall, and Linnet bunched his towel up and had a coughing fit into it.

Weld alone looked guilty.

'You again Weld.' Brother Noonan shook his head. 'What d'you think you're doing?'

'Nothing, Brother,' Weld answered.

'Nothing indeed. Well you should be doing something. It's 3.41 and if you're not downstairs in the tea queue by a quarter to four I'll have MCs for the lot of you, got it? Now scram. Weld, remain.'

As the others rushed towards the dormitory in the skipping dash that could not quite be censored as running, Weld stood before the Brother.

'Are you a Troublemaker, laddie?'

'No Brother.'

'Don't let us mark you out as a Troublemaker, or you will be sorry, very sorry. Understood?'

'Yes Brother.'

'Why are you dawdling laddie? Three minutes fourteen seconds.'

'Please, Brother, I'm meant to be at Mr Beaufinn's house. Not at Tea.'

'Are you now? Well don't just stand about talking to me.'

Weld dashed to his cubicle and started pulling on his clothes before noticing, with hollow shock, that Heavy was missing from his pillow.

'Hey Smeld.'

It was Linnet, slouching outside with Heavy in his arms, rocking the bear like an infant. 'Here's your little baby, baby bear for baby blubber ... but you're not a baby are you Weld?'

Weld stared at his bear. 'Give him back,' he pleaded.

'Quarter's not for babies, Smeld,' he said spinning Heavy by the leg. 'Next time, you're dead.' He tossed the bear up in the air and ran off. Heavy fell onto the floor with a soft thud.

Weld stood frowning and desperate, feeling like he was going to burst, wishing with all the power a human has to wish that some sort of answer would flutter down to him. But the only answer he heard was the bell for Tea, echoing along the polished corridors of the school.

Fifteen minutes to get to Beaufinn's house. Perhaps he could tell him about the Torment, find some way of asking for help.

He was a grown-up. He knew everything.

# Thirty

Valentine was still in the bedroom when he returned, lying in bed with the curtains drawn, staring at the ceiling.

'Have you been in bed all day?'

'I suppose so, haven't quite got up yet. What time is it?' she answered, not turning to him.

'Midday at least,' Max said. 'Are you ill?'

'No, just having a lie-in, that's all.' Her voice was so faint it was as if she were hardly there.

A silence yawned between them, Max not knowing what to do and Valentine looking into the air, at nothing.

'Where've you been?' she said, turning to him.

'Nowhere ... just walking around.' He turned and exited the room, his lie lingering like an odour.

Valentine turned back to the ceiling. After a while, she heard the slap, slap of octopus against rock and pulled herself out of bed to join him.

'Did you get wine?' she asked as Max, waist deep in water, beat the octopus against the rock.

'Ah ... no,' Max replied, 'didn't quite make it to the village.'

'Where did you buy it from then?'

Max dropped the creature on the flat side of a rock and sank under the water, bubbling breath through his nose and mouth.

'Where did you get the octopus Max?' Tine asked when he surfaced for air. 'You didn't catch it, did you?'

Max took the octopus up again and slapped it hard against the rock. 'Actually, I did.'

'Really?'

'Yes.'

Tine squealed and jumped into the water next to him.

'My brave hunter,' she said, squeezing him. 'Describe the battle.'

Max described a new swimming spot where spits of rock stretched into the turquoise water like fingers. He'd seen the beast clinging to a rock and had grappled with it. Somehow, he'd managed to turn its head inside out the way Valentine had once told him.

She was pleased with the story, delighted to be able to snap out of her torpor. She offered advice and encouragement while Max boiled and grilled the beast for lunch and they toasted his success with the last bottle of wine – most of which was drunk by Max.

After lunch, Tine deflected Max's half-hearted attempts at sex by stroking his head, dragging her fingernails through the salty crust of his scalp until, mesmerised by her affection and heavy with the wine, Max fell asleep on her chest.

He woke to find her shaking him.

'Max,' she whispered. 'Wake up Max.'

'I'm asleep,' Max groaned.

'There's someone here, prowling around . . . It's him.' She pushed and pulled him until he opened his eyes.

'Who?' He yawned.

'Listen.'

Max pulled himself up and listened for a few seconds then fell back.

'It's just the wind. I'll check in a little while.'

'He's fucking here, Max, I've been awake, listening.' Her tautness constricted her words.

Max sat up and saw that Valentine's face was strained, her eyes darting and hypervigilant.

'What's going on?'

One of her hands was twisted in the sheet, the other grasped a pair of scissors like a dagger.

'What are you doing Valentine?'

'It's Khalib. I've been watching and listening for an hour, for fucking days. Every noise, every bloody movement. You think I'm paranoid, I know, you've been looking at me like I am, but now he's here. He's really here.'

'He's harmless, just a lonely weirdo,' Max said with more conviction that he felt.

Tine's fear said differently.

'. . . isn't he?'

'He's trying to get in Max. I heard him scraping at the door and then he crept to the window and tried to force it open.'

Max touched her shoulders. They were cold with sweat. He drew her to him. She froze as they heard a noise. Whoever it was was no more than an arm's length from them, separated only by the walls of the house. Max put a finger to his lips, spikes of adrenalin pulsing through him. The noises crossed to the corner of the house. The kitchen window rattled. The heavy front door was worried back and forth on rusty hinges.

'What are we going to do?' Tine was rigid. The door ached and groaned as someone's shoulder barged against it.

Max scanned the room for something that could serve as an effective weapon: Tine's scissors, an old tennis racket, a chair . . .

Max whispered to Tine, 'Where's the metal thing?'

'What d'you mean?'

'For the shutters . . .'

'It's outside, underneath the window. Somewhere around there, I think.'

'I'm going to crawl through the window and get it, then

sneak round the front. Give me a minute – at least a minute – and then throw open the door.'

Valentine nodded.

Max scanned around for clothes – Valentine's light cotton trousers with the drawstring were nearest. He pulled them on and made for the window, then hesitated, pulled them off and searched the room until he found his jeans.

'What are you doing?' Tine asked.

Max did not bother to explain. There was something weak, nakedly boyish about wearing her thin trousers. He readied the legs of the jeans. Valentine came up behind and hugged him.

'Be careful my love.'

He brushed off her support. He did not need it. Not any more. His fear had become clarity, amphetamine sharp.

He opened the window and pulled himself through as quietly as he could. He twisted his hips round and slid his feet down the wall until they touched the leaves of the fig tree pushing against the wall and then the dry soil and angular rocks of the ground. He let himself drop and remained crouching in the bushes, listening. He could hear the door being pushed and a voice grunting. He patted around with his hands, momentarily remembering his floundering drunkenness a few nights before. His fingers closed around the dull solidity of the metal and he felt a sudden readiness for violence, an eagerness that was solid and potent.

Warning himself not to rush, he made his way from tree to bush, skirting the house. Placing each foot on the dark carpet of cypress needles and dry twigs with as much care as he could muster. His breaths were shallow and tight, but not fearful like so many breaths he'd taken in his life, shadowed with a sense of threat. Now he was hunter rather than victim and he felt strong, as if he was in a different body, the body that was meant for him.

Nearing the front of the house, he began to crawl, keeping as low as he could. He lay flat for a moment and then slowly edged up until he could see over the low wall of the terrace.

A man was there. Banging and bellowing.

Max saw the door crack open and the figure stepped back. Max realised that this was not Khalib. The figure was heavy set, freakishly broad, with forearms like Popeye and a neck like a bull. The man barged the door open and grabbed Valentine. Max leapt up and sprinted towards them, raising the metal pole above his head. The brute's arms were around her, crushing her, smothering her in the great bulk of his body. Max was about to bring the metal crashing down on his head when Valentine screamed.

'NO, Max.'

She pulled away and threw herself in front of the man, her arms protecting him.

Max dropped the bar. It clanged behind him, knocking out a chink of the lime floor with one sharp edge.

'Holy saints, what are you doing? You are mad!' the man exclaimed, pulling Valentine behind him as if she were a child. He looked at Max and then turned to Valentine and shrugged.

'Ahh, it's been so long I have forgotten the madness of love ... I suppose when I was your age I was like you – or would have been, if it hadn't been for the war and my wife. Madness. Scientists have shown this in America, crazies and lovers, there is no difference hahaha ... Let us sit down like civilised people and have some wine. I have brought good wine from the Cyclades and Kalenda, my wife – don't ask Vallei, she has a thousand complaints but in truth she has the health of a twenty-five-year-old – she has made you some *spanokopitre* and her pastry, you remember, it is so delicious it will make you weep. Truly, Glafkos in the village, he cries when he eats it – tears, as if his mother has died. How is your Papa, Vallei-mou? Still making films? I saw one, an old one, it was terrible – but there was a lovely woman in it . . . eyes like a tuna fish, she had.'

Max found himself deflating with each breath.

'It has been too long, Valentine, and look at you now, a beautiful woman and me so old. Weak, Vallei-mou, almost useless. It has no mercy, this ageing. You look pale, my boy, a walk perhaps? Please, go look in the bay where my boat is, you will see a red box, it is called an Igloo box. I bought it in Vancouver Canada. A beautiful city Vancouver, full of Greeks, and Chinese too, but Chinese who say hello, and good morning and have a nice day. Why this is? I do not know, in New York, in Athens, the Chinese people look at you like you are nothing, but in Vancouver they smile and say, good morning. Ah well . . . what was I talking of . . . As you see, old and forgetting everything . . . Please, please, a red box, young man. The wine will warm up . . . if you do not mind . . .'

Max turned and walked to their swimming spot, where a perfect little boat was tethered, secured to a tree with a masterly knot. Next to it was an enormous red cool box, dropped in the sand. Max sat on the box to regain his composure and consider the man's fortune in avoiding the submerged rock. After a while he stood and took up one of the handles of the box. It was heavier than he could have believed so he pushed and dragged it back, only lifting it when he was within sight of the house.

'Ah, there you are. Come Max, I know your name now, I know everything about you, EVERYTHING,' the man laughed as Max neared, 'even the terrible secrets and there are many . . . I am lying, of course. She speaks of you and flowers bloom, bees sing, birds also, it makes me sick with envy . . .

when I think of how the young girls of the Peloponnese would look at me ... I was as handsome as you – of course, I am Greek and we are a naturally beautiful people. Come, look Vallei-mou, you see how man he is, this boy ... the Canadian-Chinese Igloo box, it is nothing to him, like a feather.' He reached across to where Max was struggling with the box and swung it over to Valentine.

'I am sorry,' Max said as the enormous back turned to him, 'I did not catch your name.'

'Of course you are sorry, you are English ... haha ... We must shake hands now, no? Otherwise we may not talk.'

Max extended his hand but the man grasped his arm and kissed him.

'Greek, my boy. We kiss our friends and slaughter our enemies ... Come, come, you must know who I am. Every day she talks of me, no? She's my girl, my favourite in the world, I am like an uncle to her ...'

Max looked to Valentine, who was smiling for the first time in days.

'The Captain?' Max ventured.

'Of course! It is a pleasure to meet you. When did you two marry? You are not married ... I will not tell her father ... you may count on me, I do not care, I am modern. Most Greeks are not modern, the word is not even Greek, Roman I think, and so ugly ... No matter. You must look after this girl, Max, or we will become enemies and nobody lives happily with me as an enemy ... A baby she was yesterday, Max, in my arms in this very house whilst I drank brandy with Desmond, her Papa – you know him? A great friend of mine, but then *paff*, he disappears.'

The Captain placed his palm under his chin and rasped his neck in a way that caused Valentine to reach over and kiss him on the cheek.

'Thank you, my darling ... *Metaxas Twelve* it was, like honey, you can drink a bottle and feel no problems, two bottles if you are strong. But come, enough talk of drinking, let us drink and we must discuss everything.'

He opened the cool box as if it were a treasure chest. Within were bottles packed tight like arrows in a quiver, a freezing slush of ice and water around them. The Captain drew one out and produced an elegant corkscrew from his pocket. With the slick moves of a Zen archer, he flicked open the corkscrew and eased out the long cork with a sonorous pop.

'Vallei, Vallei, my princess. Rinse out these glasses and we will drink and fill the years that have passed since you were a little girl. And I must interrogate this young man and find if he is worthy of you.'

The wine was as cold as a mountain stream and delicious – the coldest thing to have passed their lips for weeks as the kerosene refrigerator rarely delivered more than a gentle chill. The sweetness of the wine washed away the memory of their recent fear. Valentine became happy and relaxed, laughing easily and skipping round the Captain, once or twice looking at Max with softened eyes.

Everybody spoke – Valentine about her father, Max of the future – and the Captain listened with gravity to the young people, but most of all it was he who spoke, laughing through story after story and glass after glass of wine.

'I love to be in my house with Kalenda but I swear I miss the wheel of my ship,' he said. 'What a thing it is to guide such a vessel, bigger than a thousand cars, a hundred planes, a thing like a village, a great island in your hands and yet always, always, at the mercy of the sea.'

Max asked the Captain about Khalib but he simply shook his head and would say no more. They drank and talked, one bottle becoming two and then three. As the sun began to set the Captain looked out towards the western sky.

'Regrettably, I must leave you two lovers to your own delicious madness.' He stood up and drained his glass, his broad face absorbing the evening light. 'I can no longer see at night. I used to be able to read Homer in the dark but now . . . ahh.' He sighed.

He pulled the remaining bottles of wine from the cooler and placed them on the table.

'These are for you. I thought we might drink them all but you young people are so much more sensible than we were. I suppose it's a good thing . . .'

They walked arm in arm on either side of the Captain, arriving at the boat to find a hibiscus sky mottled with strips of violet cloud.

'A storm will be here soon, I can feel it in my knees,' the captain said, loosing his moorings.

'Red sky at night, shepherds' . . .?' Max ventured.

'Ha. You listen to a shepherd or a Greek captain of the seas? I was trained in the latest meteorology by the greatest merchant navy in the world!'

'Sorry, it's an English thing,' Max agreed. 'By the way, watch out for the rock, there's a huge rock just under the surface.'

'I know of this rock, Max.' The Captain hesitated and then turned round. 'Do you think I could live here without knowing of it? I survived the Nazis, Max . . . and their whores, the Colonels.'

'I meant in the sea . . .' Max gestured towards the water.

'I understand, of course I do – my boy, I have been married to a woman since before you were even born. I've been married, and divorced, and then, thank God, we married again. Could I be here, now, passed the life I have lived, without knowing of such things?'

'I was just . . .' Max spluttered to explain.

'This thing in the water, it is dangerous. Not because of what it is – it is stone like every other stone, like the ground we stand on. And its shape, I have seen it … dangerous? Pah, it is nothing. No, Max, it is because it is hidden that people forget about such a thing, then it becomes dangerous. When you push it away from your mind … it is not there, you say … then it will destroy you, your boat, everything. As long as you remember it, look for the way the water moves above its point, remember its shape, know it for what it is, then it will not harm you. Vallei-mou, come kiss an old man. Max, look after my darling. I'll be back soon. Enough. I must go. Kalenda will be waiting.'

He stepped into the boat, started it with one pull on the motor, and roared off, disappearing into the twilight.

# Thirty-one

So, the Triff's on a walk, or gone to the village, or something, and days and days have passed without me seeing another soul. I am lying on my belly in the sun reading *Gormenghast*, my feet in the air like they're some creature's antennae enjoying the breeze, and I hear the hum of Captain Maris's boat coming round the cliff. We haven't seen him all year because he has been in Canada playing poker, or trying to get a friend out of prison – I can't remember which of the stories is true – so I run down to the sea as fast as I can. When he sees me he sounds *God Save Our Gracious Queen* on his klaxon, which is our secret code. I dive to the side of the sunken rock and swim as fast as I can until I am nearly at the boat. But before I reach it, he turns and heads out to sea, and then waits until I catch up, then shoots off again. This carries on until I am about to drown from exhaustion or we are, as the Captain says, 'too near Turkey'.

It's always the same, but he loves it.

The Captain brings the boat round, grabs my arm and pulls me out of the water like a little squid.

Other than my lovely Dad with his big old nose, and Jojo (who doesn't count), there's no man I love more in this or any other world than Captain Maris. He is a giant bullfrog, and if I have no waist then he's definitely got no neck – literally none. His huge wide head settles directly on his strong shoulders like a water balloon. He has an enormous belly and all this is supported by legs of such glorious stumpiness that they should belong to a giant dwarf. His whole body is matted in a thick fur, bleached gold by the sun. He's stronger than anyone and once when I was little, after one of those parties at the house that started as a glass of wine before lunch, he bet Dad 500 drachma that he could juggle me and Kiki, his niece. The Triff went crazy, of course, and Dad got the Full Treatment for even discussing it. Dad claimed he would never have actually let him juggle us, but the Captain had been weighing me in his hands and doing little practice throws and arguing about the rules of the bet before the Triff saved us.

As soon as I'm in the boat, I throw my arms around where the Captain's neck would be if he wasn't a bullfrog and hang on to him like a gibbon – partly because I love him, and partly to soak him as he never swims.

'Greeks do not get wet my darling,' he says, 'this is why we invented the boat.'

He once told me he had never taken a bath or shower in his life – but as the Triff reminds everyone, he's the biggest fibber in the whole world and the truth is, he doesn't smell one bit. When the Captain hears her say something like this he pinches my cheek with fingers as thick as my wrist.

'She says I lie,' he once said, 'what does your mother know of lies? I'll tell you the biggest lie after Fascism and Turkish Coffee ...' I wasn't sure what he meant as we didn't do Fascism till year nine, but I wanted to know.

'Toothbrushing,' he said. 'That's a lie. It is completely unnecessary to brush your teeth.'

Mum got angry, which Dad seemed to enjoy, but then he laughed and said that the Captain's teeth were as false as his stories.

Now the Captain tries to untangle me from his body because I am soaking him and the boat is bobbing about, going nowhere. But I am strong and wiry and harder to untangle than a bush baby from a bush. Eventually he shouts, 'Off, Vallei-mou, I am an old man,' and because I am merciful I release him, although it's not true, he's not that old. I take the wheel of the boat and drive it about a bit then he takes it to guide it into our little bay as it takes a bit of practice. He ties the boat to the walnut tree and we head off to the house. He's carrying a bright red cool box with something for Mum he says. I try to help him but it weighs a ton so I walk ahead. When we get to the house the Triff is not there, which he seems sad about, but I tell him she will come back soon and bring him a huge glass of retsina and nothing to eat, because the Captain doesn't eat.

I take his hat and put it on myself and sit on his knee to give him a hug because I have not seen him for a whole year, but he takes my arms from his neck and says 'Vallei-mou, please. Sit over there. You are a grown girl now. Tell me about your boyfriends.'

I'm sure he's teasing and I twist round on his knee, throw my arms around his chest and snuggle closer but he pulls me off and plonks me hard on the bench in front of him and says, in the most serious voice I've heard from him: 'Valentine. Please listen to me. Put some clothes on. Enough of these games, they are for children and you are not a child. Go and put some clothes on yourself and then come and talk to me.'

And I go inside and it's silly, I know, but I cry because he hates me. First my Dad, and then him. I run into the loo and lock the door and lean my arms against the wall and my head on my wrists and sob, and while I am crying I am aware of something strange and strong, a sharp deep smell, and when I breathe through my nose I realise it comes from me, from under my arms, it is me. I stink. Like a grown-up – sweet and curryish but more and different, and disgusting, but I sort of like it … and I wonder if this is why the Captain pushed me away, and I am so ashamed and vow to wash more, every single hour from now on. I turn on the light to run water in the sink and when the light comes on I realise that I'm practically naked. I haven't looked at myself for days and days, and here I am in front of the mirror. It's like one of those dreams where you are in school and you suddenly remember you didn't get dressed, but this is real. My skin is as brown as shoes and I really am on the way to growing breasts. My eyes are red from crying, my hair is mad and I am only wearing a swimsuit that's really knickers and so old they don't even fit any more.

I wash under my arms and as I do, I brush against my breasts with my forearms and they tingle and feel strange. I squeeze them between my fingers and it gives me pins and needles between my legs and fluttering in my belly. My heart is somehow pumping in my face and between my legs as well and I don't know quite what to do. For some reason I take Mum's lipstick and put it on my lips like I've seen her do a hundred thousand times. But then I wipe it off because it's scary or I don't know what … and I put on a T-shirt and some proper shorts and splash water on my face and go back out. But really, I want to die.

Literally.

# Thirty-two

Weld was there by four.

The little spoon with the London bus on the handle was tinkling in the china cup as Beaufinn stirred. Sometimes now he had the tea all mixed and ready, putting the sugar in for him: one, two, three. The cup was a funny one, like a cartoon, with legs like a human and a cup for a body. Easy to tip over.

'In you come my boy, in you come. No dawdling.'

The tea was as sweet and strong as the liqueur his Mummy let him taste from her glass but it was not green and thick like hers, it was brown like normal tea. He soon wasn't sure if he'd told Beaufinn about the Torment that day, or if he dreamt he did. As always with the tea, the close room grilled by the four bars of pulsing red, and the big comfy armchair, Weld sank into the cushions like thick warm treacle, deeper and deeper like a spiral until he was asleep, dreaming he was Heavy and his fur, his winter coat, the one his Mummy had put on, was being torn off and then he was being pulled open and turned inside out, the stuffing pulled out of him and pushed back in.

'Wake up, wake up, you can't sleep all day. Come on now, wake up.'

A smell of whisky. The face as big as a mountain, white hair like scorched bushes. Weld wondered dizzily if a rabbit might dash from a nostril and disappear through the undergrowth or up into an ear.

An ear full of wax, brown and greasy.

He felt sick.

'Drink your coffee, it'll get you on your feet.'

The blackness whirled, round and round. Eyes closed. Head falling.

'Up. Wake up, come on boy.'

He was being shaken.

The coffee was the darkness, was in front of him. He sucked it in. Hot. He dropped it. Brittle legs in the air. Coffee everywhere. Wet, rippling in the tray, like streams on Scottish holidays.

'You stupid little . . .' Beaufinn snatched the tray away.

'Sorry, sir.'

'Don't you sir me, you little fuck,' he roared, coffee sloshing onto the red carpet below.

Weld retracted like a whelk in its shell, pulling away into the chair, each swirl on the teacher's beard a terrible detail, the giant's hands gripping the sides of the tray, thick black hairs like streaks of soot on puffy white flesh, the red face, flecks of dried skin crushed in the wrinkles, sweat formed in horrible blisters, cardigan button holes slanting like eyes, a dense body crammed into a wheelchair, panting . . .

Beaufinn calms himself, steadies.

'No use crying over spilled coffee, haha.'

Beaufinn put the tray next to an open bottle of whisky by his chair, pulled himself in front of the armchair where the boy sat and reached out a hand, a thick white sausage hand covered in boar's bristle.

Weld flinched. Hypervigilant.

'I'll give you a note saying we worked late. Slept right through Studies and dinner – you old lazy bones. I'll call matron and ask why you're not sleeping, yes that's it. I'll give her a call tomorrow. You go straight up to your cubicle when you get in – d'you hear? Don't speak to anyone, don't go to matron. Are you hungry? Do you want one of my special toffees?'

Weld shook his head.

'Off you go then.'

As soon as the adult wheeled himself back, Weld sprang from the armchair, slid open the door, and ran out into the night without stopping.

The air was cold and dark. Sharp as knives. The path silver like ash.

Weld ran until he was at the school, up the stairs, past the blur of boys and into his bed, sealed in like a whelk, curling into his shell.

# Thirty-three

He was lovely of course and I didn't need to die.

Thank God that I didn't, because when I came out of the bathroom, praying he could not see that I'd been crying and wondering if I might be ... showing through my T-shirt he stood up and kissed me on both cheeks with his sandpaper face. 'Ah my Valentine,' he growled, 'look at you now, so beautiful. You are too old to run around like a savage – no?' Then he gave me a hug that would crack a three-foot walnut and told me that no matter what happened, even if I was old and ugly with four husbands and twenty children, I'd always be his most special girl.

We sat down together on Pa's crap bench and I offered him more retsina, but he shook his head and looked at me as if wondering whether to share a terrible confidence before producing a bottle from his cooler.

'Now you are grown up, I will tell you a secret my darling. Your mother is a wonderful woman, beautiful too, but this retsina, it is terrible, why she drinks it I do not know. For twenty years I've been throwing her wine in this very bush and your mother cannot understand why the poor thing gives no flowers ... I've begged her not to buy it ... it's probably made by Turks, they do this you know Vallei-mou, everything – olive oil, coffee – they make it in chemical factories. No, my darling princess, I've brought my own bottle. Cretan wine, delicious, the vineyard has a ghost, so they say.'

He raised a thick finger to his face and flicked it across his nose in one of his many peculiar gestures.

'Of course, there is no ghost – I'm not saying we don't have ghosts in Greece, Vallei-mou, ask Homer, Euripides, we probably invented ghosts – I'm just saying in the Boutari vineyard, there are no ghosts. I've been there myself. It is a story, to scare off thieves and enemies.'

'What enemies?'

'You would not believe it, Vallei-mou, so many: Nazis, Venetians, Turks of course ... Not so long ago, but before you or I, or even my own sweet mother was born, three hundred Cretans – many women and children – were hiding in a monastery from the Ottomans, who are Turks. A thousand soldiers, maybe more, surrounded the monastery and a man called Kostis Giamboudakis, he took explosives and blew up the whole thing. All the Turkish soldiers were killed ... A great Greek hero, now get me the corkscrew, my little nectarine.'

I gave him the corkscrew and asked what happened to all the women and children.

'Dead ...' he says, 'blown to pieces so tiny a baby octopus could eat them ... but with honour at least. Perhaps it was not such a great victory ... Ah, you are wise my Vallei. At last, here is your mother, she can smell the Boutari wine.'

The Triff was marching down the path with Jojo on her hip, her brown hair leaping, faded yellow rah-rah skirt bouncing, behind her, there he was, Khalib – a plastic bag in his hand, leaking something wet.

When the Triff caught sight of Captain Maris she began waving one hand like a great leaf caught in the wind, quickening her pace until she had to break into a sort of mad skip, her bare feet kicking back sand like clouds of pollen. Khalib slowed, loitered and disappeared into the bushes.

'What a lovely surprise, it's been so long, we've been dying

231

to see you so much that we all but forgot you existed. Hello darling, isn't that right we'd all but forgotten about him?'

'I didn't forget,' I insisted.

The Captain took the Triff's hands and pulled her towards him, pressing his frog lips onto both of her brown and freckled cheeks.

'Have you offered the Captain a drink?' the Triff asked, looking back for Khalib.

'Yes. I gave him some retsina but he said he doesn't . . .'

'. . . want to use up your precious wine.' The Captain interrupted, glaring at me and pulling his left earlobe with a great sense of meaning. 'Try some of this, my dear, I brought it for you especially. It's Cretan wine, the best . . .'

'Darling, be a gem and get a couple of glasses will you? And put some berries in a beaker of water for Khalib – he was saying something about it but I didn't really listen.'

'Khalib's run off, Mother . . . and for your information, slavery ended in 1833.'

She dashed up the path to look for him.

I sigh because there's just no point and anyway the Captain gives me a look if I'm rude to her. When I came out of the house with the glasses, the Triff is returning with the plastic bag Khalib was carrying – which, it turns out, is bulging with hundreds of little fish.

'He suddenly appeared and presented me with all these fish – a peace offering after the awful dog thing – anyway, I invited him to come and have fish soup with tomatoes and potatoes, and I'm chatting away and what not, and he sees the Captain and next thing, he's disappeared, left the bag of fish on the path. Perhaps he's been abducted by the same aliens that took you last summer?'

I glare at her to shut up.

It was ages ago. Me and a friend had been playing Operation

Random and the challenge was to get on the first bus that came, whatever it was. Jenn was meant to check what time it was so we weren't late. But she didn't, because, well she's like that. Her brain makes goldfish look deep.

The Triff is not frightened by my weed-wilting death-stare, despite the fact that I learnt it from her. She looks straight through me, I bet that she is ignoring me, or maybe her mind is already somewhere else. She smiles and sashays past me, not looking at the glass I offer her and heading into the house.

I sit down opposite Captain Maris, raising my eyebrows, to which he responds by brushing the back of his hand under his chin which makes an amazing raspy sound. Sometimes I swear he just makes these gestures up.

The Captain takes a swig of wine, places the glass back on the table, rinses the wine around his mouth, swallows, leans back on the bench – as if these were all important things he had to do – then he nods to where Khalib disappeared and asks:

'That boy, why is he here?'

'Khalib? He's always here, bringing things, helping Ma, hanging about, watching.'

'What things?'

'Fish, honey ... wood for the fire.'

'Hmm.'

'He's a good swimmer.'

'He is half fish,' Captain Maris says, looking at me without moving, his head a little cocked.

Ma appears refreshed and leafy, as if she had been spritzed, her vacuoles all full of water, energy production resuming under the Captain's admiring eye: photosynthesis, Year Eight biology. He pours her a glass, which she drinks in a few swigs, and then another, which she sips. They chat about the house and weather. He refills their glasses.

'And Desmond, he is coming soon?' he asks, lowering himself back onto the bench.

'No, he's working, or waiting for work ... I don't know, he'll probably stay in London.'

Captain Maris gives her a frog-waiting-for-a-fly look. The Triff's tendrils quiver, shimmer, like fur in wind, she retracts, more anemone than plant. I think she is going to cry.

'A favour, I beg you,' he asks suddenly, standing up and clapping his huge hands.

'Yes?'

'Give me a chair, this ... whatever you call it, it is uncomfortable.'

The Triff leaps up, relieved, and returns with a chair which the Captain settles onto with glee.

'Thank God. It was killing me this ... *bench*? Barbaric. A chair is better, a Greek invention, you know. The Arabs, they lie around in their beds smoking hashish, the Greeks sit upright like civilised people and make philosophy and drink wine.'

Ma and the Captain were soon gossiping about boring things and I go off and look at the dead fish in the sink. I think about cleaning them but they're slimy. They stink too. I walk about the house, lie on the bed, sigh, read a few pages, wash myself again and go back outside. The Captain and Mama are talking away, deep into a new bottle.

'Vallei, she does not like him,' he says, eyeing me.

'Rubbish. She's known him since she was little.'

'Who?' I ask.

'Khalib.'

'Oh yes.'

'The Captain says you don't like him. That's not true, is it?' I shrug.

'He taught you to swim, didn't he darling?' she asks.

'Yes.'

'And he found us a new spring.'

'Pah,' the Captain says.

'Captain Maris is jealous,' the Triff says to me.

'What do you say? Jealous? Of him?' the Captain replies, astonished.

'You don't like him because of the gossip, or because he's so handsome,' she accused.

'Ha, all Greeks are handsome ... but he, he is ...'

'You should be more charitable. Fr Dennisos was so cruel ... and to have no friends ...'

'Life is hard. Especially here. But he had the same education as me, a roof over his stinking head, a church roof even. He thinks only to survive, Khalib, like an animal.'

'You're so cruel, you Greeks. Have you seen his back ... those scars? And the fish he brought us ...' The Triff was getting warmed up now, if you pour too much wine onto her roots she gets spiky.

'Where do you think your angel boy gets his fish?' the Captain demands, lifting his fist, with his smallest fingers extended, 'From the market? From fishing? No. Khalib has no boat. *Dynamite*. You have heard him, no? BOOM. All the fish are destroyed and the sea also. Look at his hand. He has lost fingers.'

'You and your fish,' Triff exclaimed. She sloshes more wine into her glass, takes a swig, slamming it on the table with a force that surprises even her. 'All you think about is your bloody fish. At least he helps me and is kind. I need a strong man sometimes, to help me, do you think it's easy with the kids and here alone? You're all the fucking same ...'

The Captain puts down his glass very slowly and carefully. He stands. 'It is late and this wine is strong. I will go now.' He opens the red cooler and takes out a bag of olives and three peaches, drops of icy water clinging to their velvet pelts.

'Vallei-mou, these are for you, my darling. The olives are Kalimarta, the best you will ever taste.'

He empties the icy slush from the cooler into the plants. He nods to the Triff and heads off to his boat. I go with him, clutching his free hand.

'Are you angry?' I ask.

'Ahh Vallei-mou, I am. A little. But curing anger with wine is like putting out a fire with petroleum ... anyway, it will not last long, and my love for you, it will be for ever. Look after your mother.'

He gives me a kiss on the forehead, tosses the cooler into the boat and climbs in with a sigh of relief.

# Thirty-four

At breakfast, heavy with sleep, Weld patted his pockets for the sharp flat square of his MCs. With a panic, he realised they were not there. He made his way to his cubicle after breakfast and rummaged about the few places they might be, searching for the papal green plastic folder emblazoned in shining gold with the school crest. He pulled himself across the splintery wooden floor under the bed and then stretched under his cupboard with straining fingers. Perhaps, he told himself, the book had fallen out when he took off his trousers the night before.

He renewed his search, desperately exploring crannies, and when he had searched every spot in the small area that was his, he began again. By the time the first bell rang for class he was visualising the terrible consequences of having lost the whole booklet. He abandoned his cubicle and made his way down the stairs, wondering how he might progress through the day, through the coming weeks, without ever being asked for his MCs. It would be like walking on paper-thin glass, knowing that at some point it would shatter into razor-sharp shards.

As he pushed through the classroom door he saw Linnet observing him with a malevolent smirk. He wondered if this was the answer. Linnet had stolen his MCs to get him into trouble. Weld stopped, searching his face. Linnet glared back, then looked away and asked Davies a question – this was unusual as, since he could not Torment nor amuse Davies, Linnet generally ignored him.

Miss Trench hauled them through forty minutes of long division and, skipping the customary warnings of how far behind they all were, announced the commencement of a Geography lesson. At some point mid-way through a detailed list of the various eroded matters one might have found scraped by, carried, or pushed ahead of a glacier that had supposedly existed in Germany a hundred million years before, Trench announced that she was 'exhausted' and they were to copy out ten pages of their Geography textbook until break.

'Weld, approach the desk,' she said, holding up his book of MCs. 'Mr Beaufinn sent this with the post this morning. You left it in his house during your tuition yesterday. Clearly you are not only idle, but careless as well. Since I notice he has not debited you an MC for your forgetfulness, I will oblige.'

Confused, and overcome with a momentary relief, Weld took the newly signed folder from Trench's desk. As he sat back down he heard the faint sound of someone sucking air through their mouth – a message from Linnet that he was 'a suck' for going to extra classes.

Weld rested his cheeks on his fists and tried to picture what might have happened at Beaufinn's. His mind was cloudy with images that kept slipping like dreams as he tried to focus them. He knew his MCs could not fall out unless he took down his trousers. He wondered if he had used the lavatory in Beaufinn's house – and yet he was sure he hadn't – not after the first time he'd been in there, not even for a pee. It had been full of repellent smells and contained medical equipment – bed pans and things to do with the Handicap. Weld had sworn not go in there again. Yet how could his MC folder have fallen out unless he had? An idea began to roll into a memory, gaining momentum as a second sucking noise issued from Linnet, this time long and low, but loud enough to be heard by Miss Trench.

'Linnet, stand up. What is the meaning of this disgusting noise?'

'Please miss,' Linnet stood without fear or hesitation, 'I've got a cold and a runny nose and I was . . .'

'Silence. I don't want to hear any more repugnant details.'

Linnet drew his sleeve under his nose and snorted for extra effect.

'Use a tissue, boy. Lock yourself away in some private place and use a tissue, you repulsive, vile creature.'

'Yes, Miss.'

'And be sure to see matron during the recreation period. Perhaps she will be kind enough to quarantine you and protect the rest of us from your abhorrent germs.'

Linnet sat down grinning.

'Back to work, the rest of you. You all have a LONG HARD ROAD to travel if you want to make something of yourselves and that begins with copying out page 28.'

Weld was not on page 28. His mind was beginning to whir, revving up like one of those toy cars that are pushed along the ground, over and over again. What might have happened, what, somewhere in him, he knew what had happened, and it began wheeling with the repulsive sound of Linnet's suck, hurtling into a spin. As he closed his eyes, he was Heavy the Bear; feeling his fur, his springy softness, the 'x' of his eyes like kisses on a letter from his mother, naked as his fur was torn off. Weld felt it tear away; the air on his skin, something reaching his insides and pulling them out.

'Weld, you look decidedly queer.' Miss Trench was peering at him over her glasses.

Richard Beaufinn held him, snorting, from behind; a boar's head . . . saliva drooling down his back . . .

'WELD, what is wrong with you?'

'Nothing Miss, I . . .'

'Nothing, although an adequate description of your current achievements is not the answer to my question. You look decidedly queer. I suggest you join Linnet on a visit to the infirmary.'

Weld surfaced out of his vortex for a moment. He looked down at the Geography book on his desk, so far away, his clothes so damp and cold against his body.

Miss Trench stood up, a handkerchief over her mouth and nose as she walked to the classroom door. 'Since you have all become a breeding ground of contagion – no doubt engendered by your puerile aversion to hygiene – I insist you proceed to the playground without delay. Go. Introduce some fresh air into your fetid systems.'

The class rushed out, whooping with delight at the extra few minutes break. Weld did not run or whoop – he teetered. He stumbled to the gap away from the playground, the place where the undergrowth allowed a view of the speeding vehicles on the broad stretch of motorway below. The clattering in his mind reached an annihilating peak until he felt he might implode, but as he stared at the grey torrent of cars and motorbikes it soothed him with its linear force: the space between each vehicle seemed to balance the eddying of his mind, steadying it, still and cold, his eyes staring ahead, unblinking.

'What's it to be Smeld?' a voice challenged.

The gang, headed by Linnet, had assembled behind him.

'Are you in or out, because there's no more quarter, especially not for baby blubbing sucks . . . You're either with us or against us. Isn't that right Stelly?'

'Right,' came his lieutenant's reply.

Weld watched a fleet of spotlessly clean trucks flow past,

one after another, behind them a trail of space, their roar tailing off like the slipstream of an airplane.

'Here after Rest,' Weld said, without shifting his gaze.

The gang dispersed into the mass of noise behind him.

Images appeared and disappeared, orbiting like mute traffic. Thoughts no longer communicated in coherent sequences. Not where he was, not what had happened between his dreams, just the movement of metal and the air between. He was not a child, not a boy; he was thousands of, millions of, moments of experience, cleaving towards survival. Whatever the adult had done was not relayed to him, not recalled, not heard, not touched, nor seen; it was separate from his centre, from him, centrifuged out by the force of survival, sealed in an invisible ring – and with it all the trust and innocence that had been seized in those frenzied moments. The echoes of what had happened in the past would pulse on anonymously into the future, projecting their distorted image wherever they could. But this was not the past or the future; this was survival.

# Thirty-five

Was it the fish he kept bringing, the clearing of rocks and carrying of shopping, the berries and honeycombs he seemed to find everywhere? Perhaps it was the line of freckles under his eyes, his silent footstep that could creep up on a mole, his elegant swimming, or as I think back now, perhaps it was something in the scars from Fr Dennisos' savage beatings, those pale zips criss-crossing his muscular back. Whatever it was, the Triff spent more time with Khalib, going off for walks and swims, leaving me and Jojo to laze in the sun. When he'd stay for dinner, he'd sit silent and sullen, his gently curled hair falling in front of his face, his mouth open, his legs apart, proud.

Disgusting.

I knew then that I hated him but I did not know what it was I didn't like. His greasy mouth and noisy chewing made me feel sick. His way of sitting in Dad's chair made me furious and I hated how he'd watch me when the Triff's back was turned. I could not understand what she saw in him. I suppose he was a man and a part of this whole place she loved, like the olive trees or the house; perhaps he was a particular way into it that she longed for, something that not me or Jojo or even Dad could give her.

One night we sat by the sea after a thunderstorm and the sky was so pink it made you ache. Khalib gave her some flowers he'd picked and said, 'You are pretty, like the sea.'

Of course, she sucked this up, eyes brimming with hope or

retsina – who knows, but I felt like regurgitating the afternoon's calamari into the sea and made suitable noises but neither of them even heard me.

When he left, she asked me what was wrong, so I told her.

She said I was mean and spoiled.

'But what's *he* doing here?' I asked.

'Just helping and keeping me company.'

'What about me and Jojo, aren't we company?'

'Of course you are.' She put her arms around me, ignoring my stiffness, 'but you're not grown up.'

'And he is,' I said.

'Well . . . yes.'

She soon gave up trying to hug me and her large skinny hands were resting on my shoulders and the whole thing felt fake, like an American TV show where the grown-up is explaining something important about life to the little kid, who in real life probably has three or four psychiatrists and is already taking drugs.

I shook her off.

'He's never even been to England, he stinks, he's stupid and he thinks he's God's gift to the island.'

'Not everyone in the world has been brought up like a little queen with two adoring parents and everything they want.'

'Two adoring parents? I've got none now Dad's not here and you've got your new boyfriend.'

'Boyfriend? Me? That's a bloody laugh. It's your father you're thinking about.'

Suddenly there was the nearness of some great truth, like the heat from an animal. An animal the size of a hill.

'What do you mean?' I demanded.

'Nothing Valentine. Nothing at all . . . but he's not my new boyfriend, no.'

'I don't understand. Where's Dad? Why's he not here?' I felt like crying.

'Oh sweetie, I don't know ... I don't even think you'd understand. As for Khalib, he's nothing, but at least he's here ... Maybe you need to grow up a bit.'

I looked for her wine glass because normally when she talked like that she was drunk.

But she wasn't, not yet, and that afternoon, I grew up.

# Thirty-six

They gathered after Rest. All but Weld.

'Smeld's not here,' Stellmark offered, 'he's probably blubbing somewhere.' He looked to Linnet for confirmation.

Linnet ignored him, scanning the playground. Ibwe and Wilson prepared their affirming smirks, waiting for Linnet to define reality.

'Demain's on duty,' Linnet said, as if to himself.

'That's Fr Demain over there,' Wilson offered.

'I can see that, dur-brain,' Linnet snapped.

'D'you think Weld will come?' Stellmark asked.

Linnet did not reply. Instead he turned to his group, and with elbows out and head tilted back, he released one low cluck. Wilson and Ibwe looked at each other and then decided it was safe to laugh. Linnet clucked again and Stellmark chortled in relief. Linnet did a few turns as a chicken, extending his neck to increasing hilarity. When Stellmark – whose parents kept chickens – started scraping the ground with his feet and pecking, it was a signal that the joke had gone stale.

'I'm bored,' Wilson complained. 'Let's go. We'll get MC'd to death if they catch us.'

'Go then. It's a free country. No one needs you, but you'll miss the action cos Weld's over there,' Linnet said.

The figure of Weld was not so much moving as enlarging as he crossed the playground. He walked straight past Fr Demain, his coat rolled up under one arm, not using any of the diversionary techniques the others employed, either confident of his anonymity, or not caring. Weld scrambled up the bank and stood before the other boys, looking past them.

'You'll get us all caught, dur-brain,' Stellmark said.

'Fr Demain can't see,' Weld replied. 'He's old.'

'We've been here for hours,' Linnet complained.

'Yeah. What've you been doing – being a suck to Mr Beaufinn, I bet,' Stellmark jeered.

Before Stellmark had even finished his taunt Weld had dropped his bundle and attacked the lanky figure, knocking him to the ground and pummelling his face with his hands.

The others pulled him off.

'Steady on, Weld,' Linnet reasoned, 'he was only . . .'

'Shut up,' Weld said. 'If you or anybody else says I suck up to Beaufinn . . . I'll kill them, I'll bloody kill them.'

The boys were silent. Weld produced the penknife from his pocket. He opened the blade and crouched down to pick up his overcoat. There was something within, swaddled like a baby. He let the bundle unravel and something tumbled to the ground.

It was Heavy.

Somehow vulnerable amidst the roots, the cold damp ground, the wellington boots.

'Teddies are for babies right?' Weld said, holding up his bear. 'That's what you said.'

He placed the blade under one sausage arm and sawed upwards. With no more than the faintest tear the arm was severed. Weld repeated the action on the other arm, facing Linnet, who winced as he saw the penknife slice through the limp sponge, feeling it in his own arms. The legs were next – one, two – the bear's body slipping back and forth under the push and pull of the blade.

Heavy's eyes, two little crosses, staring up at the jagged

patch of sky between the leaves, as if taking in the space one last time.

When it came to removing the head, a better purchase was needed. Weld dug his fingers into the foam cheeks of the toy, contorting the bear's expression, sawing through the neck.

When the head had been separated Weld stood up and tossed it to Linnet.

'This is for you,' he said.

Linnet, pale with fear, took it, not daring to look.

Weld retrieved the arm from the ground and examined it, before holding it against his groin.

'No more wee-wee for Heavy the Bear,' he said, flapping it and pretending to urinate on the boys with the severed limb.

'You take it,' he threw it at Stellmark's face, 'in case someone cuts yours off when you're asleep.'

Weld spun round and crouched over the headless, limbless trunk. He stabbed between the amputated stumps of its legs and ripped it open, tearing it up to the chest and pulling out handfuls of foam.

The boys stood, silent and motionless, plumes of breath feathering the cold air.

'That's it now. I'm an Ace, right?' Weld said, staring at them.

No one spoke.

'Right Linnet? That's what you said.' Weld glared at Linnet as he rose to his feet, the penknife loose in his hand.

'I want to go,' Wilson said softly.

'No!' Weld jabbed the air with the shining blade. 'We're all Aces, that's what you said, isn't it?'

It was a threat.

Weld looked at the group for a reaction and saw with contempt that their stasis was no more than terror.

He turned and walked to the perimeter fence.

'Weld ...' Ibwe called after him.

But Weld was already pulling up the chain link fence. He pushed himself through the space beneath, scrabbling in the dirt with his hands. He propelled himself against clods of earth, edging through until the thick wire of the fence caught on his boots.

'Help,' he grunted. Only Ibwe responded. He pulled the wire from Weld's boot, then stretched his hand down to help him return. But Weld pulled away through the space. He stood up on the other side of the fence before walking down the bank towards the torrent of cars below. Ibwe leaned into the fence, his cheeks pushing against the wire, his right hand locked in the weave of metal above his head.

Weld paused at the bottom of the bank, for a moment astonished by the clattering barrage of noise and air as each car passed. Exhilarated by the speed, by the corridors of space that fleetingly appeared and then, with a rush of metal, were no more. A truck roared by on the inside lane, its wind buffeting Weld into the gorse. He walked back to the edge of the road, listening for a rhythm in the passing of cars, fear flapping like a trapped bird in his stomach. A green transit van streaked by, its passenger snagged by the image of Weld, a face squashed against the window in a silent questioning 'O'.

Weld stepped into the road, running out, his feet slapping the hard smooth surface, flying through the cacophony of horns, exalting in the dynamism, in the being alive, in the freedom, in the vital electricity searing through him. He saw the truck looming in the periphery of his vision leaping towards him as he fell onto the dull edge of the crash barrier.

The truck's horn cascaded down a scale as it passed. Weld waited, panting. An old car on the other side of the road pulled over and screeched to a halt and its driver – a man in a donkey jacket – leapt out. Weld saw three children in the back, a mum in the front; she was leaning behind her and holding the children against their seats, as if they might rush out of the car. The man was shouting to Weld in a voice like the miners had on television.

'Stay there lad.'

Weld yearned to run into the man's arms, be with his family, go wherever they were going. Within Weld a dense force began to spin again, like a star ready to explode. He dropped his eyes to the thick hexagonal bolts on the crash barrier, to the long strips of moulded metal: hard, dull and grey like winter. He ran back into the middle of the road, bisecting the linear force of the vehicles, sprinting towards the bank, a car zooming so close behind him he could feel its mirror brush his anorak, like an arrow, a bullet, the horn of a bull. Weld scrambled up the bank, boots slipping, hands grabbing at the damp vegetation.

The boys stared, catatonic with shock, faces pressed against the chain link fence.

Weld turned and looked at the man on the other side of the road. His hands were on the bonnet of the car. He saw him drop his head before squeezing his eyes together with his thumb and forefinger, then get into the car and drive off.

Weld crawled back under the fence and stood on the other side, mud on his knees, his face red. He walked past the boys towards the playground.

He said nothing.

# Thirty-seven

Max watched the boat evaporate into a smudge, a dot and then nothing but a vibration.

Valentine was frowning, her fists clenching and unclenching.

'He's right, Max,' Valentine whispered.

'What?'

'It's been hidden for too long.' Valentine was gazing across the water, shaking her head slowly, her lips moving as if remembering a prayer.

'What's wrong now?' Max asked, exasperated that her moment of joy seemed to have departed with the Captain. But Valentine had already turned away and was heading back to the house, walking and then running.

Max paced round in a circle, kicking up clouds of sand. He looked up to the vast space above him, and remembered that there was a way to explain this behaviour, a single manageable word: *women*.

For a moment it worked – made him feel heroic – but only for a moment, and all too soon he felt ridiculous, like a ham actor in some awful amateur play. He walked after her, sifting through what had happened for some sort of rationale. Tine reappeared, meeting him on the path, the bar for the shutters in both hands, her father's torn shirt stuffed under one arm.

'I've got everything. We'll do it now – then it'll be done for ever.'

'Do what? What are you talking about?'

'We can use this.' She held out the metal bar. 'We'll bang it in to the top of the rock, there's cracks and we can jam it in ... then tie this shirt on, like a flag. See?'

Max nodded. Valentine was even more drunk than he was.

'Tine, yes, of course I see, but don't you think we might be better off doing it in the morning?'

'No. We've got to do this now.'

'Tine, we're a bit drunk ... and it's dark and ...'

'NOW,' she screamed, 'it has to be fucking now. Don't you see?'

She stumbled to the edge, flustered about trying to get into the water with the bar in her hands and the shirt under her arm. Muddled by alcohol and the weight of the metal, she threw both on the ground then folded herself onto the sand, slapping the ground on either side of her.

'Fuck. Fuck ... I was fine until he came along ... I thought I'd get used to it, to us, you know? I've been trying so hard ... to be normal, act normal, like a girlfriend, to speak about things, to be with you like a proper girl, a proper woman ... but in here,' she pointed at her head, 'in fucking here ...' She jabbed at her head.

Max reached out his arms to her but she pushed him away.

'You don't know Max. In here,' she jabbed her fist between her breasts, 'I am ... in hell.'

'Why, what is it? Is it me?'

'No. It's not you. It has nothing to do with you.'

'Nothing to do with me? Then why have you been like this ... so cut off, so angry with me?'

'It's so hard to talk about ... because in a way, it *is* you. I was fine before I met you. I got by, but now, every time you ... I feel like that octopus being smashed against the rocks.'

'*Every time I what?* I don't understand, just tell me. It's me, it's not me. Tell me what it is.' Max crouched down on the sand beside her.

Tine stared at him, her eyes red.

'It's ... it's sex.'

Of course.

It made perfect sense. Terrible sense. The low murmur, the dark energy of mistrust, began its old rotation within him. Suspicions he had been trying to hide circled like a warped record, whispering, hissing. He had tried to ignore the feeling, but now there was no escape.

'I'm sorry,' he said, sitting by her in the sand, 'just ... sorry.'

The mantra gathered momentum, a message of worthlessness resonating from the very foundations of his being until it became a malevolent roar, shattering against the brittle bars of his chest.

'I thought I was doing it right.' He turned away from her. 'I thought that this was what everyone did, how everyone did it. I've never really known ...' Max stopped, unable to articulate his emptiness, not knowing whether there were words for what he wanted to say. He looked down at the ground.

'Max, what are you saying? It isn't you. It's not about you.' She turned his head so he could look into her eyes. 'It happened to *me* ... years ago. I was a child. I told you I came here last when my parents had just separated – I mean, they didn't even know they had, or they were hiding from it. Anyway Dad was in London – fucking someone probably, loads of people ... I don't know. What I do know is that it was just me and Mum and Jojo. He was so little then ...' She suddenly began to heave with dry sobs, the movement inward, as if each tear was being retracted before it could emerge.

'Tine, I don't understand ...'

'I was just a little girl Max, don't you see?'

'No. No, I don't. But I don't need to.' Max was suddenly desperate for silence. 'Let's just leave it, talk about it tomorrow.'

He started to stand up but Valentine held him back.

'No, I want to. I have to. I see now from what the Captain was saying. It will sink us otherwise, just drown what we have. That's what's been happening, it'll just suffocate the love out of everything. I have to say it. I've kept it locked up so it wouldn't hurt anyone else, not Mum, not you, not me ... but then with us ... and then *him* turning up here ... it all came back, stronger. I've never breathed a word, not even to my mother, not to anyone.'

An image materialised, the hulking figure of the Captain smothering Valentine in his thick arms, and with it, the desperate possibility that this defect, this emptiness came from something other than him. A thing Max could battle with, rather than turn and face himself.

'I hadn't even reached puberty, you know?' she whispered, 'had my period ... and then when he did that, it all started right then, the bleeding, the mess. Every fucking month it comes, and somewhere in me I remember. Then when he turned up here, it became real again, something I could not deny ... smothering me.'

Max looked at her; her sobs frightened him in a way he did not understand.

'Your period?'

'I wanted it to come, though. I wanted it to come because everyone else's had. I even prayed, talked to a God I didn't know, and begged him to let it start like everyone else's ... And then it happened, but not like it's meant to, not like the tides, or the moon ... but like a ...' she dropped her head, 'like a wound. That's it, a wound.'

Max did not want to hear any more. It was not him. That was enough.

Tine was pressing her closed eyes into her skull, pushing with her thumbs and whimpering to herself.

'Stop. Stop it, Valentine . . .' Max begged.

'No,' she screamed, 'I've got to say it out loud. He fucking did it.'

'Who? The Captain?' Max asked, hating the man, yearning to kick him in the face, smash his broad smiling face in.

'No. Khalib. Fucking Khalib.' Valentine was pulling at clumps of her own hair. 'I was a child. I didn't want it, whatever I said to myself afterwards, however much I accused, condemned myself. Of course I didn't fucking want it . . . and now I don't know how I ever can . . . Max, I feel so much for you and then when you want to fuck me . . . to get into me . . . to do what should be full of love, the whole thing ends up stinking like him. And that bit of me hates you like I hate him and I'm so frightened and angry, I just want to scream and run away. I thought I could make it all right, if I could just stop my mind with wine or concentrate on the rubbing, wanting you to do it harder and harder till you rubbed me out, till you made me disappear.'

Valentine's mouth was open but nothing more came out. She closed her teeth onto the flesh of her forearm.

'Khalib . . . raped you?'

'Mum was drunk, everything was wrong, even I could see it. It's awful when you are a child and you know that you're the only sensible one. Khalib was like a child anyway and Ma was so drunk she was laughing one minute, weeping the next – she even wet herself. They were both like demented children. She gave Khalib so much booze that lunch that he started blabbing like an animal, just blabbing nonsense. And I was outside, lying on a towel in the sun, trying not to hear, lying like a stupid little slut in my knickers. Lying there with my fingers in my ears, humming over and over with my eyes shut

254

because I didn't want to hear them or see them ... She must have kicked him out the house because ...'

A sob shuddered within Valentine, violent shocks of emotional magma straining against so many years of containment.

'Where is he ...' Max said, his voice low, cold fury flooding him with strength. 'Where is he now?'

'Every single day, I've felt him. On me. In me. All these years, I've felt this ... this ... you know how you feel when you see someone's shit or sick or blood. It's disgust, that's what it's called ... that's what I was, a disgusting little slut, a stinking dirty animal, because he covered my mouth with one stinking hand and held me down. I couldn't move, or call out. I don't know what he used, his finger, his penis, I closed my eyes, I left my body and then when I came back he was gone, leaving his filthy fucking mess all over me. That's what disgust is, isn't it – the knowledge that all of us, I, me ... I'm no more than a stinking animal ...'

Her whole body was heaving now, again and again, as if she were throwing herself against a heavy door, smashing herself against this dead weight, pressure building until, at last, something gave, and melted, tears flowing from her like a lifetime of rain on every dark afternoon there ever was.

Max stood. 'Tell me where he is,' he repeated.

He did not look at her prostrate on the ground.

'I never cried ... that's the first time,' she looked up at him, 'not since the day it happened. Not once. I've been damming it inside me, never saying it, not even to myself. Knowing that inside I'm horrible, infected with him ... but now I realise something Max.' She held out her hands. 'Shit, blood, piss, mucus ... That's what disgusts us because they scream at us that we are beasts, living, shitting, dying, but tears, Max, tears are human, there's no disgust in tears. Don't you see? We're the only ones who cry.'

He was not listening, had ceased to be aware, not the air against his face, not the sharp needles of pine or the jagged rocks that tore at his feet as he ran, not the bushes whipping across his shins, the branches scratching at his face, the force propelling him through the forest, on and on, a boulder unsettled from a mountain, smashing through everything not thick enough to hold him, while Valentine lay, her tears dripping onto the dry ground like the first drops of spring rain on cracked and arid ground, melting in, disappearing without resistance.

# Thirty-eight

I could see her. I could actually see her.

She sits up, picks up a shell and squats, listening to the rush of wind like a roaring sea. She lies in the sand, eyes closed, the sea like wind in her ear. She sits up again and then lies down, settling her head in the sand, the shell clutched to her ear, the heat of the tiny flecks of rock burning the skin on her thighs like a bath of scalding water. She lets the shell drop and lies, arms by her sides, eyes closed, red flesh burning through her eyelids. Red like her insides, swollen and burning. She understands what it is to want the earth to swallow you, engulf you. She wishes she could slip down a slit in the sand and sink, the sand close above her as if she had never been there – or scorch in the sun, dry to nothing, the flesh flaking off her bones, bleaching and crumbling in the white glare until there is nothing. Tears balloon in the corner of her eyes and fall, tapping the bleached gravel of the sand with sounds so near to nothing. Her underwear stretched like torn rigging across her knees. She kicks it off. She put her hands between her legs, in protection, in grief. She holds, as tightly as she can. She coughs out a sob that twists her body in the sand.

She is lying on her side, her hands pushed against herself as if she could hold back something within. Moving now, hinging back and forth, scraping her cheek on the tiny rocks as if she could rub out pain and memory, rub away the stink. Her tears are flowing into the indifferent spaces between stones. She shrieks through a body clenched against itself. Shrieks and digs herself into the sand.

She can see every ant scurrying around the sand beneath her as she stands; she can see each thing about them, what separates them, their tasks, their methods. She walks to the sea and sinks. She shovels up wet sand, and rubs it over her belly and thighs, scrubbing between her legs, rubbing until the skin is raw.

Her mother sits in the kitchen; empty wine bottles, broken glasses, spilled rice on the lime-washed floor like a windblown star. She sees the blood on her daughter's girl's legs . She puts her hand to her mouth in shock, then realises and grins and waves, gestures exaggerated by drunkenness.

'Oh darling, it's finally come, my baby girl a woman now.'

The girl is numb, cannot feel the trickle down her legs. Dark like the inside of a too ripe fig.

# Thirty-nine

Valentine found him, stunned by the unforgiving solidity of a tree stump, fallen, stalled in an arid meal of dust, stones and dead wood.

'Max . . .' she said. She plaited her warm fingers amidst his and raised him, drawing him back through the forest, not releasing his hand until they were in the house, where she seated him on the bed.

'I want to make it right Max. I want it back, I want it with you.'

Max stared straight ahead, his mind spinning, teetering, lurching to and fro.

Tine looked down at the dirty lime floor smeared with fresh smudges of blood.

'You've hurt yourself.'

She lifted his foot and examined it.

'You've hurt it, your sole,' she said.

He looked at her, not understanding.

'You've ripped your sole. Let me clean it – you've picked up a lot of shit from outside.'

'It's nothing,' Max said, pulling his foot away from her. He reached under the bed and found the bundle of socks, the same ones he had thrown there weeks before. He stretched one over the wounded foot.

Valentine shut the door of the bedroom and lit a candle.

Max did not speak and except for the seep of blood from the tear in his foot, there was no movement from him.

Valentine covered his mouth with hers, kissing him with a feeling that flowed from her mouth like the tears from her eyes. She rose and unbuttoned her shirt, removing it with a will she had never before known. She reached behind her back and released her bikini top, dropping it onto the crumpled heap of the shirt. She straddled his knees and pulled his mouth to her breasts, rubbing them across his lips and cheeks.

Max could not feel her, absorb her heat, let it soak through him like sunshine on skin. He could feel nothing. He was alone on a frozen night, staring through a window at the warm hearth flickering within.

She raised herself, loosed her wrap and with a nudge of her hips was naked before him, her skin a camouflage of gold and shadow in the flickering light of the candle.

Although he could not feel her, could not feel anything but the hardening crust of blood in his sock, he could see her – a woman naked. It made him hard.

She pulled off his T-shirt, kissing the insides of his arms as he lifted them, compliant as a child. She kissed the palms of his hands, traced the muscles of his shoulders with her lips, nuzzled the nest of his armpit. She pulled trousers off legs devoid of will and swung across him, reaching between her legs and wetting herself with her fingers as she descended onto him.

'This is me, this is you, this is me, this is you,' she whispered mirroring his eyes in hers and groaning as she felt his penis; pushing down and rising until she could place her hands on his chest and sit deep in his lap.

'This is my mouth, your lips,' she murmured, 'this is your neck, my hands, this is my belly, this is you, this is me, this is now, this is . . .'

Her voice caught and she wept, still moving up and down, her tears falling on his neck. She paused and pulled his face to her, searching out his eyes, but he could not hold her gaze. Something was unfurling in Tine just as something fastened in him. As she was opening he was tightening, his suffering intensifying like a beam of light in a magnifying glass.

She grasped his head in her hands and kissed his lips and held him to her chest, her thighs shaking as she enveloped him. She was every cell of herself, around him, his lips against her breast, the smell of her, the smell of him, the air on her back. The side of his face slid up and down the sweat-slicked crenellations of her breastbone, one eye smothered, the other blinking, his mind going back and forth, back and forth. Tine going up and down, up and down. The back of her thighs, her arse slapping onto his thighs, harder, faster, shorter, quicker. Somewhere he could feel the friction, rubbing him towards an end; an escape.

Tine felt him gasp without warning, contract and shiver within her. She pushed her hips down onto him until her legs were stretched open, her feet off the ground, suspended. So near to breaking free. She bore down engulfing as much of him as was possible. She rocked and ground into him, her arms locked around his head, her moans building, straining along the web-like suspensions that held her back, held her open. She pushed and rocked, opening herself further, pushing and stretching until something snapped, released, and she was falling free.

She fell forward, a smile stretching across her face, like a ballet dancer's first step after an age of injury.

# Forty

No one would find out.

St Xavier's was good at secrets.

Linnet would not tell his brother. Wilson and Ibwe wouldn't say a word – they wouldn't dare – and Stelly ... Stelly was all right once you got to know him. The truth was – even though he was tall – it wasn't his fault he was a stupid Stickman.

Weld had never imagined it was true what they said – that one day you got over homesickness – but he didn't miss his Ma at all any more. Of course, he loved her and his Pa too – he'd fight anyone who even mentioned them – but he didn't miss them, not like he used to. Missing was something that happened to somebody else.

A Mite.

A baby blubber.

Not him.

Not Weld. Max Weld.

Being wet was for people like Lao, or that Spanish boy in the year above who smelled funny. Max had turned it off, like a light switch. Lights-out.

And then there was darkness. Just like that, with the push of a switch. So why shouldn't he be able to turn it off. All that sadness, those tears, that longing for Mama, the safety of his bedroom, the door not quite closed.

As for Heavy, he was dead. Gone, like homesickness. Weld did not think about him and if he did, he'd chase that part away.

Outside, in the rain, where he couldn't be seen or heard.

Max took the bubblegum out of his mouth and flattened it in his fingers. Linnet shared his tuck with him – in fact, he was in charge now, since everyone, even Linnet, agreed Weld was the Ace of Spades. He stuck the pale pink gum on the cracked green of the door and reached under the flower pot for the key.

He still came to Beaufinn though, and everything was the same as before. Exactly the same – but he didn't need the tea, or whatever it was. It didn't really matter.

Not any more.

# Forty-one

For Valentine the following day was so infused with rec-
ollection, pain and promise that she was completely absorbed
in every moment. As for Max, if he was confused or suffering,
there were few outward signs. He was unremarkable except in
the vacuity of his expression and mechanistic quality of his
actions.

Valentine remained near the little white house; sitting,
looking, thinking and crying, tears tobogganing down her
cheeks like children in their first snowfall. She discovered old
boxes of shells, unpacked patched and faded clothes from
childhood. She breathed them in, weeping.

Max roamed outside. Tine did not know where he went
and he did not say. He returned from his excursion empty-
handed but for the dust in his clothes, the scratches on his
legs, and an expression that Valentine was too preoccupied to
understand.

She swam, prepared food, weighed heart-sized rocks in her
hand and arranged them around each of the fledgling palms.
She cleared the bathing area of sea urchins – most of which
Max cleaved and sucked at without relish. The rest he left in
the sun to die.

When not eating or searching through the woods or along
the stony paths that fell off into the sea, Max gazed at the
family copy of *Gormenghast*, unable to enter the miles of
mountain-high ballrooms, the subterranean corridors and vast
kitchens.

As night fell, Valentine attempted to talk to him. He ignored her questions. There was only one thing he wanted to know.

'Where's Khalib – where does he live?'

'Forget him, Max. What about you?'

'Forget him? Have you?'

'What do you suggest Max? Tell the police? Wake Zeno from his stupor?'

'I don't know … go to Athens, take him to court. Chuck him in jail with all the other animals.'

'Great, so I go to Athens and tell them that years and years ago, alone, with no one else around but my mother who is lying drunk a few yards away, this man did what he did … and then what? They come back here and find him scrabbling about like a abandoned dog. And what then? Three years before a trial, lawyers, judges, all in Greek. Appeals and retrials. Ambitious lawyers fighting to make their name on a salacious case. What did he do? Where did he put it? What were you wearing? Where was your mother? How many people have you had sex with? Do you take drugs? Show the court where he touched you. Why didn't you say anything at the time? And then what Max? The court believes me, the court doesn't believe me. Does anyone believe me? Guilty, not guilty – one year, ten years … where's my justice Max? Where's my voice?'

'So you let him get away with it,' Max said.

'No one gets away with anything.'

'He should be punished,' Max spat.

'Punished? Look at him, Max, look at that face, those broken teeth, that body, that life; he is the most punished creature I have ever seen.'

Max muttered unintelligibly through his teeth.

'What's wrong with you Max? Why are you being like this?'

'Me? There's nothing wrong with me. You finally tell someone, me, about this pervert fucking animal ruining your life ... and then you want me to sit here all pretty as if nothing happened.'

'Max ...'

'And I thought it was me, something wrong with me. The whole fucking time I've been going insane, thinking I was doing *it* wrong, or that you'd never slept with anyone or ...'

'Never slept with anyone? You thought I was a virgin?' Tine shook her head. 'Is that what you told yourself? I slept with *everybody*, Max, anyone who asked. I turned around and let them fuck me, erode away as much of my disgust as they could.'

'You ...' Max was shaking, his anger coming to the surface.

Valentine's eyes flooded with tears. 'Don't Max. This isn't about you, it's about me. Why are you ...'

She saw Max through her tears – his contorted face, his fists, his fear and fury, and her heart opened for that part of him she knew so well, recognised in herself. She moved over to him and rested in the space where his shoulder met his torso.

'Is there something you're not telling me Max? Something you ...'

Max got up and turned away, his eyes closed, his teeth clenched, his fists shaking.

She walked over to him and enveloped his right fist with both hands.

'This Max, your fist, it's the size of your heart. That's all I want. Your heart ... I wasn't trying to mislead you, I swear.

It was harder for me with you because I care for you. I was trying to make it different. I wanted to find some love in it all with you. Can we?'

She unclenched his hand and placed it on her breast, holding his neck. She brought his fingers to her mouth and then pushed them down between her legs.

'Please Max,' she whispered into his ear, squeezing her legs together. Pushing herself against the limp and lifeless digits of his hand.

But he did not respond; he could not respond to her, could not break the ringing in his mind. He could see her, but whatever she tried, she could not pull him to her.

If he could just do something, he told himself, do something to make it all right; if he could force hardness into his penis, everything that had happened to her, to him, might be altered. For a moment the achievement of an erection became the response to all the woes that had been visited on them – but nothing he could do, she could do, could rescue him from the screaming wheel of his mind. She stepped back and walked away. 'It doesn't matter,' she whispered.

Max lurched to the bathroom, pulling the door behind him.

He stared at his image in the mirror, trying to quiet his mind. Trapped, mired, sealed in an arc of rage. Impregnable. Unbearable.

Unbearable.

He could do nothing. He was nothing. He clenched his fist – the size of his heart, she said – he punched himself in the mouth, in the cheek; once, twice. The pain for a moment, a relief from the merciless clatter of thoughts. He turned, pulled open the door. He ran to the bedroom, fell onto the bed, and shrieked into the pillow until there was nothing left to shriek.

When he woke up, she wasn't there.

He reached out his arms like a child, but there was nothing. He reached further, patting round the mattress, panicked, suddenly awake, but where comfort should have been there was only emptiness. He leapt up and tore through the house. She was not there, nor on the terrace.

There was a note.

It was on the table, held fast by the last bottle of wine they had drunk.

She *couldn't bear it*, she wrote, she was *sorry*. She was *off to the village to make plans*. They would *talk things through* when she returned. It wasn't *his fault*, she said. *He'd done nothing*.

Nothing.

He ran to look for her at the water's edge.

She had gone, abandoned him. She knew, must know, must have glimpsed the real him.

He knew what he must do. A man must *do* or he is nothing. Must *do*.

The metal bar lay there, heavy, dull, a discarded weapon, her father's shirt crumpled beside it. He picked up the bar, weighed it in his hands, and walked into the forest. He knew what he was looking for, where he was going; he'd been searching for the place and finally found it after hours of hunting – a pathetic lean-to amongst ruins, roofed with corroded sheets of corrugated iron and scavenged scraps of plastic.

Max paused in the undergrowth, surveying the beams of driftwood within, smelling their hellish stink of rotted kelp, watching the heavy body move inside, all naked skin and matted hair.

There he was, trying to whistle, reedy air escaping through broken teeth as he sat in a jumble of blankets, more the place of an unloved dog than a bed – Khalib, cutting out a picture from an old magazine, clumsy fingers slicing through faded limbs. Behind him, nailed to a beam, was Tine's swimsuit.

'Khalib!' Max shouted, moving in front of the shack.

Khalib looked up hopefully and dashed out, a smile leering lopsidedly, his broken words of greeting becoming a yelp as he saw the metal arcing towards him. Khalib twisted away, roaring with pain and betrayal as the metal smashed into his collar bone, fracturing it like a wet twig. Max lifted the bar again but Khalib charged at him, roaring, knocking Max over and the metal out of his hands.

As Max scrambled to his feet Khalib grabbed the bar and swung it. Max scurried away, Khalib behind him grunting with the pain of his smashed collar bone, Max dodging trees and brush while Khalib smashed through like a stampeding beast. Max sprinted towards the house, hoping he could pull the door shut behind him, but Khalib was edging closer, reaching for Max as they approached the sea. Max felt Khalib's hand claw at his clothes and launched himself into the water. Khalib leapt after him, the metal bar ringing as it hit the edge. Max remembered the Captain's warning and buckled in the air, just missing the rock that loomed under the surface of the water. He heard the thud and scream as Khalib's entire body weight smashed into the summit.

Max swam to shore and clambered out of the water. He looked at Khalib's body spasming like a hooked fish. He was screaming. Max watched, detached from what he saw, from this beast clinging to the submerged mass: broken, disfigured, abandoned.

Max walked to the house, stuffed his passport, wallet and his few clothes into a bag. Then he walked past the place where Khalib had already ceased to scream. He would keep moving, not daring to look back, not stopping.

Not ever stopping.

# Forty-two

I can't really say everything's better – not yet anyway.

I haven't been able to tell the Triff. Some day I will. Sooner rather than later but I don't want her to start drinking again. 'It's only wine darling,' it only ever was wine, bottles of it, on her own, trying to fill the hole that I'm wondering if some dark thing in her knew, just fucking knew, she would find if she married my father.

That's why, even with the terrible things that happened, and me seething with anger these past months, forgetting what it's even like to smile – even with all this, I would not go back to how I was before. If I was to spend the next forty or fifty years of my life hiding from this, guarding this story, trying to protect them all – the Triff, my Dad – pretending things are the way they should have been, I'd be hiding from my life. And for what? To protect their fucked up ideas, their unexamined wastelands, so maybe I could repeat them.

And Max. I tried to see him when I got back but he didn't want to, wouldn't talk to me, couldn't – other than a clumsy apology and a desperate request that we 'let sleeping dogs lie'. I begged him to talk to me about it all, talk to someone at least. Perhaps we saw in each other something that neither of us could see in ourselves. Perhaps that was our bond.

He's worked out what he wants to do. He's joining the army ... or something. Officer training.

I keep thinking of this book I read once, where the English kept having tea during a siege in the Indian Mutiny, drinking diseased water out of broken china while their families lay about them, dying in shit and blood, pretending to have tea ... as if nothing was happening ...

I'm sorry. I didn't want to abandon him, just leave him in limbo ... but what else can I do? What can anyone do but him?

And I still think about what I saw then, what we both saw, the Captain and me, as we came round the point in the boat that evening after it all happened. The Captain was steering, one arm holding me as it had been since I'd told him what Khalib had done all those years before. He had not let go of me for a moment, not once.

Khalib was there, in the water, clinging to the rock with one exhausted, partly fingerless hand, and moaning like an injured dog. He'd been there for hours. We later found out that his hip was smashed, but even from the boat I could see his shoulder was swollen as if it belonged to some other being. When the Captain yanked him over the sides of the boat and onto the deck he screamed like a woman giving birth.

I even felt sorry for him.

The Captain didn't.

We took him back to the village though, the Captain bumping over the biggest waves he could find, and somehow we got him to the clinic. One day, Khalib might even manage to walk.

I stayed with the Captain and his wife Kalenda for the last week of the holiday. He refused to take me to the ferry the first time I said I had to go. He shook his head and cupped my face in his thick hands.

'Do not go. In my heart a place appeared the day you were born, Vallei-mou, and it has grown every day you lived.'

Kalenda nodded and said that I must live with them. They'd leave their house to me when they died, she announced, and the Captain added that, although it was not strictly right for a woman to own a boat, he might even leave her to me as well.

He swore they'd find me a husband.

'Christos the fisherman's son,' Kalenda suggested, 'he's been in love with you since you were a girl.'

'Perfect,' the Captain roared, slapping the table. 'It is decided then. Christos is a poet ... well his grandfather was, maybe he's a doctor ... will you stay?'

I shook my head.

That last afternoon, when I did finally leave, trying to get off to the port as the first storms of the end of summer announced themselves with huge gusts of wind, the Captain appeared and put his arms around me and told me he was sorry. He was sorry for every second of his life that had led to that terrible moment and if he could have been wiser and seen it, there is nothing he would not have sacrificed to keep me safe.

He did not even brush away the tears that ran down his bullfrog face.

'But it wasn't you,' I pleaded. 'You had nothing to do with it. You weren't responsible.'

'You were a child,' he said. 'Are we not all responsible?' He looked at his wife and she nodded.

'This is true,' she said.

And it is.

# Acknowledgements

Part of the inspiration for this novel came from my dear friend Julian Ozanne. My thanks to you, compadre, for this and so much more. I would also like to thank Molly Hallam for, amongst many wonderful qualities, her courage and inspiration.

I am very grateful to those who have read and advised me in the genesis of this rather difficult book, in particular my brother Crispin for his incisive notes; Noonie Zand-Goodarzi for her particular literary sensitivity; Jamie Catto for his wise council; Olivia Glazebrook, whose novel all lovers of literature eagerly await; Stephen Murray, a great Irish poet in a land of poets, whose first novel will be momentous (if he can keep himself out of the holy chapel of Tig Neachtains for long enough). Thank you to Peter McDonnel (lucky the students who have him as a teacher) for your comments and friendship. Many thanks to Kate McCreery, Robert Hill and Melissa North for their readings. Thanks to Kirsty Dunseath and the team at Weidenfeld.

For the most part, I've written this novel in other people's houses, and always with great gratitude. Thank you so much Catherine Eccles and Joe Gannon for shelter with the Devil's Mother – your kindness is much appreciated. Thank you Gail Behr my beloved friend – an evil part of me hopes there's still a little parsley floating round your kitchen. Thank you so much to Sir Jack and Sammy Leslie for a memorable summer at the Badia, and thanks to Jaqi Russel Flint and my friend Spiro.

Thank you dear Michael and Claude Davies for your ever open arms, open door and open hearts (and a kiss to you my JJ). Thank you dear Jamie Byng and Angela Huth for your friendship and support. Thank you Philip Briel and Lee Brackstone. Thank you to you Raffaella de Angelis for your counsel and the most precious gift that will last for ever. My heartfelt love to my family whose support is constant and essential like oxygen and delicious like food. To all those strangers on the road for a thousand selfless acts, I'll try and repay them wherever I can. Speaking of strangers, if you would like to communicate with me try rowantheauthor@gmail.com.

I'd like to acknowledge and recommend the *The Making of Them* by Nick Duffel, which provides an insightful and helpful analysis of the ways in which the traditional British boarding school system affects the psyche.

Finally, just as a bad teacher can mar or destroy a child's life, so a good one can plant seeds that will flower forever. I would like to thank the great teachers I have had: Isabel Hyde, Peter Hardwick, David Barlow, Aidan Day, Stuart MacFarlane and the wonderful teacher I have now, Dzongsar Khyentse Rinpoche.